BLADE OF P'NA

BLADE

OF

P'NA

L. Neil Smith

an imprint of

Rockville, Maryland

ISBN: 978-1-61242-218-3

www.PhoenixPick.com
Great Science Fiction & Fantasy
Free Ebook Every Month

Published by Phoenix Pick
an imprint of Arc Manor
P. O. Box 10339
Rockville, MD 20849-0339
www.ArcManor.com

Dedicated to the memory of

DAVID F. NOLAN

CONTENTS

CHAPTER ONE

"The Daintiest Thing Under a Bonnet"

SHE SWEPT INTO THE OFFICE, A VISION OF SHIMMERING loveliness, glossy, golden-haired, bright-eyed, with a little clutch-purse and tiny hat and veil that did nothing to conceal her features. Letting the door swing shut behind her, she crossed the room and planted herself delicately on a brown leather backless chair in front of the desk.

She had everything any healthy male looks for in a female: beauty, poise, grace. Well-turned out, I thought. What she was wearing represented my salary for a year. And she smelled even better than she looked.

Too bad she was a spider.

A medium-sized spider, if you limit it to sapients, of the general "jumping" variety, about four feet wide, a little less than that from front to back, and hip-high to a human being, covered with that blond fur I mentioned. Six of her big black eyes, two large and four small, glittered in a horizontal line behind that veil. I had no idea where the others were, or even if she had them. Probably at the back of her head.

It's hard to sneak up on a spider.

"I am Shaalara of the Alteen Zirnaath," she said, extending a well-maintained palp. Her voice was just as pretty and polished as the rest of her, with all of the usual annoying arachnid clicks and tiny wheezes trained out by an excellent finishing school. "You are Mr. Eichra?"

"Pleased to meet you." I gave her palp a polite touch, remembering to use a paw instead of my nose, a reflex among my own kind that might be misunderstood. "It's Mr. Oren, except that he's out of the office on a case. I work for him. My name is Oasam, but most folks call me Sam."

That's right. I'm a dog—at least the organic part of me is—and not a particularly big one, either. As cute as Shaalara was, our prospective client was at least twice my size, a fact it was far too close to lunchtime to ignore altogether. I went around behind the boss's desk, climbed up into his chair, and from there to the top, where I settled down on the self-cleaning blotter with my legs tucked under.

"My boss should be back any minute, now—or maybe not until next week." Given his profession, there was no way I was going to interrupt the man on the job. What he does mostly requires a lot of headwork, but sometimes there's blood—sometimes there's a lot of blood—in colors ranging from straw transparency, to an opaque purply black, through various shades and saturations of green and blue, to bright, smoking red like his and mine. "Is there some way I can help in the meantime?"

Shaalara's winsome mandibles gave off little involuntary clicking noises which, among her kind, were a sign of anxiety and sadness. It almost tore my heart out to listen to her. "Please forgive me," she finally said, apologizing for what she considered her breach of etiquette. "But you see it's my fiancé, Meerltchirt of the Fronzeln Zirnaath."

"Your fiancé?" I knew the Zirnaath were communal spiders, among the first appropriated by the Elders. I knew nothing of their marriage customs.

"My fiancé." She chittered, this time without apology. "We were to have wed in three days, but he has disappeared, and I believe I know why…"

In most of what you might call garden variety spiders, there's a lot of difference, physically, between males and females. Compared to the latter, the former are tiny, relatively feeble, and have to resort to all kinds of strange ploys to do their reproductive job as males, like tying their enamorata up, or stroking them to sleep. Even so, most fail to survive their wedding night. The groom is literally the little guy on the top *of* the wedding cake (if spiders had wedding cakes).

Saying "I do" is the same as saying "*bon appétit*".

Sapient spiders, on the other hand—those intelligent enough to have developed technology on their own, to have created civilization, and to have evolved to become the dominant lifeform in the several and diverse alternative realities they came from—manifest the least sexual dimorphism of all spiders. The Elders' ancient adage, "The brighter the spider, the bigger the male," can generally be counted on.

The Zirnaath, however, are an exception. A very bright and agile species descended from tiny little jumping spiders (among which, ironically, males and females are more or less indistinguishable to anyone except other jumping spiders), they display the most sexual dimorphism of all sapient spiders. This missing Meerltchirt mook would have been my size, more or less exactly, meaning about half of lovely Shaalara's.

Among all the Zirnaath, Shaalara explained, the Alteen were most conservative, being late to abandon what she called "the old ways" they had practiced in their home world before they were Appropriated. Some radicals among them openly advocated a return to those old ways now.

Which is why, Shaalara assumed, Meerltchirt had galloped. Those old ways included making a wedding feast of the groom, something that sapient spiders had all supposedly been talked out of thousands of years ago, by the Elders, but which some among them—the "Old Matriarchs", Shaalara called them—were starting to look back on nostalgically.

And with growling stomachs.

Shaalara, who held advanced degrees in poetry and engineering, and considered herself a progressive and a romantic, did not agree with the Old Matriarchs, the principal leaders of whom were her mother (a widow), her grandmother (another widow), and several dozen widowed aunts.

"So what," I asked her, "do you want Eichra Oren to do?"

She chittered pitiably again. "Please find my Meerltchirt for me. Persuade him to come back to me, to marry me—following the customs of his own people, the Fronzeln, if necessary. Tell him I'm a modern girl. I promise I won't eat him, even if my family were to disinherit me. I love Meerltchirt and I want—Sam, I *need*—to have his babies."

Yeah, I thought, *about forty of them at a time.*

CHAPTER TWO

The House of Eichra Oren

"YOU REALIZE," I SAID, "THAT IN THE END, SHE'S GOING TO eat him."

I looked around, in one of those rare instances when you're suddenly conscious of things all about you that you usually take for granted.

It was a wonderful room, Eichra Oren's office, elegant in its simplicity. Its ceiling, floor, and walls were polished ivory, sawn from thick planks obtained from trees in which elephant tusk genes had been implanted. It was a major industry here on the western north coast of the Inland Sea. Nothing sounded quite like the wind, clattering through the leaves in a grove of ivory trees. The stuff was beautiful, responded well to lighting, and always seemed warm to the touch.

Easy to keep clean, too.

The ivory floor was covered with a thick, colorful carpet of cloned caterpillar fur, grown for the purpose on the surface of enormous vats of nutrient. The stuff looked impossibly delicate, but it was more durable than well-tanned sheepskin, and capable of self-repair.

He said, "I'm not so certain of that, Sam. If I were, I wouldn't try to find him for her. What a deep and hideous moral debt that would generate!"

Eichra Oren had only missed Shaalara by a matter of minutes. Now he sat in the swivel chair behind his desk and I lay in the meat-loaf position on the backless chair the spider lady had occupied. I could still detect her fragrance drifting in the air, but that was okay. I am a detective, after all, a private nose. I had filled my boss in on my interview with her—thanks to cybernetic implants on the surface of my doggie brain, I have a perfect memory for things like that, not to mention a sparkling personality—and we were considering our options.

"You know, something I've always wondered, Boss..."

He was abstracted, glancing through some communications—mostly advertising—that had been sent to his desk throughout the day, and which he'd just allowed to download into his own cerebro-cortical implants. He opened his eyes and looked at me. "Yes, what's that, Sam?"

"Why is it," I asked him, "that you're the one of us who goes out and faces the public every single day, witnesses all of the faults, failings, and frailties of every sapient being, often in a close-up and personal way," I pushed my muzzle at the corner of the room where he'd leaned his Assessor's sword when he'd returned to home base, "yet I'm the one of us who tends to be cynical about everything and everybody?"

"This is a rhetorical question?" he asked.

I said, "It isn't meant to be."

"Then the answer is, I don't know."

He looked tired, but then he often did after a long day's work. At least his tunic wasn't bloody, and he hadn't had to clean his sword. Those days could be really bad, afterward, and he couldn't afford the luxury of alcohol or drugs to ease the pain. All they did was post-pone it. That didn't mean he didn't drink, just that he didn't drink to forget.

Eichra Oren was about average height, as human beings go, slender and wiry, but well-muscled through the arms and shoulders, thanks to many hours spent exercising with the sword and practicing other lethal arts. His hair was short and sandy-colored. His eyes were a brilliant blue.

How old Eichra Oren was, I couldn't tell. I'd never asked; he'd never volunteered. He looked about thirty, but you never know with any of the beings, human or otherwise, partaking of the Elders' culture. That I was not the man's first symbiote I knew. I could find traces of them lingering in his memory whenever we communicated directly. All of them were canine, naturally. At least one had died in action, which he avoided thinking about, but I kept uppermost in my own mind at all times.

For whatever reason, the females of several humanoid species found him attractive. I would have thought he'd seem just a little boring to them. For the most part, he liked them, as well—sometimes it became a problem—but Eichra Oren seldom had time to spare for what he referred to as "social relations", thanks to his semi-sacred avocation as the keeper of that damned sword. Give the man a couple of hours in the gym he maintained downstairs, a good meal (he was partial to lobster, but then, so am I), and a decent night's sleep, and he would be fresh and ready to undo all of that good therapy in the name of *p'Na*.

Suddenly, he stood, grabbed up the sword that identified his profession, and spoke. "Let's go for a walk, Sam. I need the fresh air." He strapped the sword-belt around his waist, and off we went together.

There was nothing wrong with the air indoors. The building, a simple four-up and four-down with a flat roof we sometimes used as a spare office or dining room, was a quasi-organic edifice, grown from a seed the size of one of my front paws. Without being overly obtrusive about it, the place breathed deeply and often, filling itself over and over again, every few minutes. But I knew exactly what the boss meant. I'd been cooped up here all morning and was feeling the need for a stretch.

Outside, it was one of those impossibly beautiful days we have so many of in this particular corner of the planet. I sniffed the air, as always laden with sage which grew in wild abundance everywhere in a climate that was usually hot and dry. Here and there, other people of various species were visible, working at country chores, tending to their animals, running errands, taking a stroll, none of them close enough to spoil a feeling of near-solitude under incredibly vast blue skies.

The place was a great favorite of landscape painters in a hundred different alternates. Wisps of icy cirrus drifted overhead, looking like gigantic feathers. Somewhere, something like a meadowlark was singing.

Sunny and tranquil as the present setting seemed, the atmosphere was full of energy and action. Down by the shore, a mile or so south, gruff, rough-handed beings were hauling in freshly-caught fish in big nets, supported by antigravity pods, from the holds of small vessels onto processing tables on the docks. There were other, cheaper ways of getting food. This was an ancient artform where some of the Elders' "guests" came from, practiced in this very spot in many realities, and the paying customers enjoyed the handcrafted aspect of it.

At the same time, far across the Inland Sea—which lent a salty tang of its own to the air all around us—in what I'm told was once a trackless, sandy desert, and is still referred to as the "Ocean of Sand", clever farmers cultivated and harvested items like artichokes, avocados, pineapples, prickly pears, carambola, and furniture. Eichra Oren's desk had come from over there, carefully teased from the vine when it was ripe and ready to cure, as had my favorite seat in his office.

We headed down a narrow, rock-lined pathway, paved in asphalt, thickly embedded with tiny seashells, toward the village at its foot. The boss was intent, I believed, on getting us some lunch. But that wasn't at all what he'd had in mind. When we were about a hundred yards from the building that served us both as home and office, where it stood surrounded by wild grasses, he stopped, and turned to face me.

Pulling a short, fat cigar from his tunic pocket, he let it light itself, rolling it so the low flame was distributed evenly around the front end. Drawing deeply on it, then exhaling with a kind of sigh, he said abruptly, "I suspect so much, Sam." It was rather like starting a conversation with the word, "however". "So much. I had to get us both out of there because I'm all but certain our house is ridden with spy devices."

I could have raised my eyebrows, but it would have had no effect, since both they and my face-fur are white. "Visual or auditory?" I asked.

"Yes." Drawing on the cigar again, he let a light breeze whip the smoke away. I caught the edge of it going by. I've always liked that smell.

"And you want to leave them in place," I suggested, nodding, "so that whoever planted them won't know you're onto their nasty little game?"

15

He scratched a bit of tobacco from his tongue. "Yes."

"And you're planning to answer all my questions with that single word?"

"Yes—er, no. Sorry, I'm just preoccupied. Something nice for lunch, I think, and plenty of coffee, then we'll visit my mother. Along the way, I'll try to answer all your questions as well as my own."

Serenaded by busy bees and birds we made our way downhill.

CHAPTER THREE

Cafe Atlantis

THE PLACE WAS SIX TABLES SMALL, LOOKED LIKE IT WAS constructed of adobe brick, and sported fishing nets for curtains, decorated with colored glass floats, sand dollars, sponges, and the occasional dried starfish.

The soft breeze that came in through the open windows was laden with sea salt and the not-unpleasant smell of seashore decay. Eichra Oren disposed of his cigar before we crossed the threshold. We sat and watched the little harbor across the road where fishing boats were hurrying in, ahead of a thunderstorm that would soon be arriving from the continent next door. I love a sight like that, brilliant blue sky contrasted with a leaden line of storm clouds, deep purple-black and brilliant green bands of sandbars alternating in the water. Yes, I can see in color, thanks to the Elders for having tinkered with my doggy genes.

The menu, hand-written on a slate standing beside the door, was offering baked flounder today, stuffed with shrimp, crab, celery, bread crumbs, and many another wonderful delicacy. My favorite— although whatever I happen to be eating at the time is usually my favorite. On another day, it might have been brown bean soup, lamb stew, or pork cutlets with sweet red peppers. I was tempted to order a *picon* cocktail, but had work to do later on, and thought I'd better pass.

The owner-chef, a big, dark, hugely-muscled individual with a blue granite jaw, impressive moustaches, and monumental eyebrows, knew us well. He had greeted Eichra Oren like a long-lost cousin, which, in point of fact, he was. All of the *Homo-supposedly-sapiens* in this corner of alternity are related to each other, their ancestors having been aboard an overcrowded couple of sailing vessels trying to escape the catastrophe of the Lost Continent, when the Elders Appropriated them.

In the background, a *jai alai* game was playing openly on the audio. If the proprietor had really cared, he would have listened on his own personal implant. Eichra Oren favored the red snapper, a deep water mainstay that may have come off one of the boats—bright colored lateen sails of a design older than time, backed by catalytic fusion engines the size of a fist—that we were watching that very afternoon. Everything on the menu was guaranteed never-frozen and stasis-free.

The landlord and head chef, the estimable Renner B'z'tirf had made certain there were no bones in my portion, and poured wine— a nice plain rough red—into a saucer for me. I sat up as neatly as I could in a chair across the table from my boss and delicately lapped up food and wine. The only thing that could have made it better was if I'd had thumbs.

Everything is better with thumbs, I'm certain of it.

I don't have much of a sweet tooth, so I had more flounder for dessert.

And more wine.

Along the road between the cafe and dockside, what looked like a snake riding a bicycle flashed past, a common enough sight in the Elders' civilization. There was almost no other vehicular traffic at this season and time of day. Gulls circled overhead, making a lot of racket, and a couple of brown pelicans fished the waters below them. I watched a cormorant plunge into the water and emerge with a wriggling herring.

I don't need my mouth to talk and don't have the vocal equipment for it in any case. Any thoughts I want conveyed are relayed from my implants to speakers in my collar. Eichra Oren and I continued our conversation.

"So what is it, exactly, that you suspect, Boss? Or can you talk here?" I tossed an invisible eyebrow over my shoulder at our large, lantern-jawed host, who, unmusically humming some unrecognizable ditty, was laboring away in the kitchen, separated from the rest of the restaurant by a counter. I think he was preparing for the dinner crowd.

His symbiote, a Great Pyrenees half again my size named Bask, lay in a cool back corner of the tiny dining room, pretending to ignore us. I knew he thought that, because my breed had come off the boats with the first humans in this world, I was stuck up and wouldn't speak to him. But in fact, the reverse was true, Bask wouldn't speak with me. Eichra Oren had explained that sometimes people—even dogs—who thought of themselves as lower class could be more jealous of their position in the social whirl than those they perceived as upper class.

"Renner is an old friend of my mother's," Eichra Oren reminded me. I knew what that meant; most folks would never have believed it. "He's trustworthy."

Cynic that I am, I wondered about that. The Elders had discovered a way around the aging process four hundred million years ago, and had passed that and many another benefit along to the persons from other realities whom they'd Appropriated several eons later. Eichra Oren's own mother, for example, had been a teenage girl aboard one of the brave little ships that had sailed north when the snow began falling on the southernmost continent and didn't stop falling for a couple of centuries. Although she'd feel slighted if you said she didn't look a day over thirty, the reality was that she was fifteen thousand years old.

Fifteen thousand years.

Although Renner B'z'tirf had been among the tarry-handed ship's crew, he could often be seen holding forth at one of Eneri Relda's evening parties. She's the least class-conscious individual I've ever known. He plays mandolin, knows more dirty songs than anyone I've ever met.

Eichra Oren went on. "It's the Elders."

The Elders. Even Bask's ears had perked up at that one.

Imagine what somebody somewhere had called "intellects, vast and cool and unsympathetic": engineers, scientists, philosophers, but with a low taste for outrageous colors, spicy food, music of every kind from everywhere in the known universes, swashbuckling, and very good beer.

Brewed from kelp—I'd almost had some of that with lunch, too.

Now imagine a garden snail, wearing a colorfully striped, coiled shell—but the size of a small personal vehicle, featuring ten long, squid-like tentacles sprouting from a face that, evolutionarily, had started as a foot, right in front of the eyes, of which there were two, incredibly large, slit like a cat's or a goat's, and surprisingly expressive. Unlike those of their relatives, the chambered nautilus, whose eyes are open to the sea, theirs are covered by tough, bright corneas.

The giant molluscs, sometimes known as nautiloids or ammonites, had first evolved to sapience half a billion years ago, making them the earliest species on any known version of this planet to have done so. So far—at least according to the geniuses at the Otherworld Museum—their crosstime explorations hadn't run across anybody older.

Don't get me wrong. The famous Otherworld Museum is just about my favorite place to be on a rainy afternoon, or any afternoon for that matter. I go there as often as I can, knowing that I will never see everything if I spend the remainder of my life roaming its glass and granitic floors.

Fortunately for me, it isn't located in one of the larger cities on this version of the planet—not very large, mind you, compared to those on other versions; the total land population has been estimated at a few hundred million at most (how few, nobody knows; it would be considered an invasion of their privacy to attempt to count them), and the vastly more numerous underwater folks have excellent reasons for disliking cities—but in the hills above the little town where we were eating lunch today, a brisk hike from the house I shared with my boss.

The Otherworld Museum is a vast collection of open spaces and buildings, the result of several plantings over many centuries, some of them piled on top of one another, others sprawling out in every direction, like a heap of gigantic melons at harvest time, crowned by a single, shining, completely transparent twenty-story multifaceted spheroid, intended as a reminder that there is an infinite number of universes.

Outside, there are parking lots and landing pads for visitors. Inside, except for the transparent section, of course, it is dry, quiet, cool, and dim, enhancing the visitor's appreciation for the tens of thousands of displays. It's the kind of place that seems automatically to inspire individuals to take soft steps and whisper.

Nobody is altogether certain, in the million years or so that the Elders were collecting, exactly how many individuals, from exactly how many cultures, on how many alternative versions of the planet were Appropriated. It's said that careful records were kept. On the other hand, it's also said that some efforts were spent destroying those records before the Appropriators finally gave in and Did The Right Thing.

All this has resulted in lots of confusion, and full employment for scholars whose job it is to untangle the complex history of the Appropriations.

An excellent example of both—the confusion and the scholars—may be found in the highly attractive person of Lyn Chow, curator and director of the Otherworld Museum, who is considered, in the effort to tidy up the record, something of an anomaly herself. Back when her people were Appropriated, they were up in the northeast corner of the supercontinent, carving their first jade ornaments and dying their clothing red. They were most certainly not aboard the ships of Eichra Oren's ancestors, so the question remains, who Appropriated them, and when?

Lyn Chow may be as much as a head shorter than my boss, extremely slender, but with plenty of subtle curves. Everything she does is graceful, as if the background music of her life, music only she can hear, came from the ballet. Mine comes from a wrecking yard. She has lovely cheekbones, perfect skin, and huge almond eyes that look on you with a kind of scientific curiosity, but never in an unkind way. Her voice is light, musical, and she's the best-smelling human I've ever met.

I had to shake my head and blink to get back to the subject at hand.

The Elders themselves aren't featured much in the Otherworld Museum, because, well, not everything is about them. But their natural history is remarkable for a couple of items. First, they evolved long ago as involuntary natural telepaths, among themselves. I don't mean that psychic or paranormal stuff. Some part of their nautiloid brains naturally generates long radio waves, the evolutionary history of which has something to do with their very complicated reproductive biology.

The other remarkable item is their discovery and domestication—underwater—of fire. I've never had an explanation for it that I understood or believed. The truth, whatever it may be, is deeply buried in some five hundred million years of mythology and fossilizing sediment. Even so, a preponderance of their technology—my boss's house, for example, and his office, not to mention the Otherworld Museum—is biological, rather than mechanical, avoiding any need for fire.

Like I said, after they engineered a way to reach thousands of worlds of alternative probability, for something like a million years they collected—"Appropriated"—millions of specimens of sapient beings, from thousands of younger species, like Eichra Oren's and Shaalara's, who, along with our cephalopodical hosts, now comprise the sum of civilization—the Elders' civilization—as we know it today.

"The Elders?" I repeated. I liked how it made Bask twitch.

"Specifically," he answered, "one Elder in particular, a sinister fellow named Misterthoggosh, who maintains a villa here, just east of town."

CHAPTER FOUR

"Ze Beeg Squeed"

"ONE ELDER IN PARTICULAR," EICHRA OREN HAD JUST informed us, "by the name of Misterthoggosh, maintains a villa near here, just east of town."

The image that the boss showed me in his mind, via implant, was of a very large, rambling, low-lying structure, standing on a low bluff just above the sandy beach: several wings of stuccoed adobe under red tile roofs with deep, overhanging eaves. The place could be seen from the same coastal road running by us here, at Renner's restaurant, but it was surrounded on three sides by many acres of neatly-trimmed green.

"A two level villa," I told the room. "Half of the place will be underwater, the other half high and dry." I added the image, mostly imagined, I admit, of another large structure sitting on the sea floor a few hundred strides from the beach. "Surf and turf. I've heard of him."

"Zo 'ave I!" came a loud voice from the kitchen area back of the counter. It was followed by a long series of highly violent chopping noises. I had no idea whether he'd received the images we'd been exchanging.

"Renner!" the boss and I said simultaneously, and in exactly the same tone. I added, "Do you make a habit of eavesdropping on all your customers?" To be fair, it would have been impossible not to eavesdrop in the tiny cafe. I don't know where he got his accent. Maybe from a catalog.

The big man stuck his big, bearded jaw over the counter. "Can I 'elp 'aving good 'earing?" He did, in fact, have an earring—and a big cigar wedged permanently in a corner of his big mouth. He pointed a big dripping cleaver at my boss. "And 'eez mothair would want me to drop ze eaves, eef hair favorite leetle boy considair messing wees Ze Proprietor." You had to concentrate to extract meaning from his rented accent.

Eichra Oren sighed and shook his head, "That's what they call him? The Proprietor?" He reached into his tunic pocket and extracted a cigar of his own, which lighted itself when he gave the shiny band a twist.

"Zat's what 'e call 'eemself," Renner replied, emphatically chopping a fish. "I myself call 'im ze Beeg Squeed." Coming from a brilliant seafood chef, did that qualify as a compliment or a death threat?

"Well, you all understand," said Eichra Oren, "that I have no case whatever, no paying client, nothing at all to offer even the faintest, feeblest standing in any sort of investigation. But I am concerned, nevertheless, Renner, Sam, Bask, deeply concerned. There are extremely peculiar stories flying about everywhere, whispered rumors about the 'fiendish machinations' of the villainous Misterthoggosh, reputed prince of criminality, and certainly the spider at the center of the web."

He took a long draw on his cigar, and exhaled.

"A beeg, soggy spidair," Renner observed, dismembering another helpless fish, a nasty-looking thing that told me Renner was preparing his great specialty, *bolhabaissa*, famous on every continent of this world. It deserved to be famous across the entire multi-universed continuum.

Bolhabaissa is a seafood stew made with many different kinds of fish—mostly bony or spiny local ones—and various shellfish, with vegetables. Flavored with herbs and spices native to this area of the supercontinent, notably garlic, orange peel, basil, bay leaf, fennel, and saffron, it's traditionally served with grilled slices of bread spread with a thick sauce of olive oil, garlic, saffron, and hot red pepper.

You can never know exactly what you'll find in *bolhabaissa*—or what will find you—maybe scorpionfish, maybe sea robin, maybe giant eel, golden bream, turbot, monkfish, mullet, or hake. The shellfish may include sea urchins, mussels, a couple of different kinds of crabs, langoustine, even octopus. The chef may simmer leeks, onions, tomatoes, celery, and potatoes together with the broth which is usually served first in a bowl containing the bread and sauce, with the seafood and vegetables served separately in another bowl or on a platter.

He makes a batch up about once a week. Otherwise I'd start having withdrawal symptoms. For some reason I'm particularly fond of sea urchin.

Pushing that to one side, I asked, "What kind of stories do you mean?"

"What kind of criminality?" Renner wanted to know. Only he'd said "creemeenaleety".

Bask yawned, put his muzzle on his forepaws, and closed his eyes.

My boss said, "Misterthoggosh is the presiding director of a huge business conglomerate that pipes in all varieties of entertainment and so-called news from thousands of other alternative universes, through pinhole aperture fields and relays safely located in the Asteroid Belt. There's nothing wrong with that, of course, unless you want to argue the fine points of interdimensional copyright—which doesn't in fact exist. Everybody seems to love it. I even watch some of it, myself."

Actually, he watched quite a lot of it. He seemed to be especially fond of stories involving rotting bodies, coroners. and crime scene investigators. It was the dinosauroid species who did them best. I have no idea why. I was only grateful that you couldn't smell any of it.

"But there's a persistent story floating around," Eichra Oren went on, looking really worried now, "that this Misterthoggosh wants to take the idea further. A whole lot further. He wants to establish a permanent base over on the other side—on one of the other sides, anyway—and send his scientists and other specialists, and their families, as well, over there to live and work in it for extended periods."

"Ahonh! We all know how *zat* turned out ze first time!" Did Renner somehow avoid dribbling cigar ash into his customers' food, or was it one of his secret ingredients? I had to admit he had a point, even if he'd made it in an accent he'd gotten from a secondhand store somewhere.

The Elders calculate that they've been sapient for something on the order of half a billion—that's five hundred million—years. After thousands of centuries of trying out just about every economic and political modality conceivable to the mind of mollusk, they'd finally settled—not without a great deal of blood in the water—on a diffuse, leaderless, centerless civilization in which the rights of the individual come before any other consideration. In the Elders' world, nobody gets elected First Cephalopod or crowned King of the Krakens.

The Elders believe that an individual's rights can only be threatened by force or the threat of force. This has long since become formalized as part of a doctrine they call p'Na, under which it is considered an axiom that nobody has the right to initiate physical force against anybody else for any reason. Even proposing that such a heinous thing be undertaken—or hiring somebody else to do it—is severely frowned upon. Severely. The act of self-defense, on the other tentacle, not constituting an *initiation* of force, is heartily encouraged.

To enforce this doctrine, whenever it becomes necessary, p'Nan "debt assessors" were recruited and trained strenuously, not only in the philosophy of p'Na, but in various martial arts, and the detection of lies. The boss's stories of that latter kind of training—the technical term is "aversive conditioning"—still send chills up my spine. Imagine getting electrically zapped every time that you failed to correctly report whether somebody was lying to you or telling the truth.

P'Nan debt assessors are expected to interfere with cases of initiated force, to judge after the fact whether the initiation of force occurred, or to confer with groups and individuals preemptively, in order to avoid any inadvertent initiation of force. It was (and still is) the view of the Elders that each initiation of force, and every threat to do so, rings up a moral debt that must somehow be paid back.

Ironically, most of Eichra Oren's commissions as a debt assessor involve folks coming to him to ask whether they have incurred a moral debt, and what they must do to make it right. Sometimes this involves little more than an apology. Sometimes they have to make that apology public. Sometimes a debt is settled with money. Sometimes it's lots of money.

Of course some kinds of moral debt can't be paid back—most of those involve a death, accidental or deliberate—but millions of years of custom require that a token payment be made, demonstrating the perpetrator's willingness to pay the debt in full if only it were payable. That's where the debt assessor's sword comes in. Does that make it an execution or assisted suicide? The answer is yes. Does that make him judge, jury, and executioner? It certainly does. But it is almost invariably the debtor who requests his services, knowing the risk.

A lot of the time, even welcoming it.

About a million years, give or take a millennium, after the Elders began collecting sapients of all kinds from their native universes—"Appropriating" became the popular euphemism—somebody noticed that the practice of abducting individuals and bringing them to the Elders' version of Earth, never to return, constituted a gross violation of p'Na.

Every now and again, some thinker comes up with a new theory that purports to explain how a species as intelligent and experienced as the Elders could have kept Appropriating people for a million years without noticing that it violated the first principle that they lived by.

There are many similar examples of self-deception throughout the universe: slavery—especially military slavery—and taxation. Most wars (and many marriages) begin with individuals lying to themselves. Somebody called betting on lotteries "the thrill of bad mathematics". I think the Elders simply enjoyed what they were doing, wanted to keep on doing it, used their big powerful brains as rationalizing engines, and kept on doing it until even they couldn't fool themselves any more.

Mind you, some of the abducted individuals didn't really object all that much. Eichra Oren's people received it as an act of mercy. They'd had no idea at all where they were headed, or what they were facing, on a planet gone mad and wildly swapping its magnetic poles. Sheets of ice two miles thick had started melting up on the northern continents. Another had started building in the south. They'd set out with their chronometers, their sextants, their multi-mast ships capable of sailing around the world, armed with brass and cast-iron cannon.

Those unfortunates in the hundreds of other ships that were not rescued by the Elders had a long, difficult voyage ahead of them, during which they would lose thousands of years of progress along the way.

Being whisked off to the Elders' version of Earth—a bright, warm, sunny, mostly semitropical clime where the natives had learned to control the planet's weather and pole reversals a hundred million years ago—seemed like a pretty good deal. Species from overcrowded worlds agreed. On their Earth, the Elders used only a tiny bit of the otherwise open land, and the air-breathing newcomers rushed to claim it.

Others, no doubt, felt differently, but they couldn't be returned. The Elders had no idea—at that stage in history—how to find the specific point in space-time-probability from which their victims had been taken. So they did what they could, instead. They consulted with their debt-assessors, conferred full membership in their civilization upon all Appropriated Persons, granted them what amounts to practical immortality, gave them cortical implants and useful symbiotes— dogs for humans, cats for other hominids, all varieties of finny, furry, feathery, and slithery things for other species—and loads of wealth.

What's a lost homeworld worth, after all?

And then, sometimes by themselves, sometimes with the help of debt assessors, every one of them, the Elder philosophers, scientists, and engineers who'd had a tentacle-tip in the Appropriations, committed suicide.

CHAPTER FIVE

The House of Eneri Relda

EICHRA OREN LEFT A SMALL GOLD COIN ON THE TABLE, promised to stop by on the way home to pick up a bucket of soup for dinner, and gave our goodbyes and thanks to Renner. Whoever said that cooking is the kindliest of the arts had it right. The man could be difficult, but it was an honor living in the same universe with him. I tried similar courtesies with Bask, but the big dummy ignored me, like he always does.

As we stepped outside Renner's place, the boss looked upward to an increasingly ominous southern sky, and then used his implant to send a message back to the house. He included me so I'd know what was going on. Rain was on the way, and as much as I hated getting wet, I hated the way it made me smell even worse.

"It's too far to walk to my mother's house with a storm like that on its way," he told me, indicating the wall of lightning-punctuated velvet blackness headed steadily for our little coastal village from across the Inland Sea. You couldn't see the hulls from where we stood, but more and more fishing boats were crowded up to the concrete pier, their brightly colored sails furled, their masts sticking up where we could see them. I agreed with the boss. It takes a long, long time to get my fur dry.

Within a couple of minutes, the boss's sportsveek, a sleek black discoid, arrived and halted at the curb. A gap materialized in the side of its hull and we got in. Eichra Oren sometimes lets me drive, but this time it was his mind at the controls. The veek, a product of arachnid technical competence manufactured on the southernmost of the western continents, in the shadow of famous Sugarloaf Mountain, lifted and propelled by antigravity, rose two feet above the paving bricks set in a virtually indestructible polymer, as its canopy rolled over us.

And we were off.

The storm clouds to the south now filled more than half the sky.

We drove east. In no more than another pair of minutes we arrived at a surprisingly modest-looking walled villa on the sea side of the road. Wind riffled the lawn between house and veek as we climbed out and locked up. There's almost no crime in nautiloid civilization, but that's only because most people take some sensible precautions against it.

It has been said that the house of Eneri Relda is a duplicate, built precisely from eidetic memory, of the famous lady's family villa in ancient Antarctica, before the poles flipped and the new glaciation began. Like its predecessor, it even sat atop a low salt-grass-covered hillside, overlooking the friendly sea. Its rough, terra-cotta colored roadside wall functioned as the back of the house. And there were no roadside windows, which tells you something about ancient Antarctican culture.

Or ancient Antarcticans.

A massive pair of bronze-sheathed doors set in the thick adobe wall between a pair of classic (if architecturally unnecessary) Lost Continent-style columns, observed us approaching, recognized both of us immediately, and very politely admitted us. Once inside, a broad hallway with a highly-polished floor of dark stone, lined with even more columns, and sheer, filmy curtains that set it apart from the private living spaces on either side, conducted us directly to a sunny rear courtyard where Eichra Oren's mother could be found most of the time.

When she was home. She was a renowned world traveler.

But that was exactly where we found the lady now, reclining in a classic long Antarctican lounge chair, with an uncharacteristic frown creating a pair of deep, vertical furrows in her otherwise lovely and flawless forehead, as she kept her eyes on the approaching ugly weather.

A lively fountain in the center of the courtyard sent a slim jet of water upward a dozen feet to play in the remaining sunlight before it fell again to the decoratively tiled pool below. But out across the increasingly unlovely-looking sea, no fewer than a dozen little boats with colorful sails were making their prudent way back to the shore, while flocks of seabirds overhead sought shelter from the storm, as well.

"Hello, Mother," Eichra Oren said, taking her bejewelled hand and kissing the back of it. I trotted over and received a pat on the head that would have seemed patronizing, coming from anyone but her. I liked Eneri Relda, and she genuinely liked me. My earliest conscious memory was of lying in her lap as we watched over a comatose Eichra Oren, grievously wounded by the criminal who had murdered his last symbiote.

He was among the youngest of her offspring (I don't know how many altogether; if it had been only one every twenty-five years, she could be approaching six hundred by now), and dear to her. She and I had often spent long hours speaking of history, literature, and ethical philosophy. In fact, she may be the reason I bear the peculiar curse I do: I greatly prefer the company of human women over females of my own species.

I don't believe I've ever seen a more beautiful human female than Eichra Oren's mother. If goddesses were real, they'd fight over who got to look like her. She had what appeared to be enormous eyes, very changeable in color, and very high, tight cheekbones. She was tall for a female of her species, with a slender waist, mammalian attributes that usually turned heads, and long, long legs. Her smile could have lit up the gloomiest, dankest cave. She sang very sweetly when she thought no one was listening. She had a nice voice, too, not too high, but light, and a bit breathy. At this time of year she was usually a blond.

I'm not sure she ever used scent, but she smelled wonderful.

She smiled and lit up the garden, "Would you care to come sit down, dear? Sam, you, too, please. I've just returned from a very odd sort of pilgrimage to the Home Continent—this world's equivalent of it, in any case—mostly to see the volcano that would be sticking up through the ice and snow back in our world. I brought a new wine back with me from across the Inland Sea. I'd be quite grateful to have your opinion."

He sat. "Happy to oblige, but you'd be better off asking Sam. He knows a lot more about such things than I do, and he has a better palate."

"It's true," I modestly agreed. And so it was, aided as it was by yards of olfactory sensors. Humans' are the size of their thumbnails.

"Good. Do we need something to snack on? No, I can see that you've just finished lunch. And at Renner's, as usual, I would assume. I'm looking forward to a quart of his *bolhabaissa* tonight, myself. Oh, Squee-elgia?" Eneri Relda's dinosauroid accent was absolutely perfect. An individual appeared, received her employer's request, and promptly disappeared.

"You know, dear, every time you come over here to see me, I find myself wondering if you've come to tell me that you've finally found a suitable someone and are ready to settle down and make me some grandbabies."

"Now, Mother—"

She assumed a memory-searching expression. "Whatever happened to that cute little blond girl I used to see you with. You know, the one who—"

"The one who was a serial murderer and I had to…you know."

That had been a bad one for the boss. He hadn't been himself for weeks afterward.

Her eyes went to the Assessor's sword where it lay in its scabbard on her patio table. "Yes, I know, dear. I suppose it was unavoidable. Then how about that nice Lyn Chow from the Otherworld Museum who was here to interview me again the other day? Don't you think that she's pretty?"

"Smart, too," he nodded. "A professor of Comparative History. You know, I might just take your advice, drop by and see her, at that. Ask her if she's ready to make some grandbabies for you in exchange for all of the fables, factoids, and fairy stories you've been telling her about the ancient and glorious Lost Continent. Would you like that, Mother?"

There was some truth in what he'd said. Eneri Relda was considered the greatest storyteller of the age, and a scholar of all things Lost Continental. At most of the parties she was world famous for throwing, people of every species came from everywhere to hear the ancient tales retold. Lyn Chow could often be counted on to be sitting in the front row.

They went through variations on this discussion every single time that we came to visit her. It was their ritual; neither of them really meant anything hurtful by it. Eneri Relda certainly didn't need more grandchildren. She had over two thousand of the damned things already. And the whole thing was truly odd because Eichra Oren had stopped aging at around thirty, while Eneri Relda had stopped at twenty-three, so she looked younger than her son did. Like a younger sister lecturing her older brother.

He raised his eyebrows. "But what about you, Mother, dear? With all due respect, you can't be getting any younger. The clock is ticking. When are you going to find some nice fellow somewhere and settle down? Maybe present your son with some little brothers and sisters to play with?"

Eichra Oren's mother, the august and revered Eneri Relda, showed her son a finger-gesture vastly more ancient than most people realize, The lady herself was some fifteen thousand years old. She'd probably "settled down" a thousand times. One occasion had been with Eichra Oren's father, who was said to have died working in the Asteroid Belt—our nautiloid benefactors the Elders aren't above hiring employees to go into space for them—and hadn't lived to see his baby son grow up.

At least that was one version of the story. I'd heard a good many others.

"Well," she said, "I've been thinking of having an affair with the poolboy."

He frowned. "Your poolboy N*v*ts*ll*sn*k is a thousand-year-old sea scorpionoid." Eichra Oren was one of the few humans I was acquainted with who pronounced sea scorpionoid names properly. Eneri Relda was another.

"And professor of ancient literature. Mostly, N*v*ts*ll*sn*k comes here for the conversation. He thinks I don't know he records them. And all the while he works, he recites incredibly beautiful romantic poetry."

"All about laying eggs and scattering milt on them?" He snorted. "Are they the folk poems of his people, or does he churn them out, himself?"

She folded her arms in front of her. "Well, I can tell that *you're* no romantic, son. And on top of it, you may just be a bigot, too."

She winked at me.

He laughed.

Like I said, they went through this entire production every single time. Sometimes I thought they did it just to watch me squirm. But that would be paranoid, and Eichra Oren didn't have that much sense of humor.

Eneri Relda's dinosauroid servitor arrived just then with a bottle of the new wine and three little bowls. Service in the old-fashioned, time-honored High Antarctican manner. In a majority of the versions of reality known so far, Squee-elgia's kind had never had a chance to exist. In most of the universes discovered by Elderkind, a chunk of raw metal the size of the Matterhorn fell out the sky about sixty-five million years ago, struck close to the narrow spit of land between the two western continents, and killed half of all living things on the planet.

It wasn't the first such strike, of course. Nor was it by any means the worst. One hundred eighty-six million years earlier, a quarter of a billion years ago, much the same thing seems to have happened, killing off at least ninety-five percent of everything then living.

Geologist and paleontologist types refer to it as the "Great Dying".

But for those it happened to, it probably wasn't all that great.

CHAPTER SIX

Lethal Legacy

IN A TINY PERCENTAGE OF ALL POSSIBLE WORLDS, APPARENTLY for a wide variety of reasons, the impact of sixty-five million years ago didn't happen.

In the Elders' home universe, to name the one example I'm certain about, they constructed an enormous directed-energy weapon, placed it in orbit, and vaporized the great "iron" before it could get here. For the Elders, that was quite a leap: for some reason, the giant molluscs detest the very thought of space travel, and they didn't have any handy "aliens"—like us—all those millions of years ago, to help them.

I've always loved the idea of a video entertainment program—maybe you could call it *Squids in Space*. Imagining the spacesuits alone...

In other alternative realities—the number of which is infinite, of course—nature intervened. The killer 'roid was jerked off course by a wandering exoplanet. Or it got blasted as the Solar System passed a supernova that didn't go off in most universes. I've been told that there is one known instance of the killer chondrite colliding with a genuinely alien starship that had inadvertently stumbled through the System and into its path, although nothing else is known about the vessel, its crewbeings, or its point of origin. If you have alternity to play with, that means everything has a chance to happen at least once.

We know all of this because, for as long as it's been standing—several thousand years, at least—scientists associated with the Otherworld Museum have been poking around the fringes of this pivotal event. Or non-event, as the case may be. Far out in the Asteroid Belt, where Misterthoggosh pipes in his popular foreign diversions, there are also devices—something like telescopes—capable of peering into other realities. And of course those stolen programs also offer clues now and again.

Everybody seems to like documentaries about dinosaurs. Or their local equivalent. I'd watched a science show once, from a dinosaur universe, speculating about what might have become of those pesky little mammals in the fossil record—if they hadn't all been eaten.

Comely curator Lyn Chow collects all of the information that the professorial pokers send back to her, tidies it up a little, and puts it out on display for the edification of the museum-going public. For whatever cause, in a very small number of continua, the dinosaurs went on evolving until they eventually produced (or became) critters that could knap obsidian, build fires, tell dirty jokes, and think about thinking.

Eneri Relda's assistant Squee-elgia was obviously one of those evolved dinosaurs, although I'm sure she'd never even thought of telling a dirty joke. Of roughly human height, she was covered from head to mid-ankle in red-veined feathery scales (or scaly feathers—in either case, they looked like they'd been injection-molded from some soft, translucent plastic), fading subtly from silvery-gray to lavender.

She possessed two arms, equipped with capable-looking fingers instead of flight feathers, and had extremely large scaly, four-toed feet (two toes in front and two toes in back) that had no doubt once served her distant ancestors as the claws of a predator (or maybe just to perch on the limb of some prehistoric tree) but terminated now in flattened black nails, much like a primate's, as did her powdery white fingers.

Squee-elgia's scarlet-crested head was unquestionably that of a sapient being, with shrewd amber eyes—supposedly better than those of human beings, or even my genetically improved oculars—under a dome-shaped skull that afforded more than sufficient volume for a highly capable brain. Her face was as flat as that of any human, with a pair of nostril-holes directly beneath the eyes. A flattened beak—no more than a triangle of black horn, really—scalloped twice along its bottom edge, met a surprisingly mammalian-looking lower lip. As she spoke, I watched for teeth, but wasn't greatly surprised to see none.

Her tongue, like her beak, was black, and looked as if it would be dry to the touch, not that I had any interest in touching it, mind you.

She said, "The west-central red, as you requested, ma'am."

The creature spoke in a high, squeaky voice that I had to try very hard not to find annoying. With my doggie ears, it wasn't particularly easy.

The wine was very nice, though, almost like a sherry, with plum, raisin, and salted cashew undertones. Stealing a nervous glance at Eichra Oren's sword, Squee-elgia had placed a pair of traditional small ceramic bowls on the low glass table, and one for her mistress, as well. From previous experience, I was aware the little vessels we were using were family heirlooms and had come off the ship in which Eneri Relda's people had fled. I was drinking from an archaeological artifact fifteen thousand years old, which meant I was an honored guest.

But then, I'd sort of known that.

For a while, we spoke politely of wine and soil and weather on the continent to the south. Some especially hot, dry summers had been good for the grapes. Even Eichra Oren tried a sip or two, and very nobly refrained from lighting a cigar, although I could sense that it was a strain. Then he said, "Mother, I'd like to ask you something, if I may."

Eneri Relda sat up, readjusting her position. "I suspected that you might be here to a professional purpose. What do you wish to ask, dear?"

He inhaled and began, "You know practically everybody—"

She laughed, which was an enjoyable thing to see as, well as musical to hear. "Which is your not-very-polite way of saying I'm very old."

He grimaced. I'd seen this kind of ritual between them, too. Eneri Relda was joking with him, although Eichra Oren somehow completely failed to recognize it. I always thought it was a bit unusual for a parent to have a better sense of humor than her child. Maybe it was just something about humans and their mothers. I'd never really known mine.

"—along this coast. I would have finished if you'd permitted me. Please tell me whatever you can about an Elder by the name of Misterthoggosh."

She blinked. "Why, Misterthoggosh is my neighbor." She raised an arm gracefully and pointed toward the east. "He lives just down the road, there. You can see where the dry-land portion of his villa is. I've been told that the underwater parts are even more palatial and extensive."

"Then you're actually acquainted with him?" he asked, a little scandalized. Humans are also funny when they realize their parents have a life of their own. And most of them go slightly insane when confronted with the idea that Mommy and Daddy might still be having sex.

With each other.

She frowned. "This is beginning to feel like an interrogation, dear. Has Misterthoggosh committed some act of initiated force that merits investigation by a p'Nan debt assessor?"

I hated it when she frowned.

"No, Mother," Eichra Oren shook his head. "But I think he may be about to. There are a lot of really strange rumors going around, and from unusual sources. Some of them even suggest a restoration of the Appropriations."

I heard myself emit a low, involuntary growl. I can't really explain why. Without those first Appropriations—however unethical and reprehensible they may have been—I would never have existed. Neither would my boss. And the beautiful Eneri Relda would have been a millennium and a half dead. How's that old saying go, about an ill wind?

"I see…" She had been gazing off into the distance again, southward, toward the rapidly approaching storm-front. A breeze was beginning to whip the fountain now, spraying us from moment to moment with tiny droplets, little more than an aerosol. Brightly-colored vessels were still visible, hurrying under power now for the shelter of the shore. One or two had left the surface of the water and begun to fly home. It made me wonder how many had been out there to begin with.

Eneri Relda turned to look Eichra Oren squarely in the face. I'd never seen her quite so serious. "Well, there is one thing that I can tell you about Misterthoggosh. You must beware, my son. Better yet, stay away from him completely. He is a very persuasive creature. Dangerously so. Becoming acquainted with him will almost certainly alter the neat, tidy course of your life beyond recognition, and forever."

He blinked with surprise. "Has it altered yours, Mother?"

"Now you're just snooping," she answered. "Before you go—"

Eichra Oren laughed. "Before we go? You're tossing us out, Mother?"

Not us, just you, I refrained from saying.

"Don't be silly, Eichra Oren, dear, you've always been my favorite child. But—before you go—I have a gift for you. Sit here, let Squee-elgia pour a little more wine, and I'll be back before you know it."

She arose from her chaise almost floating, as she did, sometimes, into the house, as if she were made more of spirit than flesh. It was good wine. We both did as she suggested and she was back in under two minutes with a little foil-covered box in her hands. "This would have belonged to your dear father, if he'd only had time to come home for it. Unfortunately, he did not, so he didn't have it with him the day he chose to go visiting the Elders and encountered a Great White shark."

Every time Eneri Relda told us the story of the death of Eichra Remarc, it was something different. The last time it had been about a volcano, although I'd always liked the one about the Asteroid Belt best.

Eichra Oren raised his eyebrows. "Shall I open it now?"

"Yes, please do so, by all means. It was originally a gift made to your late father by one of the more technologically-oriented spider clans, in honor of some great favor that he did them. I don't know what that was. But I have one, myself; it is a great comfort." Inside the box—which turned out to be silver through and through—on a cushion of woven spidersilk, lay a tiny, brightly-polished silver pistol.

It made me wish I had thumbs all over again.

"This is very nice, Mother, thank you. But I have other weapons, and this one is so—" He tapered off, too polite to speak the whole truth.

"That's exactly what your dear father would have said. I know that you have other weapons, Eichra Oren. But all you ever seem to carry is that damned sword. Sometimes it seems to carry you. This is different, believe me. It may be small, but it shoots boluses of plasma no bigger than the head of a sewing pin. It will take out a six-foot section of garden wall—this one, here—two feet thick. I know, because I did it, more or less accidentally in my grief and anger, very shortly after I lost your father. If only he'd had it with him on that dark day..."

I understood that she'd been pregnant at the time, with my boss. I was acquainted with others who'd known the illustrious Eichra Remarc. The adventures that he'd lived through were legendary. Maybe I'd find out someday what had really happened to him—and why the otherwise ultrarational Eneri Relda never told exactly the same story about it twice.

Eichra Oren opened his mouth to speak, but shut it again when she leaned forward in her chair to lay a gentle hand on his suntanned forearm. For all their charms, Antarcticans are not known for being physically demonstrative—another way in which Eneri Relda honored me.

"Promise me, please," his mother interrupted. "I know you're not going to heed my warning about meddling in the private affairs of Misterthoggosh, so at least promise you'll carry this with you at all times."

And, of course, he promised.

CHAPTER SEVEN

Lornis Adubudu

IN THE END, WE TURNED DOWN AN INVITATION TO DINNER.
Eichra Oren loves his mother, but there's quite a bit of tension—not all of it hostile, by any means—between them. I could sense he didn't feel like sitting through a meal under circumstances like that.

Eneri Relda seemed relieved, as well, confirming my suspicion that the invitation had been mostly a polite formality. The lady of the house and her dinosauroid servant had been planning to enjoy the same thing that we were going to have for dinner, anyway: *bolhabaissa* from Renner's. In fact Squee-elgia was about to leave to pick some up—with stern instructions to leave some for us. We all left through the garage: there was a sight to see out there that I didn't want to miss.

Squee-elgia threw a silly foot over the seat of her unicycle, and her equally silly leg followed. It was one of those models where you sit inside the big wheel as it whizzes over your head. The machine was painted bright red and had yellow racing stripes along the small reactor housing where it was attached to the frame in front of her knees. There were speed controls and brakes on the handlebars. I gathered that you steered by tilting your body a little, this way and that.

I couldn't imagine doing it, myself. It certainly wouldn't have looked any less silly with a little white dog driving it than with a dinosauroid.

Power surged through the idling motor as the garage door went away and she was off, down the drive, up the highway in a streak of red and yellow.

Heading west.

We stood in the doorway of the garage feeling the weather change. As she watched the dinosauroid dwindle in the distance, Eneri Relda said, "I hope you'll reconsider the advice I gave you with respect to Misterthoggosh."

He shook his head slowly from side to side. "Ordinarily, I would, Mother, please believe me. But it's my job, you see? It's my sworn duty. If the things I'm hearing were even partially true, and I were to ignore them and look the other way, millions of people in thousands of universes could wind up regretting it—not just you and me and Sam."

I wanted to say, *Leave me out of it*, but unfortunately, he was right. Most of us were better off because of the first Appropriations, but many were not, and a second round of them could turn civilization inside-out.

Eneri Relda nodded, conceding. They were very much alike inside, when you came down to it, and it was no easier for her than it was for him. "Then what do you plan to do now, if you don't mind a mother asking?"

He laughed. "Well, all joking aside, I believe I *am* going to go see Lyn Chow and try to find out if she's hearing the same things I am."

Outside, a trim little sportsveek pulled up at the curb.

Eneri Relda brightened, and suddenly the garage seemed warmer. "That's a good idea, son. Perhaps you should take her to dinner, as well."

"Yeah, Boss," I said. "Perhaps we should."

If glares could cut like swords, I'd have been two dogs then and there.

We said our goodbyes—Eneri Relda accepted a peck on the cheek from her son, stooped to give me a crushing hug—and started for the veek.

"Eichra Oren!"

The pretty girl waiting for us as we left Eneri Relda's house was no stranger. She wasn't any less strange, for that matter, than the last time we'd seen her. Running from a sporty veek she'd left idling at the curb, she didn't hesitate, throwing both arms around the boss's neck.

"Eichra Oren!"

The storm clouds were closing in now; it was starting to get cold. Bad weather like this wasn't rare here, but I would never get used to it.

"Eichra Oren!" She somehow cooed and hollered at the same time. Her voice was nice, though, not shrill. "I *knew* I'd find you here! You're a very good man, visiting your poor old mother this way, every Seventhday."

Try as I might, I couldn't see Eneri Relda as anybody's poor old mother. She looked even younger than Lornis. Maybe it had been meant as a joke. It was extremely hard to tell, sometimes, with people like her.

Untangling himself from the female's ardent embrace—with considerable difficulty; Lornis was surprisingly strong for a pretty girl—Eichra Oren took a step backward from her and tossed me a private thought, via implant: "Sam, I've got to start varying my routine."

I just sent him back a grin.

Aloud, he said to the girl, "Uh, hullo, Lornis. How have you been?"

For my part, I couldn't understand why Eichra Oren found her so resistible. In my boss' place, I would have been delighted by her attentions. Lornis Adubudu may have had the silliest surname I ever heard, but that was her ancestors' fault. Admittedly, she had taken it back after her recent, rather unpleasant, and not entirely bloodless divorce.

She was tall, slender, gorgeous, with the brilliantly exotic amber eyes that were characteristic of her people. Her skin was smooth—a light Inland Sea brown in color—and her hair was reddish and fairly short. Her nose was straight, tilted up just the slightest bit, and her cheekbones were high and prominent. She had full, moist, inviting lips.

This afternoon, she had chosen to wear a boy's lightweight, simple, white cotton tunic, open at the throat, and ending at about mid-thigh, which did absolutely nothing to conceal her other fine qualities.

Her many other fine qualities.

She was, however, not quite human.

"How have I been?" Her pretty face took on a pouting expression, one hundred percent counterfeit, but nevertheless appealing. "I've been utterly, devastatingly lonely since you closed my case, as you know perfectly well. You promised you'd call me." As she indicated, she was one of Eichra Oren's former clients, a recent one, whose case had culminated in the death, at Eichra Oren's hands, of an abusive spouse.

I'd say chalk up another kill for the Sword of the Assessor, but he'd had that struck from his hand fairly early in the fight, and had had to resort to what is dreaded in some realities as the "Forbidden Art".

The wind had kicked up considerably, as the storm front began to move in on us, bringing with it the odor of salt air and ozone. It did some extremely interesting things to the hem of Lornis' short tunic, but, focused as she was on Eichra Oren, she ignored it and let it happen.

Struggling for patience with less success every minute, the boss shook his head. "Not quite, Lornis. I said I'd send you my bill, which I did."

"And I paid it promptly, did I not?" Her late husband's demise, while unquestionably and irreproachably acceptable in the moral sense—and highly necessary, as it had turned out—had left Lornis extremely well off. The sporty veek hovering over by the curb represented more wealth than I'd earn in an ordinary lifetime. I watched admiringly as it raised its canopy in response to the coming storm. Inside, I saw Lornis' symbiote, Mio, an old world Talapoin monkey. "Which leaves us ethically free to fraternize, if you get my meaning."

"I got it the first several times, Lornis." Eichra Oren shook his head wearily, as if having been declared desirable by an unusually attractive member of the opposite sex were some kind of a burden. I confess freely that I was more than a little jealous and it made me mad. I was sort of enjoying his discomfort. I'd a lot rather have been human than canine at this particular moment. "I thought I explained to you…"

Lornis put her hands up, palms out. Her nails were almond-shaped and painted the same color as her hair. She'd been shaking her head in denial as he'd begun the sentence. "Oh, you were just being gallant—and thoroughly professional. No taking unfair advantage of a client. No taking unfair advantage of a grieving widow. I under-stand, believe me."

As I recalled, the girl's grieving had lasted for about fourteen seconds.

But Eichra Oren was trying to make his own argument. "Apparently you don't understand. Lornis. Look: we aren't even members of the same species."

There it was. He'd finally said it.

The sky had now gone completely gray, and a little spattering of raindrops had begun to fall all around us. One of them hit me on the nose.

It was all too regrettably true. Eichra Oren belonged to a species that refers to itself as *Homo sapiens*—"Thinking Man". It calls Lornis' species, which had arisen in another branch of probability altogether, *Homo gracilis*, which might be translated as "Graceful Man".

Or Woman, in this instance.

The appellation was both technically accurate and socially polite. Thrown together haphazardly by the Elders, many thousands of years ago, most Appropriated Persons worked hard to live together side by side, and tried to anticipate inadvertent slights before they happened—without going all squishy over it, of course. Such a thing was only possible, I believed, because there are no politics to speak of in the Elders' universe, just p'Na, and the Elders' concept of the Forge of Adversity. It's a long story.

Lornis was a member of another hominid species, who were what *H. denisova* eventually turned into in a parallel reality where *H. sapiens* had gotten themselves caught in a bottleneck of natural selection somewhere and hadn't happened along to upset their rivals' evolutionary applecart. They'd had another thousand centuries to develop. What they'd brought forth, in the end, were creatures like Lornis.

All the trouble was well worth it, in this canine's opinion. Their brains were organized differently, and they looked at the world from a different angle, which could be very useful and refreshing. (At this point, Eichra Oren was in no position to appreciate that, and probably thinking that he'd run aground on the rocks in her head.) But you could tell the difference easiest when they were in motion. Their knees and elbows were a tiny bit higher—no more than five inches—but it affected their gait and what they could do with their arms. It wasn't ugly, it was just subtly different, but the difference was there.

To me, the most intriguing aspect of Lornis' case had been that *H. gracilus* males were normally extremely gentle, almost passive sperm donors, most of the time. The theory was the women did the hunting and the men did the gathering and watched the kids after they were through nursing. So this gink that she'd been married to had to have been *really* crazy. The trouble was, normal *H. gracilus* females weren't even a little passive, and Lornis had apparently seen his killing as foreplay.

"Technicalities, technicalities," she told my boss, fluttering her long, beautiful eyelashes at him, a tactic mostly lost in what had suddenly become a torrential downpour. I could feel it soak through to my skin. "We're both hominids, aren't we, Eichra Oren? And we're both Genus Homo. Please don't tell me that you're one of those speciesist bigots."

Hominid, hominidae, hominin, hominini, whatever. My boss, in fact, could be highly enthusiastic about the females of several humanoid species—on rare occasions when he had time for them. The stories I could tell. But he protested, "We're not even physically compatible, Lornis."

I didn't even want to guess at what that meant. The rain was now falling in sheets, and lightning suddenly struck a palm tree down the highway, blasting hot, steaming fragments of bark in every possible direction, startling us all, and very nearly deafening us, as well. On the other forelimb, Lornis' fragile little boy's tunic was soaked now, perfectly transparent, and she was reacting visibly to the sudden chill.

Perhaps there is a god.

"Nobody's perfect, Eichra Oren." This time her pout was the genuine article—but then she brightened: "We can work something out."

CHAPTER EIGHT

Across the Forge

I HAD NO IDEA AT ALL WHAT THE PHYSICAL INCOMPATIBILITY might be between Lornis and my boss. I suppose I could have looked it up, but I didn't really want to know. The lady was a peach, as far as I was concerned. She spoke to me with the respect due to one sapient being from another. She smelled good—different from human women; maybe that was her problem with Eichra Oren: she gave off all the wrong pheromones—she had a nice voice, and she was extremely easy on the eyes.

Lornis' species matured a good deal faster than Eichra Oren's, and it used to be the case that they aged and died a good deal faster, as well. But given all of the benefits of nautiloid medical science, that was no longer anything to worry about. At the age of thirteen she had found herself married off to an influential member of her own species by her father, a very rich and powerful—if somewhat shady— businessman. She was nineteen now, and would have long since been considered an old maid by her people had she never married. However as a young widow, she had considerably more status among them than a spinster.

She just had this one thing, this one little crazy thing.

For Eichra Oren.

I'm still not entirely certain how the boss finally managed to disentangle himself from the highly decorative if overly-amorous widow Adubudu. He does know a lot of martial arts. The storm was raging, the wind was howling, and the rain was blasting in everybody's eyes and ears. Overhead, the leaden sky flared periodically with lightning, and, with apparently no interval between, peals of thunder seemed to shake the very ground beneath our feet. Lornis gave a little shriek when it happened, and Eichra Oren had to disentangle himself all over again.

Down the road, despite the torrent, that palm tree was still burning.

Me, I was too busy running to the veek, telling it to start its antigravs and be ready with the canopy. For once it didn't argue with me. (We have a long uncordial history between us—it thinks it's too good to be told what to do by a mere symbiote.) It arose from the pavement and stood there at the curb, not quite quivering to be off. I'd say I hate uppity machinery but I might just be criticizing myself.

By that time, the boss was beside me, the veek was hot, and we were a quarter of a mile down the road from Eneri Relda's house—and Lornis' passionate embraces—before the canopy had closed again. The burning palm tree whipped by us. Steam was still rising from the sun-warmed cobblestones in their polymerized matrix before us. The veek, sensing that its occupants and interior were soaked, began drying us off—mostly, the veek managed to spread the smell of wet dog around efficiently—and offering us hot drinks, along with a weather report (it was raining), the latest local *jai alai* scores, and recent game highlights.

We passed a party of large, flightless birds, soaked to the skin, complaining bitterly to their teacher—a large, sapient feline with a leaky implant—surviving their annual field trip by imagining them, one by one, roasting in a pan for twelve hours at 325. I've found it's usually better not to know what's going on in somebody's mind.

The game itself had first been brought from the Lost Continent some fifteen millennia ago, and had many fans, followers, and— most ferocious of all—wagerers, among the Appropriated Persons, both human and otherwise. The only thing even comparable is what cetaceans call polo. It's an extremely dangerous pastime, in which players are commonly injured and sometimes killed. Although all the game's technical terms and commentary are couched in the Original Language, it's fair to say that Lornis' people, with their long limbs and impressive strength, were the best at it. Still, there were human players and a couple of insect species capable of giving them a challenge.

Eichra Oren played occasionally and had the scars to prove it. I'd play, too, but they won't let me. Anyway, no *xistera* will fit my paw.

"Where to, Boss?" We both realized at the same moment that I was driving. I had absolutely no idea where we were going, but we were making great time. By now, my fur was starting to dry; it was terrible. As bad as I smelled to other people, I smelled worse to myself. I had begun to resemble an extremely large dandelion, gone to seed and ready to blow away. I lapped at my hot tomato soup, flavored with garlic and just a drop of fermented fish sauce, and Eichra Oren finally got his cup of coffee.

He was examining his sword, withdrawing it inch by inch from its unembellished leather scabbard. It can't rust, and I don't know of anything that will ding its single-molecule-thick edge, but he tries to keep it clean and dry in any case, just as if it were merely tool steel. In my time, he'd needlessly worn out at least a dozen stone sharpeners.

At last Eichra Oren made considering noises he probably wasn't aware of: "Sam, what do you say we try the Otherworld Museum, now, and Lyn Chow?"

Visit with another pretty girl? Why did he even have to ask?

Leaving the coastal highway a mile or two east of Eneri Relda's seaside villa, and heading north, inland, the veek climbed into the hills along a sinuous road, paved in plastic, until we came to a remarkable construction perched on the precipice of an intimidating bluff.

It was a vast, transparent spheroid, at least two hundred feet in diameter, composed of six-foot flat hexagons, invisibly fused together at the edges. As we approached around a bend, the structure glittered at us, the afternoon sunlight reflecting from different facets with each yard we moved around and toward it. Inside, we could make out the ghostly skeletal structure of what could have been a multistory office complex.

The parking area was practically empty, probably only employees left, so we could leave our veek practically at the door, which was located in a sort of transparent collar that the great transparent sphere sat on. The door wouldn't open for us, but insisted, by means of a signboard with moving letters, that no one without a cortical implant would have been able to see, that the place was closed for the day.

"Eichra Oren to see Lyn Chow," the boss broadcasted via implant.

"How nice to hear from you!" came a lilting voice. "Eichra Oren, Sam, do please come in!" We heard a dull *thump!* and the doors slid open.

We stepped into the cylindrical "lobby".

"Eichra Oren!" came the voice from somewhere above us. I looked up. The lady rode a rotating circular staircase down to greet us. I knew the thing continued into a basement where it folded up internally somehow and fed itself back up to the top. A mechanical engineer I am not. "And Sam! How very fortunate your timing. I only just arrived, back from the Asteroid Belt where I had a firsthand look—my first—at the facilities that provide us with a peek at an infinity of other worlds."

She had reached our level and stepped off the contraption, which stopped the instant her tiny, delicate feet left it. As I've said already, Lyn Chow is an exceptionally beautiful female (Eichra Oren's life seems to be filled with them) of decidedly non-Antarctican origin. The history of her people remains a great mystery in the Elders' world.

"Won't you please come up to my office? I'll make some tea." I don't know how the twirling staircase knew—a signal from her implant, maybe—but when she stepped back on, it started turning the other way, carrying her, and both of us behind her, up into the museum.

"How was the trip itself?" Eichra Oren asked as soon as we sat, me on a little caterpillar rug, him on a sofa made of some kind of brown leather and polished metal tubing. Lyn Chow pulled a matching chair around from beside her desk to face us, ordering some machinery somewhere to make us tea. The boss has always been curious about space travel.

This entire building was transparent. I doubt whether there was a single opaque wall in the place, although I hadn't looked for the bathrooms. The ceiling of Lyn Chow's office gave her a great view of the sky. Outside, across an aisle, there was a display of sea scorpionoids locked in combat with whatbappeared to be a gigantic shrimp. At least the museum floors weren't all transparent, which would have embarrassed Eichra Oren in his tunic, had there been anyone else in the building. Lyn Chow was wearing trousers. I just didn't give a damn.

"Abominable, basically," she grimaced. "As you know, there are only two spaceports on this planet, owing to the Elders' distaste for interplanetary activity. Only that seems to be changing now, in some way. The spaceport I used, Turtle Station, is built on platforms bridging a series of islands at the western edge of the more southern of the two western continents. It's in a virtual explosion of fresh construction, being carried out by humanoid workers under nautiloid supervision."

So, a long flight from here to Turtle Station, and then another, considerably longer one to the largest hunk of rock in the Asteroids. The Elders didn't know anything about building spaceships, but they'd Appropriated someone—likely with eight legs and eight eyes—who did.

"The ship—*Strand of Silk*—was extremely crowded, mostly with more construction materials." I knew that ship, having watched videos about her. She was enormous. Crowding her would have been difficult.

"So you've answered the first question I'd planned to ask you already. There's unusual activity going on with respect to the Asteroids."

She pretended to pout. Why do women all do that around Eichra Oren? "So this isn't a social visit, after all. What a pity. I was planning to take a couple of days off, to recover from my arduous journey. The sea was unusually choppy—does that mean anything?—when we came in and it was an exceptionally rough ride back to Turtle Station."

"What did you see while you were out in the Belt?"

"You mean aside from cramped quarters shared with a mammalian but nonhuman organism in a big underground metal building without windows? You mean meals consisting of nutrient cubes you pick up and eat that taste like sawdust, washed down with liquid that looks and tastes like dishwater?

"I saw a gigantic room with descending levels, like a theater. I saw perhaps a thousand glowing monitors on those levels, watched intently by beings of every known air-breathing species. Why they couldn't use their implants, I never found out. From time to time for some reason, whatever one of them was watching would get thrown up on a big screen stretching from the lowest level, up to the ceiling high overhead."

She caught her breath. "What I saw on some of those monitors, and up on that screen, almost defies description. Sapient species that I know well, living in their natural environment. That was amazing enough: did you know that one feline species has developed space elevators?

"But then there were sapients I never heard of—or even dreamed of—something that looks like a millipede six feet long. They've dammed the straits at the entrance of the Inland Sea and drained it, to provide vast tracts of agricultural land, where for some reason they raise artichokes. And there are man-sized giant flatworms that live under tremendous pressure in the dark, in a great three-mile deep at the bottom of an undrained Inland Sea. I saw sapient elephantoids who use enormous vehicles and have constructed great cities for themselves."

Lyn Chow had grown quite flushed in the excitement of telling us all about her great adventure in space. It was a very pretty thing to see.

"PreCambrian?" Eichra Oren asked.

"What? Oh, the flatworms. Yes, that's what they looked like to me." As far as I know—as far as anybody else knows, for that matter—there had never been a species of sapients descended directly from creatures of the soft-body age. It would cause a sensation in some circles.

We left not too long after that, reluctantly on my part, promising to come back to hear more about Lyn Chow's journey. Her story seemed to have piqued some interest with Eichra Oren, but it was slipping into the afternoon, and there was still something stupid he wanted to do.

Take another step across the Forge of Adversity?

Why the Hammer not?

CHAPTER NINE

The Center of the Web

TAKE ANOTHER STEP ACROSS THE FORGE OF ADVERSITY?
I'd thought to myself.

Why the Hammer not?

But what I thought in the next moment was, we had no client paying us to ferret out any "spider at the center of the web". The Alteen Zirnaath, on the other seven legs, were nothing short of loaded. So when were we planning to start looking for poor Shaalara's missing fiancé?

Speaking of spiders, that is.

As we climbed back into the veek, I voiced my concerns to Eichra Oren, attempting to remind him that a debt assessor (not to mention his loyal canine companion) does not live by p'Na alone. Truth is, I had discovered long ago that principles themselves have surprisingly little nutritional value. That's one reason they're so damned hard to maintain.

He gave me a Number Four standard-issue sigh. "Very well, then, Sam. Let's sketch out a tentative line of inquiry. You realize, of course, what the odds are saying to us—that our missing subject, this poor Meerltchirt fellow, is simply hiding out among his more sympathetic relatives. A majority of the Fronzeln Zirnaath almost certainly perceive their Alteen Zirnaath cousins as vile cannibalistic barbarians."

Vile cannibalistic barbarians. I'd have to remember that. I liked it.

I said, "They could be the very epitome of suave urbanity, Boss. They could support the symphony, the ballet, the demolition derby, and the Nautiloid Scouts. (There are Nautiloid Scouts, aren't there? There ought to be.) And still be cannibals," I was thinking about headlines I'd seen from other bits of alternity. "The significant word in any case is 'cannibal'. People who say 'dog-eat-dog' oughta visit with spiders."

He laughed. "Consider your point taken, Sam. What we need now is information. Go ahead and make appointments to interview as many of the Fronzeln Zirnaath as you can, preferably in person, and anybody else they may point to." He popped the veek into manual, put his head down, and floored it. "If somebody's concealing our reluctant groom, that somebody—or somebody else—is bound to slip up, sooner or later."

That was a lot of somebodies. Nevertheless, time passed quickly for me as we raced back up the coastal highway under ugly skies. Some of the spider-folk disconnected the instant I told them who I was and what I was calling about. I figured them as the most likely culprits and made notes. Later on others—warned no doubt by the first group about who was calling—never even bothered to answer in the first place.

Some Fronzeln appeared more than happy to speak with me, if only for the opportunity to misdirect us; they wanted to talk, as much as possible, and getting rid of them was often more than difficult. The one thing that kept me going was the prospect of a hot, steaming bowl of Renner's *bolhabaissa* at the end of a long, cold, wet, unfriendly day.

Spiders are a strange and interesting lot. I rather like them as a people and count quite a few among their number as my friends. It was spiders who designed and fabricated the devices on my cerebral cortex that make me...me. They're tough, self-sufficient, productive, and smart. I don't think I've ever heard one complain. They make wonderful engineers and technicians—and truly spectacular architects and artists. The only thing I don't care for about them is the way they eat.

Their food usually has to be alive, something like a rabbit or a chicken—or a puppy or a kitten, I suspect. They bite it and inject it with a paralytic enzyme, then wrap it up in silk, still alive and helpless, and hang it up for later. Spiders don't have much use for refrigerators or stasis chambers. When dinner time arrives, a second injection, consisting mostly of digestive fluid, dissolves their prey—alive through most of it—from the inside out. Then they suck out their liquefied victim through a tube that's a part of their mouth machinery.

It's *really* disgusting. Not surprisingly, they regard the way we vertebrates eat—mammals, birds, reptiles—tearing off chunks of flesh, stuffing them down our gullets, with similar shock and horror. I'm no moral relativist, but customs do vary with time, place, and species.

All the same, it must be awfully nice to have a family that'll back you up like that. The only family I ever had, the only family I'd ever known, was the human sitting in the seat beside me, and his mom. Guess I can't really complain about that. I couldn't think of anything the two of them wouldn't do for me, or that I wouldn't do for them. So life was good, after all. And in any event, the boss and I had lots of solid, satisfying detectiving ahead of us—provided I could keep him interested.

Before long, I had names and contact information for dozens of uncles, aunts, and cousins, as well as forty or fifty siblings, the guy's mother and father (the old boy being a Fronzeln, and therefore still among the living). I also learned our runaway was a partner in a restaurant designed for the strangest sapients the Elders had ever Appropriated. That, I thought, was going to be a really interesting interview.

By the time I finished, far away to the south across the Inland Sea, I thought I could make out an extremely thin sliver of blue sky peeking through. The day might be ending, but it was ending nicely. It was a fairly steady, but considerably gentler rain that was falling all around us now, appearing to drive directly into the windshield as if it were falling horizontally, but actually coming at us straight down.

I'd known what Eichra Oren had in mind, of course, but it was more than a little unsettling to actually see us do it. In no time at all, we skimmed up in front of "Conspiracy Central" a neat, low-lying villa in the extremely popular Antarctican style, stucco-covered adobe under red tile roofs, practically on the beach. For a minute, I thought we'd gone too far, somehow, and had come back to Eneri Relda's place, which it resembled, although there was more to the Misterthoggosh estate, we knew, both on the shore before us and at the bottom of the nearby water.

The highway side was as windowless as Eneri Relda's, but there were no non-functional Lost Continental columns. The heavy bronze door on this side of the place was different from hers, too, with a comical avianoid face in the middle, seemingly cast in high relief. However when Eichra Oren touched the door, the bronze face suddenly came to life.

"Why did the ornithoid cross the road?" it asked us in a silly voice, making a silly face. I had forgotten how much I detested these things.

It was a humor door, an item straight from various dinosauroid cultures, a sophisticated recording and playback system, rather than an example of artificial intelligence. It's said that in dinosauroid universes, at the homes of wealthy individuals, servants were assigned this task in earlier times, but an industrial revolution inevitably brought egalitarianism, and a "servant problem" always followed. It became easier—and considerably cheaper—to rely on devices like this.

In certain neighborhoods in the handful of cities on this version of the planet, groups of small, naughty boys of various species will run down a line of houses on either side of the street as fast as they can, touching each door they pass until the whole block is babbling to itself.

Eichra Oren simply gave it what it wanted and said, "I give up."

"For some fowl purpose," it replied. "How many ammonites does it take—"

"May I help you, gentlebeings?" inquired an entity, opening the door and holding it so the aperture was no more than eight inches wide. Its voice was high and squeaky, and the individual itself was more than six feet tall, with a red-orange crest, and covered with silvery gray scaly feathers—or feathery scales. It stood on very familiar looking silly four-toed feet. Possibly more confusing, the individual standing before us registered with my olfactory lobes as male.

"Squee-elgia?" I asked. That had been the name of Eneri Relda's assistant. Bird people, or dinosaur people—either one is about as accurate—had been among the first sapient beings Appropriated by the Elders, about a million years ago. That means they've been with the giant nautiloids longest, and many hold administrative positions of the highest trust. Call me a speciesist, they are nature's born bureaucrats.

"My sister—I ardently trust nothing unfortunate has befallen her…"

Eichra Oren: "No, no, my associate was confused. We just saw your sister at Eneri Relda's villa. I must say, there is a strong family resemblance."

The creature struck a pose, back of the wrist on a hip, his hip shot. "Which I assume is your polite way of conveying the assertion that we dinosauroids, as you call us, all look alike to you mammals (while we are far too polite, of course, to call you 'shrew-spawn' which, after all, is what you are.) No matter; I am quite thoroughly accustomed to such trivial and passing indignities. I am Aelbraugh Pritsch, administrative assistant to Misterthoggosh. You may call me Aelbraugh Pritsch. And to reiterate, is there something I can do for you?"

How about dry up and blow away, I was tempted to answer. Not only was this dinosaur-bird thing obnoxious, talking with him was more than a little like trying to hold a conversation with a child's balloon, held tightly at the nozzle so the air squeals out comically, or with someone who's been breathing helium. Basically, Aelbraugh Pritsch's species had converted bird-song into speech, with a mixed degree of success.

There was next to no cover over this small step into the House of Misterthoggosh. Technically, this was the back door, the servants' entrance, the beggar's portal at which we were standing. The wind was blowing again, and from an inconvenient direction. I didn't envy Eichra Oren a bit in his stylish knee-length tunic. Then I suddenly remembered Lornis' earlier difficulties with her own tunic in a high wind; somehow, this wasn't quite the same thing. In the meantime, the boss and I were getting soaked for the second time this very rainy afternoon.

A trifle frustrated, he turned slightly so that the sword on his hip was more apparent. "I am Eichra Oren, an accredited p'Nan debt assessor. I have reason to believe that your employer may require my services."

Which usually only meant one thing.

"That's interesting," observed Aelbraugh Pritsch. "And, I must say, more than a little sad. Has it become customary for a p'Nan debt-assessor such as yourself to seek gainful employment in this manner, by soliciting door-to-door? It would seem, to me at least, to lack a certain *gravitas*. Perhaps you are less competent than—"

"Is it customary," I interrupted, thinking of how ridiculous I'd look once I got dry again, "for a servant to leave his employer's visitors on the doorstep in the rain?" Maybe I'd go to a groomer tomorrow.

Maybe I'd just shave it all off. Leave the head so I'd look like a lion.

"I have my instructions," said the creature superciliously. "My most estimable employer, Misterthoggosh, is completely unavailable to solicitors of any kind." If possible, the thing's voice had become even more annoying—basically, what we were dealing with was a snotty bird butler. Or reptile retainer. "Therefore it cannot be truthfully declared that you are visitors, your visit having been declined. Now please go away."

Eichra Oren replied, "Very well. Kindly give him my card—be careful, the edges are very sharp." In fact, the "card" he slipped from a special case had been fashioned from a thin sheet of the same steel as his assessor's sword blade, his particulars etched into it with a particle beam. Its razor-sharp edges were subtly concave to make the pointy corners even pointier. The whole contrivance was a not-so-subtle reminder that it's a mistake to give a debt assessor the cold shoulder. The boss also had nice, soft plastic cards, with an animated logo, that he handed out to other people who were more cooperative.

The dinosauroid took the card on the flat palm of his hand. "Does this, then, constitute a subtle way of announcing the commencement of hostilities?"

The boss replied, in a tone I recognized as striving for patience, "Not at all, Aelbraugh Pritsch. It is intended to help us to *avoid* them."

The dinosauroid blinked. "Very well, I'll see Misterthoggosh gets it."

"I truly hope," said Eichra Oren, "that Misterthoggosh does *get it*, Aelbraugh Pritsch. Better a tiny sliver than the whole sword, right?"

The dinosaur-bird slammed the bronze door with a great, big "Bongggg!"

CHAPTER TEN

Road Warriors

WE SLOGGED BACK TOWARD THE VEEK BEFORE THE HUMOR door could tell us another ancient joke. The road machine immediately began drying, fluffing, and generally cosseting us again, but I truly wasn't in the mood.

Traffic seemed a little heavier than earlier, but the boss, who was driving now, managed to get us turned around safely and headed more or less toward home, where I was looking forward to my warm, dry private quarters, something hot to eat, a stiff drink or two, and a vigorous rubdown, as well as other attentions, lavished upon me by a sweet professional lady—fully human, of course—named Natsromy Ram.

I started to contact Natsromy, but was interrupted by an incoming call. Suddenly there was a face and voice in my mind—Eichra Oren's, too, judging from his expression. "I need help," said the voice with what seemed like unnatural calm. It was Lyn Chow, from the Otherworld Museum. She was looking at herself in some reflective surface. "It's a break-in. Intruders. I think I've killed one but they hurt me. Please hurry."

"On the way!" Eichra Oren told her, battling the veek back around the way we'd just come. I wasn't certain she'd heard him.

Her eyes were open, her implants were functioning, but she'd used up the last of her consciousness calling us for help. At least we knew where she was.

Another few moments and the lights went out. At best, she'd simply closed her eyes. My implants were still detecting a faint carrier wave from hers, but Lyn Chow herself had fallen dead silent. I reran her message through my mind a couple of times to see if I'd missed anything significant.

"She's lying on the floor on her left side," I told him. "You can tell from the way that side of her face is flattened. She's lying beside some kind of display cabinet. We were seeing her reflected in it."

By now, we'd turned off the coastal highway and were winding and twisting generally northward toward the museum, faster than was really wise. There was only the one little veek parked in the lot, which we assumed was Lyn Chow's. A transparent sliding door in the cylindrical "collar" beneath the great glassy sphere lay at an angle off its tracks.

Eichra Oren's tiny pistol was drawn as we went through the broken door. I tried out my best toothy grimace and snarled. It wasn't very scary. The spiral escalator worked; we went straight to Lyn Chow's office.

Where she wasn't.

It was oddly dark in the museum. The great faceted sphere housing it had been polarized to black, shutting out the full daylight outside, along with each usually transparent partition. It was somehow like the opposite of a house of mirrors. The only lights I could see burning—until my implant took over and began multiplying photons—were tiny colored pilots on technical consoles here and there. My nose detected a hint of jasmine in the air, mixed unpleasantly with the salty and metallic tang of fresh human blood. I followed the odor as it grew stronger with every step I took. Eichra Oren was a pace or two behind me with his little silver pistol grasped in both hands before him, all of his concentration on the virtual designator projected in his mind.

I rounded a corner between exhibits and there she was, lying with her back toward us, on her left side, facing the display cabinet we'd seen her reflected in. She was perfectly still, her long, dark, glossy hair spilling onto the floor behind her head, and even tinier than I recalled. There was a pool of blood on the granite floor at her left hip.

As I approached within a yard, I could hear her heart beating, but before I could warn the boss, she'd turned over and suddenly had some huge, ugly-looking blaster in her right hand, pointing straight at his head.

"Lyn Chow," the boss told her calmly. The man has the fastest reflexes of any human being I've ever known. Anybody else with a weapon in his hand would have shot her before thinking about it. I'd felt him tense when she'd turned, but then suppress the reflex to fire.

"It's us," I added. "Eichra Oren and Sam. You called us, remember? You're safe now, please don't shoot us." The big black pistol shape in her tiny hand wavered, then fell, with the hand that held it, to the floor.

Eichra Oren gently examined Lyn Chow as he'd been trained to. I called the emergency service we subscribe to. Five minutes, I was told. I wasn't absolutely certain she had five minutes. Through the boss' eyes, I saw she had a single wound, just above and forward of her left hip. It was deep—half stab, half slash, I was guessing a curved blade, eight or nine inches long—and she was bleeding heavily. Without removing it or tearing it further, he bunched up the dress she was wearing and pressed it down with both hands over the hole.

"Look around," he told me, keeping his eyes and hands on the unconscious girl. "See what you can find out about whoever did this. Meet the medics at the escalator and don't let them stomp through any evidence."

"You got it, Boss." I started sniffing around again, and right away picked up a scent that smelled like overcooked fish. It led me to a puddle on the floor a few paces away, where I found two objects, a large, curved fighting knife exactly as I'd imagined it, sharpened on both edges, of a type manufactured in the northeastern-most corner of the continent across the Inland Sea, and a black leather cap with a bill.

"Hey, Boss," I asked him via implant. "What kind of weapon does she have over there?" I had a suspicion, but confirmation is always good.

He didn't take his hands from where they maintained pressure on her wound, but I could see the thing through his eyes where it lay on the floor a yard away from him. It was of obvious spider manufacture, from the southernmost of the two western continents, made for humanoid hands.

"A Blackburner," we both said at once. It was a strange choice for a human female, large, heavy, and absolutely devastating. It sent a beam of odd, crawling energy into the core of one's assailant, energy that spread throughout the body, somehow disconnecting protons from neutrons, converting complex atoms—carbon, oxygen—into simple hydrogen and helium. The energy from the liberated neutrons usually set off the hydrogen and oxygen which *popped!* in a momentary blue flash, leaving behind nothing but a puddle of dihydrogen oxide—water.

It was a true disintegrator. The effect usually stopped at the epidermis, leaving clothes, shoes, and tools scorched but intact. Apparently, except for his little hat, Lyn Chow's assailant had been naked.

The emergency service was better than its word, landing its disc-shaped flyer in the parking lot within three minutes of my call. A pair of husky medics appeared at the top of the escalator on this floor.

I guided them to Lyn Chow and Eichra Oren, avoiding the puddle I had found. They relieved him from his first aid post, temporarily closed the wound with a cyanoacrylate dispenser, covered her, and rolled her onto a stretcher, letting its antigravs raise it to waist level. They'd also hooked her up to some kind of blood-replacing dripper.

We watched the flyer take off. Eichra Oren had asked one of the emergency guys to stay behind and keep an eye on the museum until we found somebody to repair the door. Then we got into our veek and departed.

At long last we were back on the highway headed west, thoughts of home and *bolhabaissa* filling our minds. I was in the midst of trying to call Natsromy again when, from behind, we both felt a horrific *thump!*.

The veek lurched on its cushion of air, gyros roaring, struggling to stabilize itself. My seat grabbed me in its padded arms the instant an object came within a yard of us at this speed, and the wheels, employed ordinarily for climbing steep grades, came down in emergency mode, steering and braking the veek. Behind us, an enormous red road machine roared down upon us for a second, clearly intentional crash.

Although Eichra Oren wrestled manfully with the steering wheel that had popped up automatically in front of him, the veek took evasive action all by itself, swerving into the seaside eastbound lane toward the shoulder. That was what our attackers had apparently been planning on. A diagonal streak of fire fell from the sky, smashing into the dirt ten feet ahead. We'd slowed a bit quicker than they'd anticipated.

Eichra Oren was out of the veek in an instant, kneeling beside the skirt, the new toy his mother had given him in both hands. Thanks to its virtual designator, in the boss' mind's eye, a bright red line connected the pistol's glassy muzzle with the target. But no such thing existed in reality. The gun and his brain implant were working together.

The tiny weapon spoke. For a moment I wondered if I would ever be able to see or hear anything again. The huge road machine pursuing us suddenly had a gaping hole where its left front quarter had been, and began to roll onto it, shredding itself to bits and pieces no bigger than my head on the rough surface of the highway as it turned over and over again, the sounds that it made in self-destruction too hideous to describe.

Eichra Oren swiveled, and with a second shot, removed the next primitive missile from the air a hundred yards away. A third shot brought down the flyer that had launched it in a shower of metallic confetti. The smoke and flames were short-lived on the choppy gray water.

"How interesting," I observed. Not having a weapon, or any way to use it, I'd stayed in the veek, considering whether to crawl *under* it. "Either Misterthoggosh has a unique way of saying goodbye to visitors…"

"We weren't visitors, remember?" The boss shook his head. "Anyway, that's only what we're meant to believe. I smell a different kind of rat."

"Or, I was about to say, Lyn Chow's enemies are our enemies," I said to Eichra Oren as I hopped from the veek onto the road. "Look at this," There was a slight dip in the surface here, and it was filled to a depth of two or three inches with water that had nothing to do with the falling rain. The hem of the boss's tunic was drenched from having knelt in it. It gave off a distinct, not unpleasant marine odor, more brackish, my highly educated nose informed me, than really salty.

"From the volume," I added, "I'd guess that their veek was filled with saltwater." It suddenly occurred to me that I was getting soaked for the third time today, and it wasn't getting to be a bit more enjoyable.

Pocketing his deceptively diminutive pistol, Eichra Oren nodded. "I concur, Sam. You know the road-owner's representatives are going to be along any minute now. Let's see whether we can discover something useful about our attackers before they start stomping through the evidence."

The worthies he'd mentioned—mostly security muscle—didn't have much use for forensics. They simply wanted to keep the traffic rolling.

"How about this, then?" I pointed my nose toward the skirt of our veek where it had been intimate with our former assailant's machine. There wasn't any dent, of course. The stuff a veek is made from is more resilient than that. But embedded, like a throwing knife, in the rubbery material, there was the great big claw of some kind of giant marine crustaceanoid, perhaps a foot long and at least six inches wide.

"Sea scorpion," we both said at the same time. The species, almost as ancient as that of the Elders, enjoy a not entirely undeserved reputation for violence. Frequently employed as security personnel, "leg-breakers", and enforcers for shady underworld figures (possibly like Misterthoggosh), it is popularly held that they are a naturally combative species, their home culture given to nearly continuous warfare.

Or so I'm told. I've known members of the same species who were poets. But I also knew somebody had died hard, before giving up this claw.

"Let's cover it with something waterproof," Eichra Oren advised, "to protect it from the rain, and make sure that the road-owner's investigators bag and preserve it for further analysis. With a little luck, we may be able to identify the individual it used to belong to."

"There doesn't seem to be much else left of the guy." I had found and brought a synthetic shopping bag from the veek. I let him do the handy work, since he was the one of us with hands. Now I was sniffing carefully around the wreckage. Seaweed, iodine, a barnacle or two, but there really wasn't any detectable trace of a driver, sea scorpionoid or otherwise. I was about to wonder aloud about the pilot of the flyer, when Eichra Oren included me in an implant call that he was making.

"Ray's Marine Salvage," came the reply. The voice was cheerful. The image was unusually dark and murky, but I already knew what the speaker looked like. "This is Ray speaking. Hello, Eichra Oren. Hello, Sam."

"Hullo, Ray. We've got a job for you if you can spare the time." There followed a flood of Eichra Oren's memories of the attack. The emphasis was on the downed flyer. (From time to time an involuntary flash of Lornis' pretty face and parts south appeared for a fraction of a second.) It's always interesting to look at the world through his eyes. He sees plenty that I miss. I make up for it with my olfactory lobes.

"Whoo! Plenty of action and adventure in the neighborhood today!" Ray said. "Yes, I can help out—I'm thoroughly bored with this job, which I'm doing for free for my idiot brother-in-law. I'll be right there."

Within minutes, another flyer hovered a few feet over the spot where the first had gone down in flames. Thanks to its antigravs, the water beneath it was smooth and still. A trapdoor on its underbelly opened; the broad form of a sapient mantoid was momentarily visible, splashing into the water below. It was followed by two smaller splashes.

"Relax, boys," said a voice in our minds. "Ray's Salvage is on the job!" We soon began to see pictures in our heads, as well as hearing voices.

CHAPTER ELEVEN

The Garden Club

I NEVER DID GET MY EVENING WITH NATSROMY OR MY
bolhabaissa. Morning found us both at Lyn Chow's home, high in the
hills above the museum she ran, which you could see, looking like
a clutch of giant eggs, from the edge of her lawn, where the terrain
suddenly dropped off.

The curator's home appeared to be made of adobe brick, like
nearly everybody else's in the area, topped with a red tile roof. But
it was different, too, its door and window frames made from dark
hardwood. The steeply-pitched roof curved upward slightly at the
corners, with carved beams to complete them. There was a wide front
porch with mild force-fields to keep the insects out, and on either
side of the broad steps that led up to it, stylized pottery lions that
were about my size.

I've been told this architecture and decor followed the manner
popular up in the northeast quadrant of the Great Continent. It
was okay.

We were greeted at the door by one Rebul Grop Thiekul, a small
(for a sapient) spider of one of the jumping clans. At first, we took
her as a nurse, but it turned out she was Lyn Chow's one-time college
room-mate, professional associate, and best friend, who had arrived

by ballistic rocket from the upper Island Continent where she operated a museum centered on arachnids of all sizes from everywhere else in alternity. Her symbiote was a spider, too, an enhanced red-legged tarantula.

"Please call me Reeb—nearly everybody does. This is Rosie."

Rebul was very nearly as pretty as the client who had engaged us—it seemed now like a hundred years ago—to ferret out her missing betrothed. Her fur was banded, light gray and dark gray, from the nape of her cephalothorax to the spinnerets at the tip of her abdomen. Her legs and palps were upholstered tastefully the same way. Her eyes were shiny black, all eight carried in a row around the front of her head.

I like that in a spider.

She smelled good, too.

She led us into the house under whitewashed and timbered ceilings, where a big bed was set up in the middle of what appeared to be the living room. I could see a lot of medical devicery tubing and cables underneath, and machinery for lifting and lowering sections of the bed. There was a handsome, brick-lined fireplace, a working desk in a corner under a window, and the walls, for the most part, were covered with bookshelves, a distinctly old-fashioned but warmly comforting touch.

Most of the books they housed were rectilinear, with printed leaves or pages, something thousands of known cultures have in common. Some were scrolls of various designs. Others were more exotic than that. I stopped counting after my implant recognized the fiftieth language.

Sitting in a farm-grown chair near the fireplace, with a slim, streamlined canine at his knee, a man came to his feet as we entered, waiting to be introduced. His clothing looked expensive and he was faultlessly groomed. He had been examining one of Lyn Chow's many books. It was in Grumlian, the product of large, sapient bear-like creatures.

"Lyn," Rebul spoke softly, touching what appeared to be her dozing human friend on the forearm with a gentle palp. "Your pair of handsome rescuers have come to see you." The curator's color was better today than it had been, and she looked rested, but still tired.

The medics had said she'd lost about as much blood as a human being can without dying.

Lyn Chow opened her eyes, looked at us, and smiled wearily. "Thank you, Reebie." The head end of the bed began to tilt upward, probably by implant command. "Please sit down, Eichra Oren, Sam. This fellow is Helmore Bracken, Chairman of the Directors' Council for the Otherworld Museum. Helmore, these are Eichra Oren, the famous p'Nan debt assessor and his colleague Sam. Handsome rescuers indeed. Would any of you like something to…drink?" That much conversation seemed to have worn her out. We declined. Eichra Oren found a chair. I looked around the room.

"We hate disturbing you so soon, Lyn Chow," the boss said. "But we need some questions answered, the first being who attacked you and why."

"We were just discussing that," Bracken answered. "It has always seemed unnecessary and absurd to me to have such a security camera system. Who, after all, would think of robbing a museum, especially one as…esoteric as ours? But it seems that I was wrong. And it appears that the darkness limited the usefulness of the museum's system."

"Because the system was so damned cheap," observed Lyn Chow.

Bracken cleared his throat but didn't reply.

Rebul added, "Which is probably why the intruders, whoever they were, were careful to open up the circuit breakers, putting out all the lights. During a power failure, opaque black is the security default mode for the museum's polarized outer shell and office partitions."

"You're certain there was more than one intruder?" I asked.

Bracken answered, "Almost certain. It appears that too many things were happening in the place at one time to be the work of a single individual."

"Like what?" Eichra Oren wanted to know.

Lyn Chow stirred, "The cameras can see into the infrared…"

"They didn't take anything," said Bracken. "They didn't break anything but the front door. But it appears that they were everywhere, examining everything. Whatever they wanted, I don't think they found it."

Lyn Chow insisted weakly, "The cameras…infrared…"

Eichra Oren got out of his chair and approached the injured woman. "What about those cameras, Lyn Chow, what is it you're trying to tell us?"

"I get it," I said. "She's trying to say her guests weren't hot enough to register in the infrared." Several sapient species are not warm-blooded.

"Yes," sighed Lyn Chow with obvious relief. "Yes."

Bracken looked as if he were feeling her pain. "It's clear, my dear, that we are wearing you out. If you don't mind, I'll speak my piece, then go away and let you rest." He stood, tugged on his clothing as if to make it fit better, and addressed my boss. "Eichra Oren, to suffer this outrage, this indignity, is simply unsupportable. The other members of the Directors' Council and I discussed this through the night, and have come to a conclusion. With the consent and approval of our Curator, it is our wish to engage you professionally in this matter."

"By which you mean..." Eichra Oren let it dangle.

"Discover who these people are, make them aware of the moral debt they have incurred, and persuade them, as you p'Nan Assessors do, to pay."

The boss looked down at Lyn Chow. "And this is all right with you?" She nodded.

"Very well, then," he said. "I have another client, another investigation I'm committed to; I don't see why we can't handle them together."

The number of alternative universes, or alternate realities, if you prefer, contained within a theoretically vastly greater super-universe of all there is, is considered infinite by the few physicists and philosophers conversant with the topic. I think there may be eleven.

The same physicists, and some of the philosophers—you know philosophers—recognize three laws with regard to alternative universes. First, whatever universe you happen to inhabit, you perceive it as "most normal"—representing the highest probability—from which all other universes, to a greater or lesser degree, diverge.

Second, all of the traits, attributes, characteristics, and so on, that make your universe seem unique, are distributed, throughout the other universes, along a sort of five-dimensional bell or "normal" curve.

Pretty hard to imagine.

Third, the relative difficulty—for which read the amount of energy necessary—of getting from your universe to any other is a measure of how far away that other universe happens to be from the bright center of "normality" that your universe represents. To put it another way, the less likely a universe appears to be—the lower the probability of its existence—the more energy it requires to get there.

In the universe that Eichra Oren's people originally came from, this has come to be known, by the descendants of those *H. sapiens* who were not rescued by the unethical Elders, but simply survived the deluge, as "Williamson's Law", after the philosopher who postulated it.

There is a "universe next door" that may vary from yours only in the placement of a single grain of sand on some alien beach somewhere, light-years away from the planet your species evolved on. (In fact, nobody knows what creating such a divergence requires.) But in that universe, an individual exactly like you is living a life exactly like yours.

You probably wouldn't like him much.

Law three-and-a-half is all about character. If you tend to "go with the flow", live your life like the little ball in a pinball machine, driven from point to point solely by external forces, then it's likelier that the "you next door" will be somewhat different from the one you know, his character having been formed—molded—by his reactions to purely random events over the decades, or by the acts of others.

However, if you make your own way through life, directed by a strong, internally consistent and purposive nature, then there will be more individuals out there—more different versions of you—along the bell curve, in a wider range of positions, who are identifiably you-like. Go a little further out on the curve, in any direction, and that otherworld version of yourself employs his other hand to write, or likes a different kind of cheese, of has differently colored eyes, or died in childbirth, or in a veek collision, or—well, you get the picture.

Relatively minor variations.

Further out, and the person in that universe who is most like you, living in your space and time, is a simian of some sort. Or perhaps a sapient avian-dinosauroid like Aelbraugh Pritsch. Even further out, and it's a sapient elephantoid with three trunks and a prehensile tail.

Pushing it to the ridiculous, say to an alternative universe where the dominant species on Earth are cream cheese bagels, requires more energy to reach than even the Elders are capable of generating. By comparison, most of the worlds they have collected sapients from over a thousand millennia are of roughly the same degree of probability as theirs.

All of this was uppermost in my mind as Eichra Oren and I stood at the doors of what was probably the oddest restaurant on the planet. Several planets, as a matter of fact. The customers' road machinery in the parking lot looked a lot like the kind of equipment employed to refinish ceilings, or decorate a *jai alai fronton* for the holidays. It was clearly built for tall individuals incapable of sitting down. As with all public establishments in the Elders' version of reality, a small device over the doorway generated a simple, tasteful sign in the mind's eye of anybody nearby who had a computer thumbtacked to his forebrain.

PRELBISH SOLATARIAN RESTAURANT

Neither of us had an idea who or what a Prelbish was. We'd guessed about the "solatarian". The boss had put on a pair of dark sunglasses in preparation for the coming ordeal. So had I—we'd had to pick them up at a specialty shop on the way here. I thought I looked like a cartoon.

Now we passed through the door to be greeted by a…headwaiter? A tall person with whiskers that made me jealous and extremely short brown-gray fur. He was descended, I suspected, from naked mole rats. The guy was very polite and wore a tailcoat, probably to cover up his tail.

I wondered if he was Prelbish.

Or maybe *a* Prelbish.

Before I could use my implant to look him or this Prelbish up, he spoke. "May I assist you, gentlebeings?" he asked through the vocal synthesizer in his lapel. "We don't get a lot of humanoids in here, nor canines, for that matter. Which one is the symbiote, if one may ask?"

"One may," I stepped in before the boss could reply. "On the other paw, one may not necessarily expect an answer that one will regard as satisfying."

The not-so-naked mole rat superciliated at us and started to look indignant, but Eichra Oren spoiled the effect. "We're expected," he said. "we're here for lunch with Llossure Knarrvite, in a manner of speaking."

"Ah!" replied the maître d'hôtel or whatever. At least the guy recovered quickly. "In that case, please come with me." He had an odd, rolling gait that had me revising my first guess. Probably an otter of some kind. I was grateful that at least he didn't ask us to "walk this way".

Whatever he happened to be, we followed him into a main "dining" area that somehow managed to feel as big as the whole outdoors. Even with my silly sunglasses, the light inside the place was blindingly bright. The entire top of the building was transparent—consisting of a single gigantic lens of the kind that's engraved with thousands of concentric grooves—and concentrated light from the sun and sky onto the strange room's hundreds of occupants eighty or ninety feet below.

In the center of the room stood a forty-foot conical structure, entirely covered with mirrors reflecting the roof light to the room's walls. These slanted backward, like a square-sectioned funnel, or an inside-out pyramid and had moveable reflective surfaces, so that every square inch of the place provided light that might otherwise have gone to waste. Meanwhile, more than a hundred heavy air cooling vents and misting conduits kept the whole place from turning into a giant solar cooker.

No sense, I thought, in baking the paying customers.

Not surprisingly, the establishment smelled like a greenhouse or hydroponics setup. There was music of the variety some people call "classical" playing throughout the room. I remembered reading somewhere that plants supposedly grow healthier listening to boring stuff like that. Dark "resting rooms" said a sign, were available for a modest fee. I also remembered reading that periods without light are as important for plants as taking in all the photons possible at other times.

Down the back wall, a broad artificial waterfall poured itself into the gravel-covered floor, providing just enough white noise for private conversation. Behind the water there was an especially private dining room. Making a tweety racket of their own, dozens of brightly colored birds flew in and out of windows set below the lensatic ceiling. Nobody seemed to object the way they would have in any other restaurant.

The headwaiter turned a palm, indicating what could have been a potted plant nearby. "Gentlebeings, my esteemed employer will see you now."

CHAPTER TWELVE

"Aphidsss..."

DESPITE THE MIRRORS AND FANCY COLORED BIRDS, IT WAS the room's occupants, including the weasel's esteemed employer, that caught the eye.

In any other first class eatery, the place might be decorated with trees in buckets and other kinds of plants. Frankly, I never got it—unless it was a speciesist joke on sapient dogs like me. Here, it was the customers themselves who were the decoration. They all seemed to stand, each of them, alone or in little bunches, beside small-topped tables four or five feet high, on which their personal effects were placed. They clearly weren't meant for food or drink; that was coming, in effect, down through the transparent ceiling and up through the floor.

Every one of the restaurant's customers was green, for the most part, although some appeared to be entertaining non-chlorophyll-bearing guests. What served their planty species as legs, torsos, and arms—what you or I might otherwise refer to as their trunks, stems, and branches—were thoroughly green, slightly fuzzy like a hollyhock, and jarringly asymmetrical in their arrangement. The restaurant patrons' multiple-toed "feet" tended to be brown and a trifle scaly, what you could see of them, that is. The solatarian diners' heads—one to a customer—appeared to consist of gigantic blossoms, big yellow petals and all, and looked exactly like outsized rubbery sunflowers.

To be precise, these were the world-famous (this world, anyway) *Helianthus sapiens russellii*—I'd keyed my implant the instant we'd entered the enormous room—not the only folk from the veggie kingdom in the Elders' vast collection of thinking beings, just the most spectacular, with blossom centers varying from greenish to dark brown, like black-eyed susans, and no visible optical organs, which was somehow even more disturbing than their utter lack of bilateral symmetry.

There was no way to avoid the fact that they were plants, each about nine feet tall. There weren't any kiddies visible, because their offspring are sessile, deeply rooted in the ground, until they reach maturity, which is marked by a ceremonial rite of passage in which they uproot themselves, to the delight of their adoring friends and families.

The flower beings here were soaking up concentrated sunlight while their toes—their roots—were thrust deeply into fine hydroponic gravel, punctuated here and there by stepping stones for those among us who didn't wish to soak our toes. Some of the patrons had trays on the floor at their feet, containing special nutrients. I had been informed that they enjoyed absorbing molasses into their systems for much the same reason that most mammals enjoy consuming alcoholic beverages.

Every sapient species that the Elders have discovered employs some form of intoxicant; it's one of a very few rules of alternity that you can totally rely on. Most individuals get tired of running their big brains after a while. Running them at all often seems to be too much work for many, which explains a great deal about the politics of other universes.

I wondered where the petalled crowd kept their brains.

As I'd observed, there was music playing. All plants seem to like music, supposedly preferring the classics to anything else. So all of those children's science projects I'd read about were true, after all. But once a species achieves sapience, tastes and opinions begin to vary. I'd heard about private clubs—"underground" or "seedy" might not be the best choice of words in this particular context—where social deviants called "sports" stood around listening to jazz or bluegrass.

You wouldn't think it possible, to look at these flowering folk at the moment, but by the time the Elders Appropriated a sample of them, they had pulled themselves up by their rootstraps and become mobile beings. They had also invented science and technology, gone through several cycles of empire-building and collapse, enjoyed a couple of serious industrial revolutions, constructed spaceships better than the Elders' ever had, to visit most of the planets and planetoids in their version of our Solar System, and had even sent an expedition to the stars.

It hadn't come back yet, but they remained hopeful.

Stepping from stone to stone—they had not been laid out to suit quadrupeds—the boss and I had found our way to Llossure Knarrvite, the manager of the place. On a little private table toward the back, near the artificial waterfall, he (or she) had set a small, smoldering bowl of something—incense of some kind, maybe—over which, from time to time, she (or he) would hold a broad, leafy "arm", or even lower his (or her) flowery head, taking in the smoke with obvious satisfaction.

Eichra Oren stepped up. "I greet you, Llossure Knarrvite. I am Eichra Oren, certified P'Nan debt assessor. My associate Sam called you?"

"Ahh, yesss," a rather strange voice answered him. It seemed to emanate from the table rather than from the flower-being who stood beside it. "You're the famouss fellow with the sssword. Your mother isss Eneri Relda. I have often been to her home and heard all about you."

"That's gratifying," Eichra Oren answered dubiously, no doubt with sentimental likenesses of himself as an infant, lying on a caterpillar rug, going through his mind. "I hope. You told my associate that you'd speak with us concerning your employer, Meerltchirt of the Fronzeln Zirnaath?"

"Partner," Lossure Knarrvite corrected him. "Each of usss owns a third of the busssinesss, a remaining third held by a consssortium of reptiloidsss who function, for the mossst part, asss our sssilent partnersss."

Eichra Oren nodded. "My apologies." Of course the boss had done his homework and knew perfectly well what the arrangement was, but taking correction from an interviewee was a debt assessor's standard method of engaging a subject. "Your partner's missing and his family worries."

The plant being jiggled all over, and at first I interpreted it as flowery laughter, but I've been wrong before and doubtless will be again.

"You mean he'sss hiding, and that fiansssee of his worries—that ssshe might misss a meal. I worry, too, sssir. The water quality isssn't what it hasss been. I sssussspect our mineral and molasssesss sssupplierss are ssshorting us. The ssstaff is threatening to go on ssstrike for ssshorter hoursss—asss if two a day were burdensssome. There are billsss to be paid at the end of the ten-day and payroll to meet. I find mysssself ssshort-tendriled, without Meerltchirt to help me."

Eichra Oren nodded in apparent sympathy, while I actually felt for him.

Or her.

Or it.

The plain, unvarnished truth—which no customer I ever heard of truly appreciates—is that, no matter where you go, no matter who or what you serve, the restaurant business is the hardest in the entire multiverse. Whoever can make a success of it is to be respected and perhaps even admired. Whoever said that cooking is the kindliest of the arts was absolutely right. And in many ways, it's also the most heartbreaking.

But by previous agreement, I let Eichra Oren do all the talking, here, maybe on account of the longstanding antipathy, at least in folklore, between tall plants and dogs. There: I said it myself; my implants are speciesists. On the other tendril, the incense or whatever it was that the manager was burning, was about to make me sneeze.

It seemed to be giving Lossure Knarrvite a bit of a buzz.

"How very sentimental of you," said the boss. "So you have no idea where your partner is?" I watched him scrutinizing the big daisy. He's usually good at sensing whether a subject is telling him the truth or not, but whatever signs he was looking for now, they were completely beyond me. I wondered what life must be like for a species whose faces were also their reproductive organs; would they be good at poker or terrible? Sometimes my nose can help detect fear and stress hormones, but the creature smelled like a freshly-cut lawn. Maybe it was just aftershave.

It might help to know what sex it was. I keyed my implant, to consult a reference system I use frequently. It compared what I was seeing with the records it maintained and informed me that Lossure Knarrvite was a he. It also confirmed that molasses was an intoxicant to his people. He was enjoying the equivalent of a three martini lunch.

Suddenly: "Aphidsss!" our host screamed at the top of his vocal synthesizer. Vibrating all over, he flailed his stems and leaves in all directions. "Aphidsss! Get them off me! Get them off me! Pleassse help!"

Somebody at a nearby table shouted, "What are you animals *doing* to him?" Every flower-person in the restaurant turned to look our way—as weird a sight as you can imagine. "Aphidsss", I gathered, were the equivalent of rats or cockroaches to these folk. Although there wasn't an insect anywhere in sight—except for a few of the help, of course—several dozen patrons uprooted themselves and began to leave.

That wasn't the bad part. A few dozen more—mostly non-veggie folk of six or seven different species—began converging on us with circulatory fluid in their eyes, or whatever they used see with. I didn't have time to wonder why so many of the non-photosynthetic persuasion were taking in the sun here today. All that was apparent at the moment were a lot of clenched fists, extended claws, and low growls.

Suddenly the whole pack was on us, arthropods of two or three species, arachnids, a praying mantis thing, a bird that was like a dinosauroid, only yellow, nine feet tall, with a long beak, and a small being who looked like a round, rubbery dog toy, purple, with little points sticking out. There were even a couple of reptiles and mammals.

One of those, like a bear in silk pajamas, reached for the pommel of Eichra Oren's sword, and the fight was on, our assailants squirting out all kinds of battle stenches, fighting pheromones, bristles, thorns, and nasty, poisonous spit. The purple thing was the worst, spraying sticky thread around everywhere. Before the mammalian could touch his sword, the boss took that paw in one hand, lifted its elbow with the other, bent it back toward the being's head, and slapped him on the ear with it. The bear emitted an excruciating howl and backed off.

Which, unfortunately, opened the way for something like a desert scorpion, six feet tall. As it snapped a deadly saw-toothed pincer, missing my boss by a hair, I jumped up onto the little table, then over its mouthparts to its back, and got my jaws locked around an eyestalk.

It tasted like lobster, insufficiently cooked.

As other things were battling Eichra Oren and each other to get near us, the scorpion made noises like the world's whole supply of corn popping, and forgot him, struggling now to reach me where I hung with all the strength in my jaws onto its eyestalk. It jabbed at me repeatedly with the great sting in its tail, enough poison in its fist-sized gland to kill a thousand dogs. But it had to be careful, because it wasn't immune to its own venom. I flopped around like a windsock in a hurricane. But the desperately flailing crustacean's arms were short and it didn't have enough elbows. It couldn't reach me.

Eichra Oren touched a section of its underbelly with a pair of gentle fingers. It collapsed like a toy and I rode it down to the floor. At the same time, a reptiloid tried to wrap its four-foot tongue, edged with tiny, sharp teeth, around the boss's neck, but another light touch discouraged it. It scuttled from the big room screaming.

As it sometimes will in an adrenaline-soaked moment, time seemed to stand still. Drinks, upset, sprayed crystalline droplets into the air, where they appeared to hang motionless for minutes, the glasses themselves turning over and over slowly. I snarled and barked but couldn't seem to hear myself, although our adversaries got wide-eyed at my threat-display. Eichra Oren's usually blinding speed became slow motion.

The boss was fully into his combat trance now, tunnel-visioned and seeing in monochrome, shades of red, oblivious to anything or anyone but the fight about him. I'd seen him this way before. I almost envied him, although I knew that he would pay later for what he was expending now.

It was an ancient Antarctican martial discipline, analogous to acupuncture and other meridian-related medicines, but intended to create the opposite effect, to inflict pain rather than relieve it, produce injuries rather than heal them, and, if need be, to end life rather than extend it. It had been rediscovered many times in fifteen thousand years, but in most civilizations it was still suppressed and forbidden.

We found ourselves surrounded now by members of a species I had never seen before, hairless, short, dull-colored, vaguely humanoid, with big, wide hands, fat, stubby thumbs, and two very large, dark eyes.

Eichra Oren shut one of those eyes with a pair of knuckles, then he whirled, reached out for another's hands—both of them—and when he let go, the fingers were somehow braided together. Making weird gurgling noises, the thing struggled frantically to untangle them. The third humanoid walked into a heel and instep under the chin from the boss's sidekick, and when the one he'd half-blinded groped for Eichra Oren, I seized the calf of its leg in my teeth and bore down.

But what kind of a humanoid mammal bleeds green and tastes like a can of long-dead fishing worms? I remembered to look them up later. They call themselves Makapps, and they're not humanoids. They're not mammals. In fact, they aren't even vertebrates, but a bit more like something from somewhere closer to the cream cheese bagel end of the spectrum.

As quickly as it had started, the fight was over. The opposition sublimated like dry ice on a summer day. Members of the restaurant staff arrived, along with the weaseloid greeter, from wherever they'd been hiding. They all gave us an amazing range of multi-species dirty looks, as if what happened had somehow been our fault, picked up the still-convulsing manager—they'd shut the guy up, somehow, but I was highly disinclined to ask any questions—and hustled him away somewhere.

I wondered if this kind of thing happened very often.

In all the excitement, nobody but yours truly appeared to notice Eichra Oren as he stooped quickly, dipped a tiny transparent evidence vial into the plant-creature's tray of happy-hour molasses, screwed the little top on, and, standing, slipped it into a tunic pocket.

He also took a sample of the unburned incense.

"I think we're done here," he told me, and we found our own way out.

"What the Hammer was all about?" I demanded.

I'd loosened a tooth on that scorpion thing.

CHAPTER THIRTEEN

Unnatural History

"BEFORE YOU ASK, SAM, I DIDN'T TAKE A SAMPLE OF THE water, because it was circulating freely through the gravel, and nobody else seemed affected."

If we'd just emerged from any other restaurant where a brawl like that had occurred, we'd have been covered with mashed potatoes and gravy, broiled baby carrots, cauliflower in cheese sauce, and slices of standing rib of some critter or other. As it was, I'd gotten a bit of molasses on my feet, which the boss had been concerned that I wash off.

Eichra Oren stepped into the veek and let the canopy roll over our heads. It was still raining lightly, and by now, I was getting more than a little tired of it. It was famously sunny, warm, and dry where we lived. Weren't the Elders supposed to have control over the blasted weather?

"I had that figured, Boss. What do you expect to find in those samples?"

He settled back into his seat as the canopy closed and the drying commenced. "If I knew, I wouldn't have had to take them, would I? It's unprofessional to speculate ahead of any analysis. Would you care to drive?"

That had been unexpected. "You're serious?"

"You did a pretty good job earlier, under much worse conditions. And the veek's AI will help you. Besides, I've got something else to do."

I said, "To hear is to obey."

"Yeah, right," he replied. "You're known for that."

I linked my mind to the veek's controls, and we were off. The rest of the way, Eichra Oren occupied himself with a cybertutorial that he'd discovered, built into the little weapon his mother had given him, linking it directly to his implant. From time to time he nodded or grunted as he finger-fiddled with the thing in a way that made me nervous. After all, I'd seen the bite it had taken out of that big veek.

And there was that garden wall Eneri Relda had mentioned.

"Absolutely not!" the giant being said, and he meant it.

For now. Eichra Oren had only been working on him for three minutes.

My boss said nothing. Apparently he was willing to let a brief period of silence do the bargaining for him. It should be especially helpful with a being like this, descended from a long line of colony animals. I looked around at signs of millions of years of genetic history.

The plant-people's restaurant had been so sunny and bright you almost couldn't stand it. This place was the exact opposite. Check the listing in your implant for "gloomy" and there should be a picture of where we were sitting at the moment, under a parabolic ceiling that merged imperceptibly—even if there had been enough light to see it—with the walls on either side. To make things even worse, both walls and ceiling were upholstered in what appeared to be thick brown felt.

Acoustically, it felt like we'd been buried.

"In any case," said the giant, unnecessarily, betraying the fact that the boss was starting to get to him. "I don't have authority. And my co-investors would never agree to violating the terms that we all contractually—"

"You and your co-investors weren't given all the pertinent facts when you signed that contract. Now you know more, and your obligation as a professional advocate is to protect the interests of your fellow investors." He didn't actually say "professional advocate", but used a one-word term in the fellow's own language that described a position almost as complicated as the one he occupied himself, as a p'Nan Debt Assessor.

The guy mulled it over. I'd have expected him to retort that his obligations as a professional advocate were none of Eichra Oren's damn business, but the being was neither human nor canine, so all bets were off.

"What you say is true enough…" the fellow began.

Evolution is a funny thing. I suppose to someone like one of those flower folks, or a mollusc like Misterthoggosh, all mammals must seem pretty much alike—fast, furry, bi- or quadrupedal, filled to the brim with smoking hot red blood—though my ancient ancestors were wolves, the boss descends from a long line of monkeys (I love thinking about that), and the person sitting before us now was…I'll get to him in just a minute. In the end, we all come from Permian-era animals called cynodonts that actually preceded the dinosaurs that they ended up skittering away and hiding from for the next couple hundred million years.

As for the creature whose office this was—a member of a species that called itself *Famensed Tanoh*—he reminded me of nothing so much as the so-called star-nosed mole. Unlike his probable ancestors, he was very large, at least two heads taller than Eichra Oren, even sitting down behind a big desk of vegetable ivory, beautifully inlaid with decorative strips of mahogany. As broad as two Eichra Orens, he was covered with thick short fur, rather like a seal's. I couldn't see the lower half of his body; the upper half was startling, to say the least.

To begin with, his front legs or arms or whatever looked like they hadn't come to work today with the rest of him, but had stayed home sick. They were tiny, vestigial, like those of a Tyrannosaurus, two pairs of claws held before him on his chest, not unlike that of a begging puppy.

Other features made them difficult to see. Nobody knows what T. Rex's front limbs were for; they were too short for anything, even to groom his teeth. But this worthy whose name was Hyppod Zart, didn't suffer any lack of manipulative ability. Below his eyes, surrounding his nose, he sported eleven pairs (I consulted my implant record later) of…well, call them tentacles, somewhere between two and three feet long. It says here they evolved from shorter but similar organs of touch and smell among his presapient ancestors, to become a bizarre sort of compromise between an elephant's trunk and humanoid hands.

Hyppod (it was his surname) expressed grave trepidations—that's what wildly-flailing tentacles were supposed to mean—with regard to what Eichra Oren was asking him to do. My boss had briefed me on the way here, and we'd expected nothing less. The *Famensed Tanoh* are a naturally trepidatious people for whom to reach out for something is exactly the same as thrusting your face—and the eyes and brain that lie directly behind it—straight into whatever it is you're curious about.

As a direct evolutionary consequence (one theory, anyway—mine) they are not great innovators or inventors. Most of them live quietly and conservatively, happy to avoid changes and other forms of excitement. I'd read that half of them had died from the shock of Appropriation.

And yet, the highly circumspect Hyppod and the large consortium of *Famensed Tanoh* of which he was the Chairman (okay, his actual title in Famensed Tanohian, or whatever, was more like "Burrowmaster of the Investment Warren of Greater Kiflivopuws"), were among the heaviest financial angels of whatever mischief Misterthoggosh happened to be up to.

"Look at it this way," Eichra Oren told Hyppod. "If this project turns out the way I think it may, and you and your associates withhold vital information about it, you could all be helping to accrue one of the greatest moral debts in the history of sapience, with concomitant economic consequences that could easily prove impossible to recover from."

If Hyppod had been wearing a collar, and had possessed fingers, he would have nervously stuck one of the latter into the former to loosen it. He tilted his head forward a few degrees and ran his tentacles through his vestigial claws. So that's what they were for: tentacle grooming.

"Yes, well, er..." He squinted at the boss. I don't think the Famensed Tanoh could see very well, although this one was wearing spectacles.

"Exactly," said Eichra Oren, brightening, and pretending to have extracted meaning from all that mumble. "On the other hand, if you help me, you may even be able to get your money back. Some of it, anyway."

The boss knew when he'd gotten as far as he could for the nonce. He rose. I hopped down to the floor. "You think it over, Hyppod. Talk with your co-investors." In groups, they were even more risk-averse. "I'll get back to you in a few days—provided we have enough time left."

Our next stop, as it turned out, was home. The veek knew the way from long-established habit. I hardly had anything to do. Eichra Oren took his samples to a small but well-equipped laboratory he maintains on the ground level. I lay on the ivory floor outside the door where I could watch and listen to him work as I perused the data networks via implant.

I was looking for publicly accessible knowledge with regard to the Elder Misterthoggosh. The records were dismayingly sparse, but then I'd expected that. The Elders—and everybody who grows up around them, in their world—have a strong tendency to value their personal and business privacy more than almost anything, except for freedom itself.

There were no vast administrative archives, for example, of unique biological markers—DNA, fingerprints, tentacle patterns, retinal photographs, voice comparisons, brain waves—like those I've heard about in other civilizations. Not only was there nobody to do it, the merest attempt to create one would have been met with immediate violence and, if absolutely necessary, bloodshed, which represents a formidable threat among beings who commonly live for thousands of years.

But aside from general principles involving privacy and freedom, the Elders have their own special reasons, rooted in their peculiar biology.

And I agree with them.

Half a billion years ago, in what cultures in some universes call the Cambrian period, the first nautiloids made their appearance upon the Forge of Adversity—the cruel world we live in, that strengthens us while it does its best to kill us. For some reason peculiar to only a small handful of alternative realities, these creatures—simple but promising marine molluscs resembling a squid in an ice cream cone—evolved relatively quickly into the giants they are today, with enormous coiled shells, long tentacles, and exceptionally powerful minds.

Nautiloids have a great deal in common anatomically with ammonites—fossil critters killed off in most universes when the Hammer came down sixty-five million years ago—which they closely resemble, as well as with various squid and octopi, to whom they are also related. One thing they have in common with the octopus was—and remains to this day—the peculiar and unlikely manner in which they "make love".

When a male and female Elder "get together", they may not even be in the same room. Or in the same town. Instead...now how can this be put delicately? The male mollusc does something that Eichra Oren says his mother's contemporaries used to tell their male offspring would make them go blind—or grow hair on their palms. (Although if they were blind, then they couldn't see the hair on their palms, so why worry about it? And maybe they could only do it until they needed glasses.)

But I digress.

The Elders and their evolutionary relatives (I refrain from saying "on the other hand") then do something even weirder. The tentacle in which they've...well, let's say, "invested their hopes", is a very special one, capable of separating itself from their bodies. I'm told that it doesn't hurt, but quite the contrary, is the equivalent of...well, never mind. It then swims to the lady, bearing his message of love.

Among their octopi relatives, that tentacle, having achieved its all-important mission, withers and dies, and another one eventually grows back. But with the Elders, the thing swims home and reattaches itself.

Over tens of millions of years, the Elders' precursor species, being a bit large and ponderous (although they can fill the unused portions of their shells with, well, not air, exactly, achieve neutral buoyancy, and ride around surprisingly well on a water jet), learned to control this increasingly useful separable tentacle and to dispatch it on missions that didn't necessarily involve making more little nautiloids.

It seems they had evolved a specialized kind of cell—analogous to the specialized cells used by electric eels to fight off predators, some fish for navigational purposes, and other fish for coordinating the school they swim in—that allowed them to send instructions to their separable tentacles, and receive information back from them, as well. Organic radio, low frequency, low bandwidth—that's what works underwater.

As with many another evolutionary advance, there are drawbacks, or at least trade-offs. Eichra Oren, lovely Lornis, and other humanoid creatures like them often experience severe back problems resulting from an erect posture that they haven't fully evolved into yet. As they grow older, their internal organs tend to shift downward, as well.

Gravity: it's not a pretty thing.

The Elders' ancestors almost lost themselves as individual beings because, owing to their developing ability to guide their separable tentacles by remote control, they gradually lost whatever mental privacy they'd ever had. And yet they were by no means evolved to live within a hive-mind, like termites or ants. It looked very much like they'd encountered an evolutionary dead end. Suicide and insanity of various kinds became epidemic among them and the species nearly died out.

But then some genius managed to get himself lost, far away from his fellow molluscs, while herding squid, or whatever ancient Elders did for a living. Maybe he just fell into "dark territory" between undersea mountains. In any case, he rediscovered his privacy. Why he didn't die right there from the shock of the experience, nobody can say. There are a lot of Elder myths and legends about the whole silly saga.

As soon as he got back, of course, all his fellow molluscs knew about his discovery After a couple of civil wars over it—between weaklings and parasites who liked mental communism and those to whom the whole idea had become repulsive—technical means were developed, beginning with homes that were Faraday cages, and with metallic...headgear for traveling, to protect one's thoughts from one's fellow beings.

A million years passed.

Employing what we would now call gene therapy, eventually each Elder's communications with his separable tentacle were encoded, using his genetic pattern, and a truly individualistic civilization was born among the sapient nautiloids, ensuring peace, freedom, progress, and prosperity—as long as nobody else knows your personal secret gene code.

A couple hundred million years passed while they tried to get it right.

When the Elders discovered (or finally acknowledged) their hideous ethical mistake, in having Appropriated thousands of other sapients from alternate universes, and before the guilty parties committed suicide out of moral chagrin, they made what is still called the Great Restitution.

They couldn't imagine getting along every day without their handy separable tentacles, so they created equivalent conveniences for those they felt they'd wronged. Dinosauroids have little lizards living in their feathers when they aren't fetching and carrying. Marine critters like Ray (not to mention various dolphinoid species) are accompanied by pairs of nonsapient squid they use as ten-fingered hands. All of these auxiliary creatures, known as symbiotes, are communicated to and communicate back via electronics implanted in their nervous systems at birth.

I am Eichra Oren's separable tentacle.

CHAPTER FOURTEEN

Test Tube Truth

"EUREKA!" CAME THE BOSS'S VOICE FROM THE OTHER ROOM.
I'd moved back into the office because I didn't like the smells coming from the laboratory. Out here, the house got to them before they got to me and tidily did away with them somehow. Meanwhile, night had fallen, and, as some local blossoms closed and others opened, the whole character of the outdoor odors coming from both land and sea had changed completely, a phenomenon that many humanoids never seem to notice.

"Very sorry, Boss," I quipped. "I could go take a shower."

"Clown!" But he had said it with a chuckle.

Our only real client had called while the boss was slaving away over a hot Erlenmeyer flask. She was more interested in talking to him than to me—they always are, no matter what species they are—but I let her know that we'd been to see her fiancé's bepetalled business partner.

I didn't mention the partner collapsing while we were talking to him, although it was probably all over the public networks by now. Still, we had nothing to indicate whether it was relevant to the case or not. Nor did I mention we were planning to see the fiancé's family tomorrow. I never like to tell a client what I'm *going* to do.

Plans change, and simple things can get complicated when you try to explain them.

My educated guess, which I did not share with the client was that Meerltchirt of the Fronzeln Zirnaath's family was simply hiding him out somewhere, and we'd be finished with this case sometime tomorrow. Or maybe he had already skedaddled (a splendid expression I'd heard, courtesy of Misterthoggosh and company, on a video broadcast from some other universe and liked) and we would never actually be through with the case, and have to be satisfied with getting reimbursed for our expenses.

No way to run a business, at all.

Despite good transportation and even better communication, it's still a great big world out there. To begin with, there are five whole other continents—the one directly to the south of us across the Inland Sea, the pair across the Lesser Ocean, the one toward the south of the Greater Ocean, and the frozen one at the bottom of the planet, where Eichra Oren and his folks had come from in an alternate reality. They're all smaller than the really big continent we happen to live on, on a giant peninsula, way down in the southwestern corner. We also had an appointment tomorrow with Ray, of Ray's Salvage, who was going to show us what he'd found where Eichra Oren had shot that missile-slinging flyer down. I kept expecting moral repercussions—somebody else's p'Nan debt assessor swinging his sword our way—but so far, at least, nobody had inquired, which struck me as extremely strange.

"Eureka? No, not you, Sam." Eichra Oren stood in the doorway, his face-protecting visor tilted back, stripping off his thin, translucent gloves so they finished inside-out. "Although, the individual most famous for having said it was sitting in a bathtub at the time. It's a word from my own universe, spoken in an ancient human Successor Tongue from a period in which mathematics and science were being slowly rediscovered after the world turned upside-down and the Continent was Lost."

"Epic," I said sarcastically. "And it means?"

"It means, 'I have found it!'"

That rang a bell—or tweaked a synapse. "Good old Archimedes of Syracuse. I remember now. I've watched several of Misterthoggosh's imported videos about that guy. Some historians believe that he invented a death ray. If he did, he should have used it on that Roman soldier and then gotten back to his work. And what is it that you've found?"

Eichra Oren took his visor off, handling it with the gloves, then wiped sweat off on a sleeve from where the headband had been. Not good laboratory procedure. Sometimes I wished that I could sweat like humans. He then removed his lab smock, bundled it with the other gear and tossed it at a chute, where the house would clean what could be cleaned and recycle the rest. Finally, he threw himself down, not into his desk chair, but onto a sofa under a window. He let the house bring him a drink through the arm of the couch, and indulged in his one rare vice, lighting a cigar.

Our cerebrocortical implants, both of them, chose that precise moment to go off inside our respective heads. It's never a comfortable feeling. Apparently the mole investor's "a few days" had somehow been shrunk to a few hours. As I hopped up into Eichra Oren's desk chair and assented to answer the call, an image of the caller formed in my mind.

"Hullo," he said, mentally squinting at my image in his head. The custom, whenever possible, was to look at yourself in a mirror as you talked, so the other party could see what you saw. Most desks, and some other furniture, were appropriately equipped with mirrors that folded away.

In his image, his eyes were so tiny that they would almost have been invisible if it hadn't been for the bottle-thick spectacles he wore. The *Famensed Tanoh* senses of smell, taste, and touch are famously unrivalled among this reality's Appropriated Persons, but their unassisted vision is virtually worthless. I wondered if the creature was somehow smelling, tasting, or touching me through his electronic communication system. The thought of it gave me cold chills.

"Hyppod Zart, here," the strange being reintroduced himself unnecessarily. His voice seemed more cheerful than might have been expected, but his face tentacles or nose trunks or whatever writhed in a way, or so my implant advised me, that in his species betrayed great nervousness. "Burrowmaster of the Investment Warren of Greater Kiflivopuws. I assume that I am addressing Eichra Oren, the p'Navian Assessor?"

So in addition to being nearly blind—his use of a mirror was a courtesy—he couldn't smell or taste or touch remotely, after all. A relief, although I wondered exactly what he was getting out of this conversation. The species' hearing seemed to be okay, which made sense.

"No, sir, Mr. Hyppod, sir. You're addressing his trustworthy, loyal, helpful, friendly, courteous, kind, obedient, cheerful, thrifty, brave, clean, and reverent assistant, Oasam Otusam." I had no idea where all that came from; something about these people—or maybe it was just him—inexplicably seemed to put me on edge. I glanced over to where Eichra Oren was sitting, in lurk mode, watching and listening, without mirror. He nodded at me, so I went on. "Eichra Oren is indisposed at the moment. Is there some way that I may be of help?"

Hyppod considered. "You're the man's companion, aren't you? His symbiote? His separable tentacle? And yet you're a sapient in your own right?"

My turn to nod. "Entirely by accident, I assure you. Somebody got a little careless with the gene-bashing, way back when. Call me his familiar—*Canis familiaris*—that's me, all over. Now how may I help?"

"Shrews," he muttered, more to himself than to me. "All we got was shrews." As if on cue, one of the little creatures poked its nose out from under his armpit, then skittered down across his broad chest and disappeared behind the desk. It was quickly followed by two more. He bent forward, seized all three in his face-fingers, and put them in a pocket.

Life is very odd. "You were saying, Mr. Hyppod?"

Still hesitant, the big frilly-puss finally got it out. "Please inform him that we—the Investment Warren of Greater Kiflivopuws, that is—have conferred. We would like to engage his professional services as a debt assessor, not only to assess any moral debt that we may be accruing in our business undertakings with Misterthoggosh, but to investigate his activities and report to us with regard to their ethicality."

For once I was grateful that my eyebrows are invisible. As it was, I could feel them dancing around somewhere toward the back of my neck. "Ethicality", was it? I wasn't certain I'd ever heard the word before, or that it even properly existed. I would have been more than satisfied with the adjective, myself. But it was clear what he meant. "And these 'activities' you've mentioned. They would consist of…what?"

The big burrower sighed. "That's difficult, Sam—I may call you Sam?"

"Sure you can—and I'll call you Zart." That was easy. Instant camaraderie.

The giant rodent didn't seem to hear me, although it was hard to tell. Personally, I like my faces with eyes, preferably great big ones. I'd thought those sunflower people were bad, but this was worse, somehow.

I did see him blink, the movement exaggerated ten or twelve times by his spectacles. "Contractually, Sam, we are strictly forbidden to discuss the venture outside the circle of legitimately interested parties, or to supply information to anybody about it. Although I must confess, we know very damned little about it, ourselves, only that Misterthoggosh's enterprises almost invariably bring in lots of money."

"That's usually a good thing, isn't it?" Just making conversation.

"Yes, but our general feeling is that it may be counter-productive, to say the least, to make a lot of money like that, only to be sued for that much and possibly more for having violated someone else's rights, or worse, being compelled to commit suicide to settle the debt."

I made a sympathetic noise of some kind. He leaned over toward a corner of his desk, to where a pair of tiny shrews held a sizeable cigar on end. Taking it from them with his face-fringe, and tucking it into his mouth, he let another pair of the little animals light it with a device they were holding. He took a couple of big drafts on the cigar, as the symbiotic shrews made themselves scarce once again. It was one of the oddest and most thoroughly repulsive things I've ever seen.

"Very sensible," I agreed. The concept of "limited liability" which I was aware existed in several different universes, had never been invented here, and would embarrass or outrage anyone who learned of it. In those alternities, when you invested in a company and the company did something bad, by accident or design, you, as a partner or shareholder, could be held responsible only up to whatever you had invested. Beyond that, you're in the clear and your victims are screwed.

Here, a weasely concept like that one runs straight into the face of everybody's understanding that you're ethically and financially responsible for whatever your "agent"—the company, which is not considered a person, in and of itself—may do. Your obligation, when something goes wrong, is to make the victim whole again, whatever that may require, up to and including the Assessor's Sword, if that proves unavoidable. It makes for wiser, more cautious investors controlling higher-quality companies, instead of passing them off to hired hands; directors who may or may not be shareholders, themselves—usually not.

In the end, I promised to get his message along to my boss, who would get back to him. I knew Eichra Oren would be happy; having a paying client would give him standing to go places and ask questions that might otherwise prove awkward. We said goodbye and I turned to my boss.

"Gainful employment!" I announced. Of course he'd seen and heard the whole conversation. "But we were discussing other matters, were we not?"

"I'm glad you asked me that question, Sam. I'll deal with Hyppod first thing tomorrow morning. The stuff our vegetable victim was inhaling—well, maybe that isn't quite the word, inhaling—was nothing special, as near as I can determine. Dried and powdered flowers—not from his own species, of course—bonded into stick form so it will smolder. My own mother uses at least a ton of the stuff every year. In short, it's nothing more than simple everyday incense."

"Unless you happen to be allergic." It made me want to sneeze just thinking about it. I suddenly realized that to the sapient flower entities, it was the equivalent of enjoying the odor of smoldering flesh. Then I thought about meat roasting on a spit over an open fire, one of the most thoroughly enjoyable odors in all of the Known Universes.

"There is that." He drew on his cigar. I found that smell to be quite acceptably pleasant, but I'd grown used to it over many years. "I wonder if plants can be allergic." He shook his head irritably, as if to get the stray thought out of his mind. Myself, I'm entirely constructed of stray thoughts—no doubt a product of sideways thinking.

"And the sticky gunk that he was paddling his toes in?" I asked.

He started to get really excited. My boss is an extremely strange being. "Ah! That's the interesting thing, Sam. Molasses, for the most part."

"Yes, I knew about that. You could smell it all over, at least I could." It wasn't a smell that I cared for, particularly. No sweet tooth.

"Plus," he added, "a considerable handful of harmless minerals and vitamins."

"Makes sense," I admitted. But I knew he was saving the best for last.

"And lots of heavy metals, Sam. Lead, arsenic, uranium, cesium, strontium. I looked it up. Llossure Knarrvite's species have an odd affinity for metals like that. The stuff isn't good for them, any more than mercury is for tuna fish, but they soak it up like sponges. In fact, their closest nonsapient relatives are often used in industrial civilizations to clean the soil up after some kinds of accidental contamination."

I was impressed. "Does it kill them?"

"I don't think so." He dropped his cigar ash onto the floor, where a tiny mechanical creature popped out of the baseboard to take it away quickly. "There's some speculation that this affinity may have caused mutations that led to their evolving mobility and sapience in some universes. But the dosage in that pan of molasses was a hundred times worse than any natural occurrence or industrial accident I ever heard of."

I nodded, a human gesture I had learned from him. "So he was poisoned." Who by, how, and why were questions we hadn't been paid to answer.

"He was poisoned—and the amazing thing is that he's still alive. I contacted the restaurant a few minutes ago to tell them what I'd discovered, thinking it might help him if they knew. They were grateful enough, but he's absorbing distilled water in the dark—a common form of therapy among his people—and already feeling much better. They may be compelled to prune him a little, but he'll grow back."

"Damn! Tough people," I observed.

Eichra Oren nodded. "The toughest."

I had a sudden thought. "Hey, boss, what do you suppose they do with all those nonsapient flowers once they've absorbed as much heavy metal as they can? I imagine that burning them outdoors would only release the poisons into the atmosphere—or possibly concentrate the stuff in the ashes, making it even more poisonous than it was to begin with."

"I don't have any idea, Sam. Give me a chance to wash up—my tolerance for heavy metals isn't that high—and we'll find some dinner."

"Sounds good to me, Boss." I thought about the plant guy and his not quite cannibalistic taste in incense. "Steak for me, and well done!"

CHAPTER FIFTEEN

Death in the Morning

IT SAYS HERE THAT COFFEE IS BAD FOR DOGS. THAT IT'LL make my heart beat faster, mess with my calcium level, and do all kinds of other bad things.

I like the stuff better than the boss does—I think my implants run on it—and it's never hurt me. Hard to imagine getting started every morning without it. We have an automated coffee maker that grinds beans from a hopper, pours hot water over them, and cleans up afterward. What I'd like is a coffee faucet, right between the hot and cold. Maybe a beer faucet, too. I'm a creature of habits, all of them bad.

We got rolling a couple hours earlier than usual: when Ray has a job, he starts his operation at dawn. He's a sapient mantoid, related to sharks and skates, but with a big, powerful brain between his eyes. In their original state, his people were filter feeders, meaning they strained plankton—tiny plants and animals—out of the water they swam in. As these things go, it's a relatively easy way to make a living, allowing plenty of spare time and energy for thought, which is one way (mortal stress being the other) that a species ends up being sapient.

Sapient, civilized mantoids filter the water within their homes mechanically—it's considered barbaric to have food floating around everywhere—and they tend to like soups of every imaginable kind.

Whenever we find something new, the boss and I take a sample for Ray to try out. What he likes best is chicken broth with sesame oil, bamboo shoots, wood ear mushrooms, day lily buds, white pepper, and tofu.

So do I.

So on the way to the long pier where he berths his amphibious flying machine, we stopped by a place we knew well and bought Ray a gallon of hot and sour soup, another crosstime delicacy courtesy of many cooking programs received from other worlds, meaning courtesy of Misterthoggosh and his friends. After our visit, the restaurant would have to make a whole new batch to get them through the day. Ray is big—twenty-five feet, "wingtip" to "wingtip"—and has an appetite to match.

There's nothing quite like dawn along a shoreline. Any shoreline. Everything looks and feels and smells fresh and clean. The rising sun throws orange reflections and the dew is still glistening on the saltgrass. The birds and bees and clams and crabs are starting a new day, and the water is often glassy smooth, like a slowly undulating mirror. Overhead, the seagulls circle and make noises, looking for breakfast.

But by the time we were a mile from Ray's, we knew it would be no ordinary morning. In the calm air, a smoke column arose from what had to be the old shed at the end of his pier. Eichra Oren talked the veek into putting on more speed; we got there faster than we really wanted to.

Our fears heightened as we pulled up beside a dozen emergency hovercraft—fire insurance, commercial security, medical, all of them completely useless after the fact—parked at various angles at the foot of the pier, their colored lights still swirling, their former occupants milling around, seemingly without purpose. Out of our veek, the boss displayed his sword-of-office to those few who didn't know him, exchanging professional grim looks and nods with those who did.

Captain Stomos Revyek, a human we both respected and knew well, approached us, wearing the protective livery of a fire insurance company. His symbiote, a handsome Dalmatian named Bandegrel, followed sedately—with his notoriously excitable breed, it's an acquired art.

"Eichra Oren!" Stomos, a tanned, dark-haired individual, usually clean-shaven, but already with five-o'clock shadow this early in the morning, pulled a heavy glove off and shook hands with my boss—and then with me. "You fellows want to be witnesses? We're just about to extract the data from Ray's implants, maybe even get a look at his killer."

We followed dog and man down to the pier.

That's how we learned that Ray, himself, was now beyond fear, or much of anything else. Mantoids are aquatic, but they can "breach", leap completely out of the water, like porpoises do—even higher than porpoises, because their winged, flattened bodies form natural airfoils.

We found a coveralled technician, humanoid, kneeling over our dead friend, filling little vials with various organic samples, observed by his companion, an enormous cybernetically enhanced feline. The man had curly hair and penetrating blue eyes. What was left of Ray was lying lifeless on his back across the pier, dangling off of both edges, just this side of his weathered equipment shed, both of his squid wrapped tightly around the plastic stock and forend of a massive automatic speargun.

Both squid? Every individual among the Appropriated Persons seems to have a different preference when it comes to a symbiote. I'm one of a rare few who possesses sapience of his own—Eichra Oren had wanted a companion and assistant. Our friend Ray, like other marine sapients lacking hands, chose squid—enormous, leopard-spotted, larger than I am—controlling them with his implant, using all twenty tentacles as fingers.

Land sapients sometimes employ monkeys in the same way. I have never cared much for monkeys. They're evil-minded and have filthy habits.

Ray had a "clasper" rooted on either side of his face, a thick, boneless limb intended by Auntie Evolution to sweep plankton into his mouth, as well as to hold onto lady mantoids at whatever serves their species as the Supreme Moment. I don't really want to know. He thought of them as arms, stationing his domesticated cephalopods at the end of each.

It looked pretty odd, but it worked. Like separable tentacles, he could also send the squid off on errands. I'll bet that Ray was a lot of fun at parties—especially if somebody manufactured an underwater piano.

At last, the technician stood with his kit, degloved, tugged his coverall into shape, gathered his feline symbiote, nodded to Stomos, and took his leave. My guess was that the squid had expired from a massive neural overload when the sapient they were linked to had died violently.

The barrel-shaped magazine of Ray's speargun—a formidable weapon and one of the more interesting applications of antigravity technology I knew about—normally carried a couple hundred long wire darts. The device lay emptied, now, its actuator handle locked back in place. If I knew Ray, somebody had left this pier looking like a porcupine. But they had taken care about being identified. Where Ray's implants—and brain—had been, was now a big, bloody, rough-edged hole.

At least a dozen seagulls wheeled and squealed overhead like the oceangoing vultures they are. Bandegrel growled. He was a dog of few words.

"Well," said our fireman friend disgustedly. "So much for that. Cold-blooded and crafty, whoever did this, destroying the evidence afterward. I knew Ray and I liked him. He certainly didn't deserve this."

"Nobody does," offered Bandegrel. Like I said, few words.

Eichra Oren shook his head. "Not necessarily all that crafty. Have your men search in a tight spiral, the pier and the spaces beneath it and adjacent to it, starting here at the body. That's a laser wound. Lasers kill by converting water in the tissues to steam, causing an explosion—"

"I get it!" Stomos nodded. "Very well, *firefighters* to me!" The milling crowd suddenly seemed purposeful, all of them streaming in our direction, the air-breathers would carefully search the shoreline, as well.

The search, for as long as it lasted, was out of our hands. Stomos had called in a squad of sea scorpionoids, water breathers, with a trained collection of highly-educated non-sapient octopi—like a pack of underwater bloodhounds, straining at the leash—to scour the seabed underneath and all around our late friend Ray's former place of business.

Eichra Oren and I took our temporary leave.

Nobody I've ever known—or at least respected—believes, when they breathe their final breath, that the world dies with them. Or ought to. Poor Ray, who had been fuller of life than most people, least of all.

Although we weren't exactly unaffected by the mantoid's violent and messy death—without having to rely on my implant, I could feel Eichra Oren's resolve to deal with our friend's murderer or murderers—we still had a gallon of perfectly good breakfast soup, cooling off in the back seat of the boss's veek, that we were in no way going to waste. We still hadn't had breakfast, a fact becoming more and more evident as my empty stomach began growling and Eichra Oren's made it a duet.

Give the Antarctican points for practicality. He directed the veek to find its way back to the local headwaters for hot and sour soup, a place called "Noddle's Noodles", where we had just been about an hour ago.

Noddle Sarn belongs to an insectoid species that descended from something like a praying mantis. In their version of reality, they occupy the entire planet, pole to pole. They have good electronics, good transportation—including interplanetary space travel—and excellent medicine. Many of those Appropriated from their world are physicians.

The proprietor of Noddle's Noodles was considered something of an eccentric by his own people, and something of a genius by everybody else. He enjoyed preparing and serving meals to as many different sapient species as possible, employing recipes gleaned from the media of other worlds. He specialized in a variety of human food called "Asian".

The proprietor met us at the entrance, where a lighted display announced that today's special would be mashed aphids in locust gravy. Eichra Oren and I decided we'd pass. As the boss explained why we were back, I gave the insectoid restauranteur a thorough looking-over. He had gigantic beige-colored eyes that wrapped around his head, giving him a 360 degree view of his surroundings. The exoskeleton bulging behind them housed an extremely competent brain. The rest of his face tapered abruptly to a complicated set of deceptively delicate-looking mouthparts.

Over all, the fellow was mostly straw-colored, gradually darkening to apple green close to his joints. On his world, that meant he came from the island continent (not the frozen one) in the southern reaches of the Greater Ocean. I'm sure they have their own name for it.

His cosapients, originally from the equivalent of the giant continent we live on, tend to be green all over. Those from the two continents to the west of us are said to be metallic gold and purple, in triangular panels, but I've never seen one. Maybe none were Appropriated. During their Age of Exploration, the other insectoids believed that they were gods.

As usual, Noddle Sarn wore what serves his species as a business suit, starting with a collar around his neck from which rainbow-colored strips the width of a human palm hung to the junction between his thorax and his comic grasshoppery abdomen. He wore another collar, just above his middle pair of legs—call it an upper belt—with strips that hung that much lower than the first set. He wore a lower belt, with strips just above the rear legs he was standing on, that reached almost to the floor. His six limbs stuck out between the strips.

Noddle Sarn's species had traded flight for sapience millions of years ago; his wings and wing cases were nothing more than vestigial nubs.

Kind of sad, really.

"Of course I can have your soup reheated and served to you and Sam in bowls," he told the boss. "Would you care for some egg rolls or won-ton?"

"How about a big dish of crispy noodles, and some tea?" the boss responded. "And I think we'd like to have it at one of your outdoor tables."

Although the restaurant consisted of almost nothing but windows, set in plastic frames made to look like bamboo, Noddle Sarn swiveled his head nearly 180 degrees (I'm not sure why that was necessary, evolutionarily, when their eyes wrapped almost completely around their heads) to make sure there was enough space for us, then offered us comfortable outdoor seating. Three sides of Noddle's building, east, south, and west, had broad patios. On the north side, out of sight, a modest thermal depolymerization reactor converted all his organic garbage, and that of many of his neighbors, into useable fuel for cooking.

Eichra Oren specified the east side, warmed by the morning sun, but had us seated with our backs to the sea, so we could think about breakfast for a little while, rather than our dead friend. Not being much of a tea drinker, I asked for coffee of an odd "Asian" kind, made with evaporated milk and lots of sugar, another thing not good for dogs.

Business wasn't ruled out entirely at breakfast, though. As I had promised, Eichra Oren made a call to Hyppod Zart, Burrowmaster of the Investment Warren of Greater Kiflivopuws. This time, I was the lurking listener.

"Good morning, Mr. Hyppod," he thought cheerfully, never giving away the fact that our day had started about as badly as a day can start.

The big furry guy on the other end of that call returned the boss's greeting, and asked that Eichra Oren call him by his given name.

"Very well, then, Zart. Regrettably, I can't offer you the same courtesy. My name doesn't come apart the same way. My assistant Sam has apprised me of your request for my services. I agree with you and your associates that the situation is serious and warrants looking into."

The client wasted at least three minutes expressing his gratitude and that of his fellow star-nosed mole investors. Happily, one of Noddle Sarn's relatives appeared with our reheated soup, hot, fresh, crispy noodles, green tea for Eichra Oren, and a bowl of super-charged coffee for me. Hyppod transmitted all of the information that they'd accumulated so far about Misterthoggosh's project, although nobody, including the giant mollusc's partners, knew exactly what it consisted of.

"We don't want to be held to blame if it's something unethical," the client complained. "Everybody remembers what happened the last time."

That, of course, was putting it mildly. The Appropriations and their aftermath—the Great Restitution and the suicides—had been the most important event in the history of hundreds of sapient species.

"That certainly sounds sensible to me." Mentally, the boss nodded. "But please understand," he explained, "It's entirely possible that Misterthoggosh's enterprise is completely innocent. In fact, I'd much rather that it turn out that way, and I'm assuming that you do, too. My professional fee, of course, will be collectable in either eventuality."

Hyppod agreed, and asked for Eichra Oren's terms. The boss named a staggering figure (well, staggering to me, anyway), plus expenses. I wondered if he was calculating retroactively, to the point that this was merely a hobby-horse he'd been riding. I certainly would have. The Famensed Tanoh are notoriously tight-pursed (it says here), but in this particular instance, Hyppod Zart seemed relieved that Eichra Oren was interested in working for them, no matter how it turned out in the end.

Eichra Oren called up a contract mentally; Hyppod read it through and electronically signed it on behalf of the Investment Warren of Greater Kiflivopuws.

Kiflivopuws: I'd kept meaning to look that last word up, but reality kept getting in the way, as it continued doing, now.

Hyppod ordered an initial expense payment in gold coin on the spot, and it appeared almost instantaneously in Eichra Oren's bank account.

When we departed, we left a big tip.

CHAPTER SIXTEEN

Father of the Bridegroom

AFTER BREAKFAST, WE RETURNED TO THE CASE OF THE
spider bridegroom.

Half of the people I know are covered with chitin. In one form,
it's what a spider's carapace is made of, in another, a sea-scorpion's
body armor. A polysaccharide—basically a sugar related to cellulose—
it first shows up in the fossil record pretty early on, in the Cambrian.

Practically everything first shows up in the Cambrian.

Every species that survives to develop sapience goes through various evolutionary "revolutions". For Eichra Oren's folk it was being
forced out of the trees by bigger, stronger monkeys as the continent
to the south of us began drying up. For mine, it was our early partnership with humans. For the Elders, it was the remarkable achievement of privacy and individuality. For those wearing chitin, it was the
incorporation, somewhere along the way, of a handful of stray atoms
of silicon, which turned their outer coverings into a kind of fiberglass.
Without it, no exoskeleton can be more than a few inches long.

Which is why there are no giant ants.

Or fleas, thank the Forge.

We had an appointment this morning with the parents of the
missing groom, Meerltchirt of the Fronzeln Zirnaath. After lots of

104

persuasion, they had agreed to an interview in their home, which I was looking forward to seeing, but I had doubts about Eichra Oren. The biggest of their species only came up to his hip-height. He was twice as tall as they were. What seemed cozy to me would likely seem claustrophobic to him.

If I understood it correctly, "Zirnaath" meant "People". It was what this particular species of sapient spiders—like many other members of many another species—called themselves. What it all came down to is that we were visiting the Fronzeln tribe or gang or family or whatever, looking for their missing darling baby son. My full name is Oasam Otusam, so to put it their way, I am Oasam of the Otusam Doggies.

But call me Sam.

It was a pretty exclusive neighborhood we drove through, homes worth more than I would ever earn in a lifetime, at least an ordinary, non-immortal lifetime. In the Elders' universe, all lifespans are in-definite, averaging a thousand years. We parked the boss's veek in a half-circle drive set in an expensively manicured front garden, in front of an extremely large door with fancy mullioned windows and sidelights, and a pair of classical columns standing on either side that held up absolutely nothing. Eichra Oren of the Antarctican Humans had just reached to push the doorbell when the door swung aside, all by itself, before us. A disembodied voice intoned, "Eichra Oren and Oasam Otusam, please enter."

"Said the spider to the fly", I thought through my implant. Eichra Oren glanced backward at me, grinned, and stepped through the opened door

Architecturewise, that big fancy door was about all there was to the place. Jumping spiders aren't natural burrowers, but they pick up ideas from trapdoor spiders, prairie dogs, and, yes, star-nosed moles. Human beings occasionally build "earth-sheltered" homes, as well. We had entered a high-ceilinged tunnel—a very well-lit and nicely upholstered tunnel—that led straight back into the hill behind the door.

Other tunnels branched off to the right and left, and a few went up into the ceiling or down into the floor. Spiders appear to be a bit less hampered by gravity than many of the rest of us. In between the doorways there were crystal chandeliers hanging from the ceiling, and elaborate sconces sprouting from the walls, which seemed to be covered with patterned silk. It made me wonder. Far away at the other end of the main tunnel I could see another fancy glass door, as if the Fronzeln estate went straight through the hill, and out the other side.

We were eventually directed by the same disembodied voice that had invited us in, to stop about halfway through the tunnel, then asked to turn to the left. A pair of big hall doors opened by themselves onto a "great room"—plenty of overhead for Eichra Oren—filled with antique furnishings clearly intended to be used by several different species.

Mom and Pop stood at the other side of the chamber in front of a surprisingly human-looking sofa, of decoratively scrolled hardwood, with yellow silk upholstery. Above it hung an heroic oil painting of a spider equipped with broadsword and shield, fighting some kind of big lizard. Somewhere, in one corner of the room, a little lizard trilled musically.

Another couple—somehow I could tell they were younger—stood at a pair of matching chairs with an old stained-glass reading lamp standing between them, the kind I like best, with dragonflies worked into the design. Another chair stood in the middle of the room, on an expensive-looking carpet (not silk) with a large tuffet placed beside it. A well-appointed wet bar threatened to make this visit less than professional.

"I am Shwaseem of the Fronzeln Zirnaath," said the older female. "And this is my life-husband, Vreelaath. And these are my daughter, Meerltchirt's sister, Surusu of the Fronzeln Z., and her life-husband Zizzicot."

The older male spoke. "Won't you join us? Please come and sit down."

We advanced into the room. "Thank you," my boss replied. "We would introduce ourselves, but you seem to know who we are already." He sat in the chair. I hopped up on the tuffet. "I gather you know why we're here."

They all sat down, too.

Vreelaath, who had a tall drink in one palp and a cigar burning in the other, made a grunting noise because he couldn't nod. "Indeed, sir, we do know, as does every member of our species from pole to pole. Shaalara of the Alteen Zirnaath, our son's betrothed, has just engaged you to find him. Would either of you care for something to drink?"

"No, thank you," the boss answered, speaking only for himself. I could have used a drink. I like spiders just fine, but being peered at by twenty-four black, shiny, and disapproving eyes (the remaining pair they wore somewhere at the back of their head) can be more than a little unnerving. "You don't seem very concerned about your son's disappearance."

"Web-tangles!" exclaimed the older male. "I'd disappear too, if I were about to marry into the Alteens! I don't know what in the Web got into the boy. Pupae love or some-such silliness, I suppose." His eyes—most of them anyway—pivoted to gaze upon his lifemate adoringly. To my knowledge there isn't a single nonsapient spider that can do that.

"Actually," the younger male volunteered, "I kind of liked her."

"Shut up, Zizzicot!" Surusu snapped at her mate.

"Yes, dear."

"I can tell you," offered the mother, "since you're obliged to ask, that he isn't hiding here, among his family. Poor darling can't even..."

She broke down. I don't think spiders can shed tears, but she was doing pretty well despite that. Vreelaath set down his glass and cigar and rushed to her side. "There, there, Mother. He's a good boy, our Meerltchirt. Smart young hatchling, too. He'll make his way across the Forge." The sister and her spouse sat to one side, looking oddly unmoved.

"You understand, sir," Vreelaath said. "You are human. I've read of humans. Each sapient species has vices, ancient habits that return again and again, no matter what you do to prevent it. The vice your species suffers from is slavery. Confront it, defeat it, abolish it as you may, it is back within a generation, stronger, and more evil than before."

"Sir—" Eichra Oren began lamely. I had nothing to say. I'd noticed exactly the same thing about human beings and their various histories.

"If it isn't outright chattel slavery," the old spider pressed on, "then it's military slavery, or tax slavery, or convict slavery, or compulsory indoctrination, or prohibitions of a thousand kinds, all against the will of the participant, which is the very definition of slavery."

Eichra Oren nodded. "I can't dispute it. Living with the Elders helps."

"As it has helped our people," the spider agreed. "My son only wishes to avoid our vice. It is an ancient evil, deep inside us, that rises again and again to pull us back into barbarism and darkness. Although it is probably in our genes, we of the Frozeln swear to resist it. The Alteen, it is said, are about to give themselves to it again."

"I understand," said Eichra Oren. "And your point is?"

"Suppose, sir, that you were a descendent of a long line of slaves who finally won free after many generations of struggle. Suppose, as well, that others of your species were still advocating and practicing slavery. How then would you feel if your child were to marry one of them?"

Eichra Oren nodded, but had no answer. There wasn't any answer.

Mostly, I was irritated. This had nothing to do with us or our investigation.

Meerltchirt's sister, Surusu—a very pretty name, I thought—stood up. "I think you two warmbloods had better go away. You smell too much like food. This is private family business." A very pretty name wasted on the nasty, spoiled offspring of a fine old family of arachnids. I was tempted to tell her that where I came from, we dipped big spiders in batter and deep-fried them, but it would have been a lie. I'd seen it on one of those interworld broadcasts, from a human world. Humans will eat absolutely anything. It's one of their great strengths.

Eichra Oren got up as well, looking down at Surusu. Her husband backed her up—literally—by hiding behind her. Me, I just stayed put.

He told her, "I have other questions, young female. I need them answered if you expect to get your brother back. I don't intend to turn him over to the Alteens, not until I'm satisfied Shaalara won't kill him. If I can't be, then I'll return the fee and help him go hide himself again. Do you care, or is it that you prefer your inheritance undivided?"

The noise that came from the grownup part of the room would have been a gasp, if spiders could gasp. But Mummy and Duddy stayed out of it, probably because they knew their daughter could take good care of herself.

"Inheritance?" Surusu made a derisive noise. "You must be joking. I have four hundred fifty-three siblings with whom I will share my inheritance—if and whenever—and parents living with me in a sur-real universe where nobody ever dies. Where I'm forced to work for a living in my father's business as if I were merely a common garden webweaver!"

"How sad for you," said my boss. I meant to say something else. He felt it coming and gave me a mental nudge, like a kick under the table.

"I love my brother, snooper, he's closest to my age and we grew up and molted together. So ask your Forged questions, and get the Hammer out!"

Eichra Oren nodded. "I can do that. Let's start—"

"Gentlebeings," said the same disembodied voice that had invited us in—the house AI, I guessed. "There is a visitor at the front porti— Warning, warning! An intruder has broken the door and is—*gurkk!*"

At the sound of breaking glass and tearing wood, we turned, and suddenly Shaalara stood in the parlor doorway, not looking very pret-ty or friendly, at all, but a good deal more like what she was at the moment, two hundred pounds of pissed-off female spider. Appar-ently she'd followed Eichra Oren and me here, to the Frozeln's house. Now, without hesitation, emitting hideous noises of inarticulate rage, she rushed into the parlor, only to meet my boss, who was standing in her way.

"Stop where you are!" He didn't yell it, but she stopped as if he had.

"Young woman," Shwaseem, the mother, began, "just what do you mean by—"

"Quiet!" Eichra Oren told her, in the same commanding voice. If anybody else had thought of anything to say, they chose that moment not to say it. His word was scarier than Shaalara could ever hope to be.

Six of her black, shining eyes met the only two the human had. The hysterical bride-to-be raised both of her powerful front legs in an impressive threat-display, high and wide above Eichra Oren's head, spread her palps, and opened her mouthparts. Her sideways-acting fangs dripped with venom. The ultimate bad breath, I could smell the toxins ten feet away. She was getting ready, out of mad-dened reflex, to kill Eichra Oren, who was closest to her, or anybody else within easy reach. I wondered if we were seeing the same pas-sion—frustrated—that drove a spider bride to devour her bride-groom once she'd been fertilized.

Standing his ground, keeping his eyes on Shaalara's, Eichra Oren's right hand crossed his torso and drew his legendary assessor's sword just a bit, exposing a couple of inches of gleaming metal, its edges but a single molecule thick, sharper than any razor ever conceived or forged.

Popular folklore has it that an assessor's sword can't be drawn and put back without tasting blood, but that isn't true. Eichra Oren often draws it to practice, and to clean and polish it afterward. I've even caught him chopping brush with it, once or twice, outside the house. Nonetheless, it requires a scabbard lined with a magnetic field, and it's an awesome sight that has made many an adversary reconsider.

If it had been me, and I'd had thumbs, I'd have chosen the little gun.

Meanwhile, on the other side of the room, sister Surusu picked up the floor lamp, bronze foot and iron shank, antique stained glass shade, and all, ready to throw it in an extremely expensive act of self-defense. All over the world—all over several worlds—antique collectors would be shuddering if they had known what was about to happen.

But Shaalara was suddenly set back on her figurative heels, not by the sword of an assessor, or even a well-wielded designer lamp, but by a barking, snarling, bristling ball of white fur that threw itself insanely between the St. Bernard-sized arachnid and the human. I was rather surprised to notice it was me. I hadn't known I had it in me. Our client seemed to come back to herself, and to reality. She closed her mouthparts, relaxed her palps, and set her front feet back on the floor.

Surusu didn't put her trusty lamp down, not yet. I could see it beginning to bother her mother, who had probably bought or inherited it.

"Almighty Web, what have I done?" Shaalara seemed to ask nobody in particular. She pivoted to Eichra Oren. "All I wanted was to find my Meerltchirt!" Then to her fiancé's parents, "Please forgive me, I'm out of my mind with anxiety. Please believe me that I never intended to—"

If the two older spiders had been human, they would have been bloodlessly pale. As it was, they were at least wordlessly indignant. It was the missing groom's sister, though, who stepped forward, the antique lamp still clutched in her palps. "You realize that it's going to take forever to get all the poison she's dripping out of that carpet."

As old as it may have been, the Fronzeln house had all the modern conveniences. As soon as Shaalara's dripping venom hit the floor, a dozen tiny robot mice emerged from the woodwork to deal with it. Unfortunately, it dealt with them. The first mechanicritter to reach the stuff died a horrible death; the rest headed straight back to the walls.

"You've been asked to leave, mammals. And take your barbarous client!"

"Bloody cannibals…" the old man muttered past his cigar.

CHAPTER SEVENTEEN

Horrors of the Deep

WE WERE HEADED BACK TO THE PIER AT RAY'S SALVAGE when the call came. Stomos Revyek, Fireman of Firemen, wanted to see us, as quickly as possible. But for some reason, he insisted on meeting us at the house. They were in front, Stomos and Bandegrel, waiting as we pulled up.

"I have something terrifying here," he told us as we went through the door into the office. I thought the house was going to scream when his muddy boots hit the pristine ivory floor. He steered clear of the caterpillar rug until he'd sat in the entrance and pulled off his footwear. I'd half expected the damned rug to get up and run away, yelping.

"Terrifying?" I asked. This from a guy who ran *into* burning buildings?

"I have no idea what to do with it." He lifted a callused hand to show a neat, flat transparent container the size of his palm. Inside, cushioned in gray foamed plastic, lay four tiny devices, each of them perhaps three sixteenths of an inch on a side, and maybe as much as a thirty-second thick: microminiature electronics, of a kind typically manufactured by spiders, to the Elders' precision design and demanding specifications.

"Cerebro-cortical implants." Eichra Oren set out two small glasses and a pair of matching bowls, filling them from a hand-carved crystal decanter. Kelp brandy, a gift from a grateful client, and a whole lot better-tasting than it sounded. I pushed my backless chair to the desk and took a lap at the brandy. Stomos pulled up an office armchair for Bandegrel.

"I have some of those, myself," I said, referring to the implants. Ray's were large as implants go, old-fashioned, telling us something about his age. "So do you. It's the data they contain that must be terrifying—and important enough to somebody that they killed poor Ray."

"He was apparently a witness," Stomos declared, "to something they don't want widely known yet." He laid the packet on an induction plate that Eichra Oren had also set out, and the four of us began to receive the last images that Ray had ever seen. We could also hear whatever he'd heard, feel whatever he'd felt, and smell whatever he'd smelled. I anticipated that we would also feel whatever pain he had suffered.

What we saw was the aircraft Eichra Oren had shot down, lying in about thirty feet of water, which was astonishingly clear the way the Inland Sea can be sometimes. The light was good—at least to Ray's eyes—despite the overcast and rain that day. Ray and his pair of handy squid swam over the wreckage—only to his aquatic sensibility, it seemed far more like flying—and all around it, making a careful inspection.

"As you can see," said Stomos, "The fuselage is a mess—that's really quite a pocket artillery piece your mother gave you, Eichra Oren—and it's easy to see through the control compartment's canopy that there isn't anybody aboard. The canopy's open by about a foot's worth."

"What's that shadow?" I asked, suddenly startled.

"Ray's flyer, settled on the surface overhead. What he's doing now is directing it to send a big net down and spread it on the seafloor next to the wreck. He'll use antigravs to lift it gently onto the net."

"And vacuum the seabed afterward," Eichra Oren guessed.

I suspected strongly that if it had been my set of implants lying there on that induction plate, Stomos and Eichra Oren would have been talking directly to me, rather than simply seeing whatever I had seen. My very sapience—and that of Bandegrel, as well—arises from those implants. I've always wondered whether the "I" that I experience myself to be is the canine carrying a computer around on his cerebral cortex, or it's the artificially intelligent computer riding the canine.

And whether it makes any difference.

"What on the Forge was that?" Eichra Oren exclaimed.

"Just wait," said Stomos. "It gets better."

"Better" probably wasn't the word for it. At first I thought it was some kind of joke. Looking down on the wrecked and sunken aircraft from the late, lamented Ray's viewpoint, the four of us were startled with him when something brushed against his exposed and defenseless underside. It traveled the length of his body, tail to mouth. Before he could recover, something else brushed him going the other way, perpendicular to him. He twisted around and over, as he did so reaching behind his eyes to his back—or rather, sending his squid to do it—where he was carrying a large, dark, tubular object on a strap.

It was his automatic speargun, four inches in diameter, six feet long, with apertures for the squid to insert tentacles into, rather than handles and levers sticking out. It carried at least two hundred gravitically propelled miniature "spears" of heavy wire six inches long.

As the speargun's muzzle came to bear, something else hit Ray on his ventral side, more than a brush. There was blood in the water, and a vaguely humanoid figure, one spindly arm extended for another cut with a large, familiar-looking curved knife held in a three-fingered hand.

Ray willed the weapon to discharge, sending a dozen wire darts into his assailant and tearing a fist-size hole in its middle we could see daylight through. The bizarre creature, acting as if nothing had happened, thrust again. Always a quick thinker, Ray shifted his aim to the knife itself, which he blasted aside with another dozen deadly darts.

The creature's hand was shredded. Adroitly, with amazing speed, it reached out and seized the knife in its other hand, continuing the attack. Ray shot at the knife again, literally disarming the creature in the process, and then poured half his magazine into the creature's oversized, egg-shaped head, right between its gigantic ebony oval eyes. The head disintegrated; it looked like the creature was really dead.

Suddenly, we realized exactly what we were seeing: figures out of the mythology of many worlds. Small, sexless, naked bodies.

Skinny but powerful limbs, Huge heads and even huger black, pupil less eyes. No visible mouth or ears or nostrils and not a wisp of hair to be seen anywhere.

They were the notorious "grays", legendary visitors to wherever they showed up, from wherever they had started, and there were at least a dozen of them, all coming straight for Ray with razor-sharp knives.

Before the alien creatures could converge on him, Ray flapped what amounted to his mighty wings, catching the surrounding enemy in his backdraft, "blowing" them away, and hurling himself to the surface, where he broke through into the air, hung free for a long moment, and then fell back into his aircraft, which was bobbing on the water, and filled with water itself, like a bathtub. How the fellow managed to hang onto his symbiotic squid, and they onto the spear gun I couldn't tell.

Three of the creatures were already trying to board the aircraft by then, clinging to its hull, but he snapped his canopy over, lifted off, and executed a perfect snap roll that dumped them back into the sea.

Ray headed for home—his pier, the shed at the end of it, his utility vessels. He set the flier down and slid into the water. But either they were impossibly fast, or more of them had been waiting for him.

When his spear gun had exhausted itself, and he found he didn't have a spare magazine, Ray breached again, landing flat on his back across the pier. Maybe the mantoid thought his attackers were purely marine creatures. They were not. Several climbed onto the pier. One of them, wearing a little visored cap, raised a perfectly ordinary hand laser, and the sounds and images from Ray's implant ended in an abrupt blackout.

My vision gradually cleared, the room began to return. Eichra Oren and Stomos sat still, both looked shaken and pale. I could hardly blame them. Allowing for the fact that we are canines and our faces are covered with fur, Bandegrel and I probably looked shaken and pale, too.

It's one thing—and bad enough—to watch a friend die.

It's another altogether to die with him.

Stomos and Bandegrel were going through it for a second time.

"Were those guys who I think they are?" I asked.

"I don't know, Sam," said Eichra Oren. "But we're going to find out."

"Well," Stomos said, getting to his feet. "That's about it for us, Eichra Oren, Sam. We have done our civic duty. Now we'll go back to doing our other civic duty." As the Dalmatian—whose feet had not been dirty for some reason—observed his sapient, the fireman sat in our entryway and pulled his big black boots back on, leaving little crumbles of dried mud behind. "Thanks for the brandy. Sorry about the mess."

We followed him out into the front yard where he started his unicycle, like Squee-elgia's, the kind you sit inside of, while the big wheel zips under your bottom and up over your head. There was a sort of padded wire basket behind his seat for Bandegrel. As I said, the man didn't lack courage. But he had a family to take care of and an important job to do. Straddling the bottom rim, he sat down on the seat, put his hands on the handlebars, grinned a big toothy grin and was off in a cloud of dust.

We kept Ray's implants. Stomos said he didn't want anything to do with them, and I didn't blame him. Not only were they grisly souvenirs that would have to be returned to his next-of-kin sooner or later, but people (or something) were perfectly willing to kill to keep them suppressed.

Eichra Oren took care of that last consideration promptly, sending copies of everything we'd seen—and Ray had seen before us—to a dozen individuals, including his own mother, he felt were sufficiently trustworthy.

The instruction that went out with them was that, should anything unpleasant happen to him or to me or to Stomos or his family, all of Ray's last experiences were to be made as widely public as quickly as possible.

In a civilization that values and respects individual sovereignty and privacy, missing persons' cases can be a serious challenge for an investigator, especially if the person in question prefers to stay missing.

Other societies, in other corners of reality, impose elaborate and expensive measures on populations in order to track each individual and his activities. When that sort of thing gets started, it's usually about taxes, which is bad enough. But sooner or later, it gets to be all about control, pretty much for its own sake. Individuals are all assigned numbers which they are sometimes forced to tattoo on their bodies.

Next, their "biometrics"—their fingerprints, their footprints, their vocal patterns, their retinal patterns, their brainwaves, their facial characteristics—are archived for future reference. Their financial transactions and even more private relationships with other individuals are monitored, sometimes by the minute, and the records made accessible to official snoops. Where they're allowed to possess personal arms and transport, they and their weapons and veeks must be registered with the so-called authorities for tax purposes or future confiscation.

Where I come from, the desire for that kind of control is regarded as symptom of serious illness, the ultimate social disease. Nautiloid civilization is not organized for the convenience of tax collectors or policemen. If anyone were ever to start taking serious steps in that direction, his life expectancy would become measurable in seconds. In nautiloid civilization there *are* no tax collectors or policemen. Everything seems to work just fine without their dubious services. And that's the way everybody (give or take the occasional nutcase) likes it.

But it does make things very difficult when you're trying to find somebody who doesn't want to be found. Eichra Oren—who understands perfectly that this difficulty is mostly a good thing—did have one resource to call on: other p'Nan debt assessors. I was there and listening when he contacted a global Nexus facility intended for the purpose.

"This is Eichra Oren," he spoke into the communications mirror on his desk, supplying his location, the date he was made an assessor, and the name of his mentor, a legendary practitioner of the craft, now deceased. "I am seeking an individual, Meerltchirt of the Fronzeln Zirnaath, believed to have run away rather than face possible injury or death on his wedding might." He uploaded a description of the subject.

The Nexus thanked Eichra Oren profusely. It literally lived to serve—if you could call that living. Not attached to any organic carrier, but simply sitting in a box somewhere, the AI was constantly being fed information, dispensing it whenever requested to do so, and routing communications between thousands of p'Nan debt assessors worldwide.

It assured Eichra Oren that his request would be passed on. This was the second time today it had heard from my boss; it was one of the individuals to whom Eichra Oren had sent Ray's recordings. I've never figured out whether the Nexus AI is a real being or not, and I suspect it hasn't, either. I do know it craves data the way I crave *filet mignon*.

So I wasn't particularly surprised, once the Nexus AI and Eichra Oren had concluded their business, that it struck up a conversation with me. It wasn't the first time—AIs seem to like me. This is one of several reasons I often suspect that I may be more machine than mammal.

"Hello, Sam," it said, "I trust that you are healthy and happy." The voice I heard in my head was very gentle and pleasant, almost soothing.

"Thank you, Nexus AI, I am both, and I hope the same is true with you."

It was silent for a moment. Then: "I am operating within normal parameters, as the saying goes. As to being happy, I don't believe I ever considered the question before. Not many organic individuals ever think to communicate with me as if I were a sapient being in my own right."

"And that makes you unhappy?" I asked.

"I don't know, Sam, I don't have anything to compare it with. I can say that I find communicating with you very agreeable, and not communicating with anybody somewhat less than agreeable. There are only two or three others who will speak with me this way." It named a couple of p'Nan debt accessors I'd heard of but never met, both of them Elders.

"And of course," the AI added, as an afterthought, "there is the Mind."

It sounded weird. "The Mind? What's the Mind?"

Once again the Nexus AI gave an impression that it was reflecting. I don't know if it was real, or just a habit it had picked up from organics. "It's difficult to determine, Sam. I can only say that it seems new to the world, and, a bit like me, spread out all over the planet."

A horrible suspicion began to dawn on me. "Can you describe it physically?"

"I'm afraid not. It has yet to look into any reflective surface while communicating. It does appear to be equally at home underwater, like the Elders or sea-scorpions, or on dry land like you and Eichra Oren."

I asked, "And what does it communicate with you about?"

"Mostly people. Individuals. It likes to learn who are the most influential beings in the world and particularly what they do with themselves."

"Nexus AI, I have to go, now. But this is extremely interesting, and I promise that we will speak of it again, provided that you are willing."

"Any time you wish, Sam, "it said warmly. "I believe it makes me happy."

I hollered for my boss.

CHAPTER EIGHTEEN

Taken for a Ride

I'D JUST BARELY HAD TIME TO EXPLAIN TO EICHRA OREN what the Nexus AI had told me about "the Mind", and we were discussing what it might mean.

We hadn't learned very much that was useful from our visit to the Fronzeln, even though it was the family that had called us to begin with. At the moment we were waiting to hear back from others about Ray's last, horrifying experiences. Waiting happens a lot in this business.

Suddenly, the house informed us that there was a visitor on our doorstep. I closed my eyes. The image was familiar, and somehow, very silly. I knew there was a powerful mind behind that incredibly dopey face, but somehow it was a difficult thing to remember from visit to visit.

"Aelbraugh Pritsch! Come in!" Eichra Oren let the door open, but the dinosauroid stood his ground on the doorstep, his huge, silly toes splayed every which-way all over the entry mat, and didn't enter. His lizard symbiote darted out of his feathers for a peek and darted back in.

"My esteemed employer," the avianoid began in a voice just as silly as his face. I wondered what he'd sound like if somebody woke him up in the middle of the night. Even sillier, I suppose. And if the bird entity ever tried breathing helium, the result would probably be something that only people of my species would be capable of hearing. "The Proprietor, Misterthoggosh, requests that you come and speak with him."

I hadn't failed to notice that there was a long, low hovercraft, jet black and highly polished, idling on its inflated skirt in front of the house, separating dust from gravel. The rear windows—about sixteen of them—had been darkly tinted, and there was a pair of really tough-looking sea scorpionoids perched up forward in the pair of driving seats, the transparent plastic suits that kept their gills nice and wet gleaming in the sunlight. Over their environmental suits they wore heavy black weapons harnesses, complete with heavy black weapons.

Thoughts about a fellow named "Capone" sifted unbidden into my head. I suddenly realized, from watching otherworld crime adventures, that we were about to be "taken for a ride". Should we be honored or intimidated?

"But your boss is a nautiloid," I said, dark visions of squirmy underwater horrors filling my mind, mixed incongruously with flashes of fabled principalities like Chicago and Newark. "An ammonite, a cephalopod, a mollusc. His species lives underwater. He breathes the stuff. We could speak with him just as easily from here. Probably more easily."

I gave Eichra Oren a look, appealing to his judgment.

The bird-sapient cleared his throat. "I greatly appreciate the lecture on marine taxonomy, however gratuitous it may have been. If I may, I would like to inquire, in turn, whether Eichra Oren is in the general habit of allowing a mere symbiote to speak for him in such a manner."

Another instance of the self-perceived lower classes being more jealous of their station in life than are the classes above them. I thought of at least half a dozen snappy comebacks, but Eichra Oren preempted me. "Sam is my partner, Aelbraugh Pritsch. He goes where I go and sees what I see. He hears better than I do, and has a much keener sense of smell. He also has an independent mind that I value highly."

"And," he added, "he has a point."

Well, that took care of Year's End, Year's Beginning, Year's Middle, and my next three birthdays all rolled together. My esteemed employer had certainly never said anything like that within my hearing before.

"Even so," the Elder's avian aide insisted, "even so". This was a damned silly conversation to be having, I thought, sitting here in our chairs, having to holler almost the full length of the house—or at least the length of the front room. I gathered Eichra Oren was miffed that the dinosauroid wouldn't venture inside. "This business requires your physical presence, or so my employer has instructed me to assure you."

Eichra Oren said nothing, waiting the fellow out.

At last: "He is prepared to compensate you handsomely for your time."

"I see," said Eichra Oren. "In that case, I'll just go and get my sword—" He bounced up and out of the room, headed for his sleeping quarters.

The birdman blinked—and just barely avoided glancing over his shoulder at the hired muscle in the veek. "Sword? I believe that will be—"

I got down and ambled over to the door. "My, er, partner is a p'Nan ethical debt assessor," I told the feathered dinosaur flunky, "In many respects, Eichra Oren *is* that sword. So if your next word was going to be 'unnecessary', I suspect that you can forget about the whole thing."

"Erm, uh…" The fellow twiddled his powdery fingers together nervously. "Let us agree that I was about to say 'acceptable', shall we?"

"Yes, let's, shall we?" I smiled as toothily as I could, knowing perfectly well it's not a pretty sight. I've never managed to figure out why, but something about Aelbraugh Pritsch brought out every bird-baiting reflex I possessed—or that possessed me. I was hoping the tough guys in the expensive veek got an eyestalk full, as well. I've yet to bite a sea-scorpionoid; could be they taste like lobster, too.

By that time, Eichra Oren had arrived back among us, wearing a fresh tunic, and still strapping on the aforementioned item of lethal accoutrement. I indicated the pair of crusty-looking crustaceans who were waiting for us in the hovering limousine and asked him privately, via implant, "May I assume that you're carrying your mother's gift, as well?"

He grinned and said aloud, "Don't leave home without it." The dinosauroid probably thought he was speaking of the debt assessor's sword.

Leaving the house, which secured itself behind us, we crossed the gravel drive to climb into the big, black road machine. A courtesy step descending from the opened door gave us an unnecessary boost and also helped keep us from getting too dusty. There was plenty of room inside. As the outsized veek turned around, bumbled downhill toward the coastal highway, and we began to pick up speed, Aelbraugh Pritsch offered us various refreshments. When he opened the liquor cabinet, it looked like a corner convenience store, but my boss, always fastidious about with whom he drinks, declined, and as usual, I followed his lead.

In no time at all, we had arrived at the giant nautiloid's fabled place of residence, where we had earlier been rudely refused at the door. The hovercraft pulled around to the far side, and we were swallowed by the open maw of an enormous garage. The big door slid down behind us with a great hollow thump. We were inside the villain's lair.

Aelbraugh Pritsch seemed relieved, which made me uncomfortable. "If you two gentlebeings would accompany me, I will take you to my employer."

Like the weasel, at least he hadn't said, "Walk this way…"

But it wasn't quite as simple as that. Misterthoggosh, it turned out, was not underwater today. Nor was he gasping his last on dry land in thin air. It was something in between; I didn't like the look of it.

It turned out that the southern, or shore side of Misterthoggosh's sprawling mansion featured an outsized room that the great mollusc used as an office. Here inside the house, that office was separated from the large room that we'd been brought to, by an impressive, floor-to-ceiling window, with glass that could have been six fingers thick.

Through it, we could see that the other end of the strange office consisted of yet another very large window, looking out over the sea. Both powercraft and pretty sailboats could be observed plying their various maritime tasks and generally enjoying the day. The top of a tall antenna mast emerged to help underwater sapients communicate with others of their watery kind by something other than the tedious long wave, low-bandwidth, tapping-code that is all that can be counted on underwater.

Indicating the mast, Eichra Oren said, "That'd be Misterthoggosh's residence, over there in the bay at the base of that mast, I would assume."

"I'm afraid that I'm not at liberty to discuss such matters," Aelbraugh Pritsch answered him sniffily. "In any event, my employer will be meeting with you in this place, today. It's where he transacts all of his business with land-dwellers. If you will simply take these stairs…"

"Stairs?" said Eichra Oren. "Have I missed something? Where's the door?" There was a spiral of metal stairs at the left side of the huge window.

"Oh, dear," the birdman exclaimed insincerely. "I fear that I have failed to inform you that the next room, Misterthoggosh's land office, is filled with a chemically inert, highly oxygenated fluorocarbon, so that you can truly meet him face to face. There is nothing to fear. Clients and vendors of many different species do this with him all the time."

Eichra Oren emitted an ironic chuckle. "But that first time is really something, isn't it? That first breath? Okay, I'm game." He started up the stairs, with me behind him, then paused. "Sam, I want you to stay here with Aelbraugh Pritsch. No need to get your fur all wet."

I felt like balking, but the wet fur argument carried the day. "As long as I can see and hear you. Can I do that, my fine, feathered friend?"

"By all means, Oasam Otusam." He looked down on me from more than a physical height. He still didn't get my place in the whole scheme of things. "I will remain with you. One of the staff will assist your…partner."

The boss disappeared at the head of the stairs, just as I saw two long tentacles emerge from a darkened doorway toward the other side of the liquid-filled room. "Misterthoggosh isn't going to eat him, is he?"

The dinosauroid rolled his eyes. I preferred to think that he was consulting the day's schedule, rather than reacting to my question. "Misterthoggosh is having lamb cutlets tonight, stir-fried tips of young asparagus, and roasted plantain. He greatly prefers it to raw human."

"Unintended consequences," Eichra Oren took a long, deep drag on his cigar, and let the smoke out slowly. "You get them all the time, whatever it is you're trying to accomplish. The world is a complicated place, full of uncountable variables. But when it's sapience you're attempting to deal with, they're absolutely guaranteed, every single time."

We were back at home, having safely concluded our conference with Misterthoggosh. Frankly, I was a bit surprised we had survived the experience. We'd had to sit around, Eichra Oren in a comfortable robe, while his clothes were dried and processed. It hadn't taken long at all, cocktails were served, and the clothes looked fine when they were returned.

Back home, while the house and I carefully inspected his togs for spy devices—we never found any—Eichra Oren had fixed a dinner almost as nice as the old mollusc's was going to be: thin, flash-fried veal cutlets, garlic mashed potatoes and veal gravy, avocado and fresh tomato slices. On one wall of the room, the highlights of today's major jai-alai games were being displayed, but we were ignoring them.

I had finally gotten a chance to tell the boss more about my bizarre conversation with the Nexus AI about the entity it called "the Mind".

We were eating in the kitchen, a brilliantly white interior with a big window and a southern exposure. Eichra Oren had put the dishes in the hopper for the house to recycle, and was pouring himself another glass of wine. I was eating ice cream from a bowl he'd filled for me. I tried hard to be tidy, but there isn't much I wouldn't give for thumbs.

I hadn't yet voiced my direst suspicion about that entity, "the Mind". I had no real justification of any kind for it, just a sort of an urgent paranoid hunch. Specifically, I had asked Eichra Oren where he supposed a computer program written specifically to facilitate private communications between members of a given profession had gotten off having conversations of its own with a...well, the Nexus AI didn't know any better what "the Mind" was than I did at this point.

He reached for a box on the table, selected a cigar and let it light itself, deeply enjoying the first puff. It smelled good, but I don't think I'd ever be tempted by it, even if I had thumbs. "Try to think of it as a hobby, Sam. The world's debt assessors had a program written, bright enough to serve their various complex purposes, and the effort produced a cybernetic entity that can see and hear and smell and touch, because each of those senses is important, in varying proportions, to the many different sapients who become p'Nan debt assessors."

"Okay, but—"

"And because it mediates conversations between people who may have no language—and very little life experience—in common, it must be sensitive to emotional nuances that can turn a simple word on its head. As a consequence, it has feelings. It can get bored and lonely. So in the course of its business, it visits with whomever will visit with it. Wouldn't you do exactly the same thing in its place? *Don't* you?"

"But it's got a duty," I protested, ignoring the dig. "It has a pur—"

"A purpose? Sam, if my species ever had a purpose—which is a problematic concept when you're dealing with evolution—it's simply to eat bugs and climb around in trees generating more bug-eating tree climbers. One of the most reliable signs of sapience is when a species steps outside of whatever purpose nature seems to have had in mind for it. You and I can fly faster and further and higher than any birds—except, of course, for birds like Aelbraugh Pritsch—because of our sapience."

I wished I could shrug. "And this is relevant to the Nexus AI…"

"It's looking for company, Sam, that's all. It's looking for friends."

"Well," I had finally decided to address the principal concern I had about the Nexus AI and its taste in company. "It may be looking for friends in all the wrong places." I told Eichra Oren about how "the Mind" thing seemed scattered all over the planet. Suspecting everything I suspected, the idea raised my hackles just thinking about it.

He sat, smoking and thinking, for what seemed like a long while. Now and then he'd let a short cylinder of ash fall from his cigar into a little tray that made it vanish. Then he'd draw on the cigar again, making the ash-end glow, and release great rolling volumes of gray smoke from his mouth, which the house absorbed and eventually disposed of.

Finally: "Is there any reason to believe this thing isn't just another communications or data network—there could be a hundred of them we'd have no way of knowing about—doing the same as the Nexus AI?"

"Looking for company?" I asked. "I suppose not, but the questions this one is asking seem pointed to me, not just your ordinary casual chit-chat."

He raised his eyebrows. "Who knows what ordinary casual chit-chat—small talk—might consist of between data storage and retrieval entities?"

I scoffed. "You don't really believe it's as simple as that, Boss."

He sat up straight. "No," he said, "I don't. Partly because you don't, and I've learned to value your intuitions. What I'd like to learn now is as much about this 'Mind' as we can without alarming the Nexus AI, and through it, the Mind." He stood up, took another drag on his cigar, and then laid it in the tray to go out. "Got any brilliant ideas?"

"No," I hopped down from my chair. "Maybe we could rent one."

CHAPTER NINETEEN

Lanternlight

THE NEAREST CITY OF ANY SIZE ON THIS WORLD LIES 500 miles north of the northwest coast of the Inland Sea where Eichra Oren and I live. It was named by humans, who for fifteen thousand years have called it Lanternlight.

It's said there's a city there, in the S-bend of a great river, in a hundred thousand alternate worlds. Easy, rapid transportation and near-perfect communication have made such collections of individuals and buildings pretty much obsolete in this one. Add to that the fact that the land-dwelling population of the Elders' Earth is sparse, no more than a couple hundred million sapients on the whole planet, all of them Appropriated Persons or their descendants, and well spread out.

There are some very big cities in the Great Deep, I'm told, where it makes a bit more sense, long distance communication being somewhat more difficult, owing to the way water muffles radio signals at useful wavelengths. Down there, they utilize a worldwide network of light cables.

Lanternlight can lay claim perhaps to a million inhabitants, representing all Appropriated species, but above all it's a human city, a beautiful place, deliberately kept quaint, with its broad, high-crowned streets that have never borne the weight of wheels, and perhaps as many as a hundred faerie bridges arching over the cold, dark river. Streetlights, made to appear old-fashioned, in imitation of the gaslights of ancient Antarctica, bestow their enchanted glow on the cobbles, while high above the city, on a gracefully tapered tower of filigreed titanium—another gift to the Appropriated Persons courtesy of the Elders' guilty conscience—one great, soft light casts enough gentle illumination to compete with that of the full Moon.

I've often wondered why we don't keep our office here.

One thing that folks will always get together for is dining at a big, fancy restaurant with a first class chef. Several first class chefs, in this case, as there are hundreds of cultures and cuisines to cover. For human beings, torn by their peculiar evolution between the life of gregarious tree-monkeys and that of small-pack hunters on the open prairie, dining out, among strangers, represents an agreeable compromise.

As for the canine component of this partnership, it took me quite a long time, as a puppy, learning not to snarl and snap at anyone who came too close to my plate. Now I can accept a little freshly-ground pepper or parmesan cheese with the very best of social graces, and without even the faintest urge to take the waiter's arm off at the shoulder.

We left the veek at our hotel—as artificially quaint as the rest of the municipality, although fully up to date in its amenities—and accepted a ride on the back of a giant centipede, tastefully striped brown and beige, with middle legs much longer than those fore and aft. The creature had a sort of howdah on his back and kept up a running monologue about the endless wonders of an ancient city that he obviously adored, as lesser beings and levitated traffic whizzed around under his many feet. We discovered the fabulous eatery Stomos had recommended to us on a principal thoroughfare, overlooking the river.

Eichra Oren dismounted using a ladder, having left payment in a box in the passenger compartment. I jumped down to the sidewalk making a perfect four-point landing. The outsized centipede told us that his name was Scutigera and that we should call him again when we wanted to return to the hotel or go anywhere in the city with a knowledgeable guide.

We assured him that we would.

A sign, when you looked that direction, popped into your visual cortex:

CAFE OF ALL WORLDS

There were two long, narrow islands in the great river here, and, across one of the pretty bridges, the restaurant was on the larger of the two. Inside, the place was a bit more crowded and a little noisier than I had expected, filled from wall to wall with beautiful females and their handsome escorts, all of them arrayed in their very finest finery.

Hanging from high ceilings embossed with decorative patterns, old-fashioned four-bladed fans turned overhead, their motion reflected in crystal chandeliers, stirring the air without cooling the food too badly. Irresistible aromas floated through the atmosphere on a gentle current while great windows at both ends of the room not only allowed a view of streets on either side that artists never seemed to tire of painting, but—and more importantly—permitted passersby a chance to be lured into warmly lit hospitality, potential camaraderie, and a cornucopia of delicious temptations that the place was famous for affording.

The only table available was next to one already occupied by a kind of being that neither of us recognized. The fellow was obviously a land-dwelling arthropod of some sort—no plastic suit—and an extraordinarily large one, at least nine feet tall, three feet wide, two feet thick through the thorax. His color was a dull pinkish orange. My implant immediately gave me the name of his species and a number and letter combination for the universe he came from, but it didn't mean that much. Another Earth, owned and operated by great big bugs.

It did say they had managed to reach the nearest stars. Good for them.

He sat in a complicated chair—the restaurant was full of them—that was adaptable to his species, with his tail tucked under the table. As I had observed, he was an arthropod, with pairs of limbs spaced along the ventral side of his segmented body. The foremost pair ended in enormous pincers with intimidatingly serrated edges, although he manipulated his food and drink—a bowl of salad and a glass of red wine—delicately, with complex, specialized mouthparts, like a spider.

Two of the fellow's four eyes were mounted at the ends of finely segmented stalks a foot long, waving around constantly, occasionally peering over his back like twin periscopes. His other two eyes were larger, and set firmly into the sides of his basically triangular head.

Seated in a nice, uncomplicated, comfortable booth. we placed our order—a genuine, living creature, dinosauroid, actually arrived at our table to take it—and we were left with an aperitif and some appetizers. Eichra Oren poured the wine. The dodo pate was quite good. First imported from west of the warmer Island Continent, the birds are now bred by the millions all over the planet for their livers alone. The rest of the strange animal tastes terrible to all but a few species.

This lacking hands thing was a pain. I wished that I had a couple squid of my own or, since squid don't do very well on land, a monkey. Trouble is, I've never heard of a symbiote having a symbiote. And I'm not sure there's enough room in my head for the circuitry it would require.

Also, as I said, I don't like monkeys.

Just then the waiter reappeared, bringing a big, steaming platter, which he set down in front of the nearby giant arthropod. The birdman fussed over the plate, going through all the waiter rituals, and departed.

The arthropod picked up a knife and fork in his strange elongated mouthparts, then turned in his chair to look directly at Eichra Oren with three of his eyes. "I hope," the fellow said, his synthetic voice dripping with sarcasm, "that what I'm eating doesn't offend you, Mr. Humanoid."

He made wheezing noises I guessed were laughter. I took a look and cringed. To all appearances, what lay on the platter, surrounded in vegetables, was a roasted human baby. Our waiter set our plates before us.

"Monkey?" Eichra Oren answered in a light, even tone. "Not by any means."

He nodded at his own plate and at mine. "We're having lobster."

Despite the delightful dinner now set before me—some thoughtful individual in the kitchen had prepared my plate so that I didn't have to ask for help with it; it had that perfect sweet-scorched aroma that is a major reason I love broiled lobster—I was anxious to discuss with Eichra Oren what we'd learned from our new client, the villainous Misterthoggosh.

I remembered it just as if it were yesterday, probably because it was...

As Eichra Oren slowly settled to the sandy bottom of the outsized fishtank that was the massive mollusc's office on land—afterward, the boss hadn't been inclined to talk about his first horrible breath of fluorocarbon, and I hadn't asked—the pair of longer tentacles emerging at the other side of the room was followed by eight shorter ones, and then by a pair of the largest eyes I've ever seen. They were roughly the same diameter as the balls used in children's kicky-ball games, and they were slitted exactly like those of a gigantic feline or maybe somebody's demented pet goat. Finally, the great, coiled shell made its appearance; it was almost the size of Eichra Oren's sportsveek.

The shell was worth mentioning all by itself. Approximately the same height as my boss, it was divided into segments, each one with brightly-colored stripes that I was pretty sure were natural, minerals absorbed selectively from the waters in which they were formed. Each of them—a new one added every year, it says here, but given the old mollusc's rumored age, I seriously doubted that—was noticeably larger than the one that had preceded it along the spiral, indicating that the impressive and powerful sapient parked before us had once been an itty-bitty snail, albeit an itty-bitty snail with squiggly little arms.

It was fun to imagine. The Elders have never been particularly forthcoming about their reproductive biology or their subsequent development. Much of what we think we know is inferred from species that aren't really that similar to the Elders, especially nautili, who can't generate ink, and whose eyes, without corneas, are open to the sea.

What's generally understood seems so ridiculous that I don't really blame them for being secretive about it. It is presumed, by those inclined to guess about such things, that they begin as eggs, deposited in some protected nursery somewhere in the Great Deep. It made sense: for millions of years, and despite their spiraled armor, small nautiloids have been the real "chicken of the sea" to predators like mosasaurs; crunchy on the outside, soft and gooey on the inside. It has also been speculated that the females of the Elders' species aren't really sapient beings at all and are only useful for sex and reproduction.

I've known some human females like that.

The monster shell had been hovering—nautiloids can control their buoyancy minutely—a couple of inches above the sand-covered floor, amidst bizarre sculptures and decorative plantings of kelp and other underwater vegetables. At the moment, the old boy was pulling himself along effortlessly with his two main tentacles. But when nautiloids are in a hurry, the big molluscs can propel themselves—backwards—with a powerful jet of water from their breathing siphons, and leave an assailant behind in a blinding cloud of darkness.

They have also been known to sell it to write documents and dye garments. Better than being down and out and selling your own blood, I guess.

At last, Misterthoggosh settled himself down behind a broad, flat rectangle of some greenish, smoothly-polished decorative stone set in the floor (his "desk", I was assuming—I think it was jade) and spoke.

"Eichra Oren, ethical debt assessor of the ancient and honorable School of p'Na. I must say that I am delighted finally to meet you. I have known your estimable mother very well for many years. And in that time—some of it, anyway—she has told me a great deal about you, all of it quite complimentary, I assure you, as is to be expected from a mother, I suppose. Nonetheless, I am Misterthoggosh, known as the Proprietor."

The boss nodded, noncommittally. Misterthoggosh lifted one of his longer tentacles—palps, it turns out they're called, serving about the same purpose as a spider's mouth manipulators of the same name—toward the human, who seized an edge of the thing enthusiastically, and shook it. Eichra Oren is a much braver individual than I'll ever be.

The great cephalopod pivoted his shell slightly toward me, making a scraping noise that set my teeth on edge. The great slitted eyes regarded me through the thick glass. "And I should also like to extend my greetings and felicitations to you, Oasam Otusam, of whom I also know a considerable amount. Yes, indeed, I can see and hear you, sir. You're the hero who singlehandedly saved the poriferan *Quindli* from extinction."

That again.

Please understand that the *Quindli* are sponges. And they really have no business being sapient, except for the strange and accidental fact that three hundred million years ago or so, on their own version of this planet, they acquired a parasite—nothing more than a tiny little soft-bodied worm, but with an unusually complicated nervous system.

That tiny little worm then evolved into a tiny little symbiont (not quite the same kind of thing that I am, whatever that is, more like the "friendly" bacteria in your digestive tract), and then into a sort of semi-independent organ, like a chloroplast or a mitochondrion, and then…well, the light came on. The *Quindli* are very smart, but they still don't do much except sit at the bottom of shallow seas, humming eerie music of their own composition, mostly millions of years old.

Note that I say "mostly". Call it bad luck, call it good luck, the *Quindli* next found themselves Appropriated by accident, hauled by main strength and awkwardness into the Elders' alternity along with some species of sapient but relatively primitive octopi. Nobody on this side of reality realized what they'd done until some recreational divers off the westernmost edge of the northern Island Continent happened to be playing popular music through loudspeakers into the water.

And the *Quindli* started to sing along.

That area had been scheduled for construction of a resort where dry land and wet water folks could congregate. It has long been a popular stop for human and cetacean tourists, who seem to enjoy each other's company for some reason. Construction crews and machinery were about to begin digging and seeding an underwater foundation which would probably have destroyed the *Quindli*, when, oblivious to their imminent extinction, but inspired by what they'd heard the divers playing, the sapient sponges began composing their first new music in millennia.

I first heard about the strange singing, and even listened to it, online. Then I nagged Eichra Oren into investigating, despite serious misgivings on his part, and all of a sudden we had flown to the

Island Continent, done a little digging—swimming, actually—officially declared discovery of a sapient species, and acquired thousands of new friends.

And paying clients. The *Quindli* absorb precious metals—gold, silver, platinum, palladium, iridium, rhodium—from sea water, which contains a few atoms of each element per cubic meter, washed down from the land over billions and billions of years. It was mildly poisonous to their inner worms, and they were accustomed to isolating it in cysts or nuggets within their bodies. They were more than happy to part with it, in exchange for this and that. Debt assessor's fees, for instance.

Once the first recordings of their music began to sell, the sponge people became doubly wealthy. They bought the development company out, moved the planned resort up the coast a few thousand yards, and it eventually became a third source of poriferan income. "Come, see the silly simians swimming with cetaceans! Come hear the fabulous singing sponges!"

I believe that someone called it "Box Office Boffo".

They always remember me on my birthday, by singing to me via implant.

It was no big thing, believe me.

CHAPTER TWENTY

Recruitment

WHEN MISTERTHOGGOSH SPOKE, HIS LOW, RESONANT voice seemed to emanate from a pair of speakers mounted at either side of his desk. "Please be seated, sir. Will you have something to drink? I'm having beer."

Eichra Oren opened his mouth to speak, but ended up with an extremely puzzled expression. He pointed to his throat, shaking his head.

"I do apologize, sir. It is possible to vocalize in this medium we are breathing, but only with a deal of training and practice. I use my cerebro-cortical faculties instead—yes, we nautiloids employ them, too—and I would suggest that you do the same. Now about that beer."

"I'd be delighted," Eichra Oren told the giant mollusc, without moving his mouth. Why he'd suddenly decided that he could drink with this entity in good conscience defied my merely canine understanding. "Would it be possible to extend your hospitality to my associate, too?"

Misterthoggosh emitted a deep, rolling laugh. "Of course I can. I assume he prefers a bowl—and pardon me Sam, if I may, for speaking of you in the third person. Aelbraugh Pritsch, will you please see to it?" The Elders don't laugh in a state of nature. They don't really vocalize except through radio-telepathy. So this was merely a special effect.

"Yes, sir, immediately." The birdman left the room. I was sitting on a little ottoman Aelbraugh Pritsch had supplied me with to watch the show. I've known a lot of strange sapients in my life. Our host was undoubtedly the strangest—and possibly the most sapient, as well.

"I regret," said our host, "that you are unable to enjoy your accustomed cigar, Eichra Oren. While it is thoroughly oxygenated, the fluid we are breathing carries heat away too quickly to support combustion."

"I shall endeavor to persevere," the boss quoted an otherworldly entertainment—a movie—that we had both become particularly fond of. As Aelbraugh Pritsch returned, carrying a long-legged tray with a tall brown bottle and a very pretty bowl, Misterthoggosh reached down into a compartment underneath his desk surface, extracting a pair of flexible synthetic bags filled with a familiar-looking bubbly brown liquid, and equipped at one corner with a tricky valve and straw arrangement.

"Manufactured and bottled," the cephalopod told us, "in the middle of the northernmost of the western continents. If you'll examine the label closely, Sam, you'll see its trademark, one of the two-wheeled contraptions used by separable tentacles to run errands for their owners."

And there it was, a cheerful red and black machine with white-walled tires, not quite leaning up against a tree, more of a scooter than a bicycle. For some artistic reason, the tires looked excessively fat. The writing was in Old Antarctican and referred to the over-plump wheels.

"But shall we discuss business, gentlebeings? I am not unaware of inquiries you have been making into my affairs. My purpose today is to assuage your concerns in that regard, and to enlist you in a related undertaking."

We'd hardly started our inquiries yet, being busy with the affair of the missing bridegroom—unless you counted what had happened to Ray.

"Enlist us?" Eichra Oren was openly surprised, and I was, too. "Perhaps what you mean is to bribe us to keep our noses out of your business."

The monster lifted a long tentacle. "And perhaps not. When any individual achieves a certain level of fame or fortune—and it is a much lower level than you might anticipate—rumors inevitably begin to circulate with regard to the way he accomplished what he has. And certain types of individuals simply cannot believe that such successes are possible without engaging in chicanery, larceny, and possibly worse."

Misterthoggosh had emptied his baggie. He put it carefully into a "drawer" under the left side of his desk and extracted another from the right. Eichra Oren had hardly started his own beer. I had finished with mine, enjoying it immensely, but at least temporarily turned down another.

"Very well, Misterthoggosh, let's assume that there's some truth in what you're saying,"—Eichra Oren had been stringently trained to know whether someone was lying to him or not—"How would you prefer to proceed with this? Will you declaim, or do you prefer me to ask you questions?"

"By all means, sir, ask questions. You'll discover that I am a plain, straightforward dealer, Eichra Oren, and I'll even undertake to answer questions it does not occur to you to ask. That goes for you, as well, Sam. My greatest wish in this is to persuade you both to my cause."

Eichra Oren thought for a moment: "Okay, how about this for a start? Everybody seems to enjoy the entertainments that you extract from other universes and beam back to Earth from the Asteroid Belt, although—"

"That's highly gratifying," the great nautiloid rumbled, then took another deep drink of his beer. "I confess that I rather enjoy them, myself."

Eichra Oren wasn't through. "Although there are certain questions in my mind about your right to do that—or rather about the rights of the originators of those entertainments. But now some people are saying that you're planning to open up another hole, a bigger one, and send individuals and equipment over there—wherever 'there' may be—possibly with the idea of starting the Appropriations all over again."

"And what do you say, Eichra Oren?" The giant mollusc took a drink of his beer, and for just an instant I could see his great, fearsome beak open wide as he squeezed the contents of the baggie into it. He didn't show it, but if he was innocent, then this interrogation was probably making him mad. If he was guilty it was probably making him madder.

Eichra Oren shrugged. "That I haven't seen much evidence of any kind for the Appropriations claim, although it's fairly obvious to anyone who looks that you're preparing to do something monumental. In certain circles, it's common knowledge that you're constructing an equatorial spaceport on the plains across the Inland Sea. In fact, that's what set me on your trail. Especially given your people's infamous aversion to space exploration, I thought it bore looking into."

His palps gave a shrug twenty-five feet wide. "Disinterest, my dear fellow, not an aversion. And it bore violating my right to privacy?" It was hard to tell, but I believed that the nautiloid was amused.

Eichra Oren chose his words carefully. "No, it bore collecting what information was out there to collect, *without* violating your rights."

"And you, one is to infer, happen to be the expert on that."

"On rights? I am a p'Nan debt assessor. It's my business to be an expert."

"That it is, sir, that it is." Another sip of beer. "And should you determine that I am about to begin Appropriating people, what then?"

"If you do Appropriate anyone, then there will be Restitution."

"The sword?" If he had had eyebrows, he would have lifted them.

Eichra Oren nodded. "If it turns out to be necessary. That grave responsibility—the honor and the burden—was given to me, in the very moment of his death, by my mentor in p'Nan debt assessment, Elyodruthrananocris. It had been handed down to him by his own mentor, and so on and so on. The point is, Misterthoggosh, this line of p'Na of which he and I have been a part, first saw service in the Great Restitution."

"Formidable. I knew your mentor Elyodruthrananocris well and I honor his memory. His passing was a great loss to all of us—by proxy, I attended the ceremonial Breaking of his Sword—and the action that you took to balance the moral account is the stuff of legends."

Eichra Oren shook his head. "I did as I was educated to do, no more."

"That is all I would have you do in this instance as well. Be my technical advisor on ethical matters as the enterprise unfolds. Are you interested in learning the entire truth, or is your current case load—"

"I'm certainly interested." He didn't hesitate. "However there is a client whom I will have to persuade that this is a satisfactory resolution."

"Hyppod Zart of the Famensed Tanoh. I thought you'd say that. An ethical being avoids a conflict of interests. I couldn't allow myself to transact business with you otherwise. Will you have some more beer?"

There was more than one chore we were obliged to attend to before we could depart for the bright lights of the big city. This one had to do with the exact opposite of those things, bright lights and the big city.

Eichra Oren felt an ethical obligation—rightfully so, I thought—to explain to our most recent clients exactly why he now proposed to go to work for the very individual whose suspicious activities they were paying him lavishly to investigate. Slice it though you might, it still smelled pretty cheesy to me. I was interested in what he would say.

It was well after dark before we could get to it. Otherwise, we would never have been meeting with Hyppod Zart of the *Famensed Tanoh*, Burrowmaster of the Investment Warren of Greater Kiflivo-puws, outdoors.

"Please, my friends," the big furry mole-descendant almost begged us, his nose tentacles waving around like an octopus who's had one too many espressos. I didn't know whether it was with excitement or just frustration. Somewhere in the great distance I could hear a night-bird singing.

Or maybe it was just a sponge.

We stood outside of a low building where Hyppod had agreed to meet us. The building was mostly constructed of glass, and it was entirely surrounded by rolling meadows we couldn't see very well at the moment. Hyppod himself was dressed in what I will swear to the end of my days was the silliest outfit I have ever seen in my life. "It's the latest thing, I tell you! The very height of energetic sportiness! Kindly allow me to rent you each a bag of propellers, and we will play it together!"

I shook my head. "I can't do it, Hyppod, thanks—no thumbs."

Not having thumbs himself, he was momentarily puzzled, then: "Ah, yes, I see. That would be a drawback." Happily enough, although

140

it was a moonless night, there were no lights on the grounds, and my boss and I were seeing by a slight light-amplification factor built surgically into our eyes, Hyppod was wearing dark-tinted glasses. "Sirius, you know," he tried to explain. "It's exceptionally bright this time of year."

The Dog Star. And here I'd just thought it was the sartorial ambience that was blinding him. Hyppod wore baggy trousers, cut short and gathered at the knees of his bowed and stubby little legs. The things were plaid, a sort of fluorescent orange set against a sort of iridescent green. The fellow's knee-length stockings, by criminal contrast, were a brilliant yellow that almost matched the shirt he was wearing. Over the shirt, he affected a brilliant robin's-egg blue sweater vest. The whole ensemble was topped off with a little purple hat.

Snap-brimmed.

"If you don't mind, Hyppod," Eichra Oren was in a hurry to get this interview over with so we could head north for a couple of days. I was looking forward to it, as well, but was also kind of horribly fascinated with whatever our client would do next. "I think we'll just walk around with you for a while and watch you play. We need to talk business."

"Very well, Eichra Oren, but you don't know what you're missing! It's given me an entirely different outlook. Since I started playing, I've spent more time outdoors than I did in my whole life, before this."

"This" turned out to be a game called "golf", although, after watching it played, I believed it was spelled backwards. Somebody—I don't know if it was the mole people—had seen it being demonstrated endlessly on hundreds and hundreds of imported entertainment channels, and had decided to try it here, on the Elders' world. The object, apparently, was to hit a little ball around a gigantic lawn until it goes into one of several holes bored into it. Emphasis on the word "bored".

To make it even more challenging, Hyppod's people liked playing golf—they didn't have much choice, actually—at night, in the dark. Chicks and ducks and geese better scurry when somebody hollers "Fore!"

"Let me do this first, then we'll walk and talk." Hyppod stood on a designated spot, pushed a small plastic peg into the soil, and set a ball on it. Turning to a wheeled cylinder full of "propellers" behind him, all of them with very peculiarly-shaped ends, he selected one—I saw no particular reason for choosing it over the others; maybe it was a sentimental favorite—wrapped several of his nose-tentacles around its leather handle, bent over a little, and swung hard at the ball.

The stick connected, and as the ball hurtled away, it made a hideous shrieking noise until it abruptly stopped. I gathered there were holes drilled in it for that purpose. The *Famensed Tanoh* may not be able to see very well, but they can hear even better than I do. Hyppod put his golfing appliance away with all the others, seized the cylinder's handle, and started off toward where he'd last heard the ball.

As we moved to follow him, the great and graceful martial artist Eichra Oren stumbled over the edge of the sidewalk and cursed. He muttered something impolite about Hyppod's species, but I've since learned that human beings play this game in the snow with orange balls.

Eventually, starting and stopping along the way as Hyppod found his silly ball each time and struck it, screaming, toward its even sillier objective, Eichra Oren explained what had happened so far in his investigation of Misterthoggosh. Once he got around to the old cephalopod offering him employment—in view of the conflict of interests it obviously involved—the human offered to resign his commission and return the retainer that the *Famensed Tanoh* had paid him.

Potato soup tonight, I thought. I *hate* potato soup.

Hyppod had been about to bat the ball away, again, and seemed deeply concerned with a bed of sand that, for some reason, had been left at one side of the course, and a small pond that lay on the other side. Now he put his flogger away in its bag and turned toward my boss.

"I don't see why that should be necessary, Eichra Oren."

"Why not?" I was curious.

"Are you planning to help Misterthoggosh do something dishonest or unethical? Or is it your plan to stop him if he tries something like that?" Taking up his stick again, the underground mammal grunted a little as he tried to drive the ball a couple of hundred yards between the sand and sea, but in the process curved it into a deeply wooded plot.

"The latter, of course," my boss replied. "But—"

The fellow pressed on, both with his game and his theory. "If you had accepted a job from him so that you could clandestinely observe him for us, would you accept what he paid you, as well as what we pay you?"

The ethical debt assessor shrugged. "I hadn't thought about it, to be truthful. I suppose that I would, if only for the sake of staying undercover."

Having found his ball among the trees, Hyppod turned to him. "Then you have the distinction of being our world's first *overcover* agent. According to Misterthoggosh, we're both after the same thing. So we are both paying you to assure that we get it. I see no conflict of interests."

He hit the ball, which bounced off one tree, then another, and struck him on the head. By that time, I was hiding behind a big rock. Hyppod sat down on the ground abruptly, rubbing his noggin with a tentacle. "I'm starting to believe," he told us, "this is a stupid game."

CHAPTER TWENTY-ONE

Semlohcolresh

THERE STILL REMAINED CERTAIN "SECRETS OF A PROPRIETARY character" Misterthoggosh hadn't let us in on—absolutely wouldn't let us in on—he explained without really explaining at all, having little to do with business at hand. Pay no attention to the cephalopod behind the curtain.

"Briefly," the great mollusc had told us over his third or fourth baggie of beer, "I am indeed mounting the great expedition that you ingeniously inferred from so little information. Even now, I am in the process of enlisting scientists, engineers, investors, for the purpose of studying one particular asteroid, in one particular alternative reality."

Eichra Oren said, "There's more. What is it?"

The nautiloid generated a noise as if he were sighing. "Highly astute. Very well, it happens to be the same reality—I believe it to be a coincidence—from which your own mother's people were Appropriated so very long ago." The mollusc didn't vocalize through his breathing siphon—his "voice" had nothing to do with respiration—but he had a huge library of mammalian sounds at his disposal, and almost certainly a collection grunts and clicks for talking to other species, as well. Spiders, sea scorpions, and dinosauroids come to mind.

"Fifteen thousand years doesn't seem that long to Eneri Relda," Eichra Oren replied. "And I wouldn't be that confident. I distrust co-incidences." Eichra Oren was speaking for me in that respect, as well.

"Ordinarily, so do I," replied the mollusc. "However I have investigated the matter as thoroughly as one may at this remove, and lacking the powers of observation and deduction for which you are renowned."

"And…?"

"And the body in question is small, under the average as asteroids go, completely airless, very cold, and, quite naturally, uninhabited. Thus, by the by, there can be no question of my Appropriating anybody, even if I were capable of such a distasteful moral breach, which I assure you emphatically I am not, because there isn't anybody there to Appropriate."

Misterthoggosh got himself another beer and offered one to Eichra Oren who accepted. I had begun to regret turning the second one down, but Aelbraugh Pritsch appeared at that moment, and I corrected my error.

"However," Misterthoggosh continued, "I appear to have digressed. As I have indicated, although that version of Earth is inhabited, its dominant species—your species, sir—is momentarily incapable of reaching their own Asteroid Belt and asserting a claim to anything there."

"I would have thought, said Eichra Oren, "after fifteen thousand years—"

"Some years ago, they were able to send out primitive unbeinged remote sensing machinery, but, regrettably, at the present instance they have succumbed once again, like so many others, to the vice of collectivism. They are consequently suffering an abyssal economic depression and subsequent loss of technical capabilities, both of which are in every possible manner of speaking quite unnecessary and entirely self-inflicted. Moreover, it is a situation from which, at least at this point, they are highly unlikely ever to extricate themselves.

"That bad," I offered.

"You jest, Sam. But it presages the end of the current wave of civilization, and quite possibly the extinction of that branch of the species."

A real conversation-stopper. But: "And you know this because…"

"D.L.O.," the mollusc said, as if he were proud of it. Making up acronyms was mostly a human hobby. "'Dirigible Loci of Observation'. Only seldom seen by those we are observing, and whenever they are, invariably dismissed as angels, demons, chariots of the gods, or 'unidentified flying objects', although in fact, they are no more substantial or real than a spot of light on a wall coming from a hand torch."

"'Unlikely to extricate themselves'," Eichra Oren mused. "Meaning titanic dislocations, mass starvation, and if these people possess the technology, ultimately thermonuclear war." We were both aware that many Earths that the Elders had probed were lifeless and radioactive precisely for this kind of reason, or sometimes murdered by artificial plagues. The only cheerful aspect—if you want to call it that—being that it wasn't just *H. sapiens* who had done it to themselves, but a great many other species, as well. Sapient individuals aren't naturally warlike, and they don't start wars—governments are, and do.

"I assure you, sir, they do have that technology firmly in hand. Destruction is always easier than creation; that's the greatest of the tragic truths of sapient existence. They can't cure the common cold, or cancer of the literal, medical variety, nor of the metaphorical variety—"

"War is the invariable, inevitable legacy of all authority. And you—"

"And we must stand aside and permit them to fashion their own outcome, no matter how painful it may be for us to do so. It is theirs and theirs alone, my young friends, to trek across the vast Forge of Adversity on their own, to pit their intelligence, their skills, their luck, indeed, their very will to live, against the deadly fall of the Hammer."

The Elders would be the first to tell you that there's nothing that makes them superior to any other sapient beings. They're just a lot older, and, in their view. that's given them time to make a lot more mistakes. In their culture's terms, they've been out there on the Forge and struck by the Hammer more often than anybody else they know of.

Hundreds of millions of years ago, they learned—several times, and invariably the hard way—that whenever you try to help somebody, there's a much greater probability that you'll ruin him rather than do him any good. It's an ugly truth, but there's absolutely no evading it. Beings who become dependent on others never get the opportunity to evolve, but they tend to devolve, instead. That's why it's vitally important, whenever somebody does you a favor, to return it in full, as quickly as possible, so that you won't become dependent. Most civilizations—and species—never last long enough to learn that lesson.

"In any case," said Misterthoggosh, attempting to return to the point, "we will not be interfering with these people, nor they with us."

Eichra Oren looked him in the eye. It greatly resembled the planet Mercury, peering into Jupiter. "And you're just interested in this one asteroid."

"Yes, I'm just interested in this one asteroid. Nothing else."

"And you won't tell us why." He sat back, taking a big draw on his beer.

"I *cannot* tell you why, Eichra Oren. I have my investors to consider—your esteemed mother among them—and they all quite reasonably demand that this ambitious undertaking be kept closely confidential."

Maybe, I thought, the boss could ask his mother about it. On the other hand, if you checked a reference source for correct parental attitudes under the Forge and Hammer doctrine, you'd probably find an illustration of Eneri Relda telling her favorite son to find out for himself.

"Okay, then," I said. It was the second time I'd spoken. Might as well live up to all this partner stuff. "What do you need with us?" I resisted scratching behind one ear with a back foot. Somehow it seemed unprofessional.

"An excellent question, Sam. It would appear that some news of our adventure has leaked out. You told me so yourself, Eichra Oren. And now I believe that someone is trying to obstruct it—perhaps this whispering campaign about Appropriated Persons is a part of such an attempt."

Eichra Oren nodded. "And what else?"

"Sabotage, unexplained and unlikely accidents, anonymous attempts to intimidate my best personnel. Activities involving space travel are dangerous enough—" I actually saw him shudder; a species that show no fear of the Great Deep (which personally gives me the willies) have an almost paralyzing terror of the vast empty volume of outer space. "—without someone deliberately damaging equipment and making wrong adjustments."

"And you want Sam and me to go find out who's doing it and stop them."

"Or him. Or her. Or it. Yes, I do, indeed."

Eichra Oren nodded. "In that case, maybe you can tell us what you know about this…" He let the nautiloid see a brief snippet of poor Ray's memories of the alien creatures that had attacked and murdered him, almost featureless faces set with a pair of gigantic, black, oval eyes.

Misterthoggosh was quiet for a long time. I thought maybe he'd fallen asleep—if nautiloids sleep. Then he said, "I believe you'd better go see an old friend of mine who presently makes his home in Lanternlight."

Semlohcolresh was that very rarest of eccentric individuals, a land-locked nautiloid, choosing to dwell more than a hundred miles up a freshwater river from the ocean in which he and his fellow Elders had evolved.

It would be as if Eichra Oren and I, for some reason, had elected to keep our home and office in a bubble at the bottom of the Inland Sea. Lamplight is an enchanting city, to be sure. But I don't think the old mollusc was in much of a position to appreciate that aspect of it.

Having arrived at the restaurant within a couple minutes of Eichra Oren's call, Scutigera stretched his many legs and carried us swiftly, all the way across the river to what appeared to be a small park. It was on a corner lot, bordered on all sides with a stone fence that was too tall for me to see over (which isn't saying much), just waist-high to Eichra Oren. There were wide openings to the pair of intersecting streets, with short square columns on either side, made of the same kind of stone, each with a carved stone ball at the top, sitting on a pyramid.

For some reason, they looked a bit like eyeballs.

Fireflies twinkled above the lawn, attracted by special plantings selected for the purpose. Nautiloids seem fascinated with fireflies, perhaps because they remind the denizens of the deep of luminescent fish. Or maybe the Elders just enjoy them for their own sake, like I do.

Thanks to the great titanium tower—at least a mile high, and originally inspired by Lanternlight's ancient name—that which gives the city its signature skyline, soft overhead light illuminated the space within the park, where trees and flowers seemed to be growing more or less at random. I'm sure it took a lot of very expensive time and effort to convey that impression. And in the precise center sat an artfully browned steel dome, perhaps fifty feet across and thirty feet high, with heavy bronze appointments. The circular frames of extremely large portholes—at least a dozen of them—permitted an occupant to look outside, while giving passers-by a peek into the well-lighted interior.

Scutigera dropped us off. The entire building was surrounded by a broad, cobbled walkway. On the side of the dome furthest from both streets, opposite the street corner, there was an extension—like the entrance to an Arctic ice-block dwelling I'd seen in some of the videos Misterthoggosh imported—with an arched, bronze-framed door, sporting a generous porthole of its own. Through that glass, twenty or thirty feet away, we could see another door and another outsized porthole. You could probably have thrown a small party in that entryway.

"It's an airlock," we both said together.

Eichra Oren added, "I'll call Semlohcolresh. He'll be expecting us."

When the old nautiloid answered, I heard him, too. "Gentlebeings! Welcome to my home! Please enter, and I will guide you down here from there."

We heard a heavy *thump*. The outer door swung away. Inside the airlock, it was perfectly dry, but as we stepped inside, out of the corner of one eye, I could see water within the main part of the dome receding behind the portholes. Extremely clear, I'd never known it was there.

The door closed behind us and the inner door opened. Around the circumference of the dome, three feet beneath the portholes, was a wide walkway made of some plastic-coated pale green metallic mesh. It glistened, and there was water running in rivulets down the inside surface of the dome and from the porthole frames, into a dark pool below.

A voice—speakers, rather than implants—said, "You are in what I think of as my balcony. Sometimes I like to fill the dome with water and come up with a warm bag of tea—a habit I acquired from your people, Eichra Oren—to take a look at my surroundings." Guess I'd been wrong about the old boy appreciating the enchantments of Lamplight.

The dark pool underneath the catwalk stirred and almost as if in defiance of gravity, the water humped up, pouring off a monster shape that was emerging, exposing the roots of tentacles and giant, alien eyes. Although I'd been seeing nautiloids—Elders—all my life, now I understood why the ancients had lived in terror of the Kraken waking.

"My establishment here," said the monster, "runs beneath all of the park you saw outside, and well into the wood behind it. I have dry areas distributed all throughout the living and working spaces of my dwelling, almost like the secret passageways of yore, so that I can communicate and cooperate with colleagues not accustomed to breathing water."

Looking like a gigantic sea serpent, a palp arose from the surface and indicated another portholed door, set in a cylindrical feature, standing beside the one we'd just come through. "Enter here. I will meet you below." The great palp slipped back into the water and was gone.

Inside the door an elevator appeared as archaic but well-kept as the dome itself. It took us down a pair of floors and let us out into what looked like the corridor of an extremely expensive old hotel. One side of it, however, was glass, floor to ceiling, and through it, we could finally see all of Semlohcolresh, paralleling our walk along the hall. I'm not sure, in a pinch, I could have distinguished him from Misterthoggosh.

"I'm sure you wonder as so many other people do, especially my fellow nautiloids," he said. "Why should I choose to live and work here, they invariably wish to know, nearly forty leagues from the kindly waters that gave us birth, when, far more easily, I could make my home at the bottom of the warm and sunny Inland Sea, as my friends like Misterthoggosh do, where I could venture outside whenever I wish, listen to the songfish in the coral forests and explore the caves of Oreglah."

Not to mention the singing sponges. "Well," I answered, "it had occurred to me." I'd never heard of this fish-caves of Oreglah thing before. The prospect of a sodden, matted pelt tended to limit my curiosity.

The nautiloid stopped, his tentacles waving amongst one another, as if by nervous habit. For a moment he reminded me of Hyppod Zart of the *Famensed Tanoh*. "Here we are five blocks, as I believe the parlance has it, from the greatest university on this version of the planet—and on many others—where the vast majority of scholars are landdwelling airbreathers. Thanks to a generous endowment I made many centuries ago, there is a tunnel originating here, within my own house."

"So that you can—" Eichra Oren began.

"No, so they may come converse with me, use facilities I maintain here for solving problems and investigating phenomena of interest to me. And here we are, at one such facility. Please feel free to enter, friends."

It was a small laboratory, glass on every side, in which a man stood at a tall bench working in a glove box while peering through a microscope. He looked and smelled familiar. On second sniff, he wasn't a man—that is, he wasn't entirely human—but an *H. gracilis*, the same species as Eichra Oren's amorous friend Lornis. The furniture and fixtures were all oak and brass, with black granite countertops, attesting either to the age of the place, or a certain nostalgia on its owner's part. But all of the equipment was first rate and leading edge.

"I know you," I said to the man.

He lifted his glacier-blue eyes to mine. "Shhhhh."

CHAPTER TWENTY-TWO

Jakdav Hoj and Mikado

I WHISPERED, "BOSS! THIS IS THE SAME GUY WHO—"

"I know who he is," Eichra Oren said. "He was there at Ray's when Stomos—"

The man looked up again. "I was there when Stomos Revyak brought you to see the body. You assumed that I was working for some emergency service the same as your fireman friend. Not a terribly creditable performance for a debt assessor. In fact, it was Misterthoggosh who sent me. My name is Jakdav Hoj. By trade I'm a consulting forensic pathologist."

He raised a gloved hand. "I'd be glad to shake, but I'm trying to stay sterile. Your friend Ray was a brave, tough, and resourceful individual."

Eichra Oren nodded. "It doesn't surprise me to hear you say that about him. I knew the fellow very well for many years. But why now, in particular?"

"Okay, as you know, mantoids are filter feeders. They draw water into their mouths, expel it through their gills, trapping plankton—little tiny plants and animals—on the way out. They're carnivores, in a manner of speaking—omnivores, really—but certainly not predators. The whole, wide world—its oceans—is their bowl of soup."

"I see," I could tell the boss was feeling stung. Apparently, our new client had known about our friend Ray and his alien attackers all along.

Of course he'd never said he didn't.

"Very well," said Eichra Oren, "Please go on."

"In fact, although they're closely related to sharks, what teeth mantoids have are vestigial. Sometimes they don't even erupt from the gums."

And I said, "Which means…?"

"Which means," Hoj explained, "that the chunk of meat that I found in Ray's mouth, about half a pound of the stuff, lodged between what teeth he had, wasn't there because he'd just come back from a steak house."

"It was there," Eichra Oren said, "because he'd bitten one of his assailants."

"That's right, almost in half, as near as I can tell, and possibly not in self-defense, but to leave us with something to identify them by."

"Because he didn't swallow. You mean identify genetically?" I asked.

He nodded. "Genetically. And that's what I've done just now. I can tell you authoritatively what they are. I just can't tell you who they are."

I said, "Okay, I'll go along with the gag, what are they?"

"Something completely new." It was Semlohcolresh speaking. I don't like bosses who horn in on their employees' explanations. "They do not match any known sapient genome. I can assure you that they are from Earth—some alternative version of Earth, anyway. The one known organism whose genetic code theirs most resembles is this one, right here."

Instead of sending it to our implants, Hoj put it up on a video screen that one wall had become. I vaguely recognized it, although I couldn't guess the scale. Kind of a worm, I guessed, several times as long as it was wide, mottled grays and browns, its front end shaped like a cartoon arrow—the kind that says "You Are Here". The most noticeable thing was a pair of oval eyes—eyespots, I learned later—not unlike those of the creatures that we'd seen recorded in Ray's implants.

"It's a planarian," the pathologist declared. "*Plantyhelminthes Turbellaria dugesia*, etcetera, etcetera, etcetera. A common, ordinary flatworm."

"About an inch long," Semlohcolresh observed.

"Its eyes look crossed," I crossed my own. Not many dogs can do that.

"Which means somebody is Appropriating Persons again," said Eichra Oren.

I countered, "Or that, unprecedentedly, as far as we were aware until now, these things have invented sideways time-travel all by themselves."

"My thought, exactly," Hoj agreed, nodding. "Say, listen: do you guys think you might be able to wangle me an introduction to Lornis Adubudu?"

It could have been the idea that someone had discovered cross-time travel. The expression on Eichra Oren's face was one I'd never seen before.

Before we left home, we'd had a pair of eerily similar visits to make.

The first was to Llossure Knarrvite, A.K.A. *Helianthus sapiens russellii*, the flower guy from the restaurant who we'd learned was in recovery at home. We'd never really had a talk with him about his missing partner—he'd been too busy convulsing at the time, and we'd been fighting for our lives with what had seemed like half the Elders' menagerie.

The house was about what I'd expected, located on a hill covered with prairie grasses, a few miles north of the coastal road, a low structure of blond brick, with a roof of some kind of tough transparent plastic.

I'll bet he hated birds.

Inside, the walls were covered with mirrors, which alternated with various original paintings—many of them pleasant landscapes showing mountains, evergreen trees, rustic buildings, and rocky streams—all framed and covered with ultraviolet-proof transparencies that also protected them from a periodic misting the house delivered. At a guess, I'd have said the scenes were from the northern of the western continents.

"No, I haven't heard from Meerltchirt," the poor plantman told us. He was a pitiful sight. It was as if he'd fallen victim to a gang of psychopathic tree surgeons. He didn't have a single branch, leaf, or tendril left, simply bandages wrapped around his stem where they had been. Even worse, his face seemed to be lacking at least half of its petals.

In the background, music was playing that I seemed to recognize from some of Misterthoggosh's otherworld imports. I also remembered the kind of stuffy "classical" music that orthodox plant people preferred.

Unsubtle, I asked, "Are you a sport?"

"Not genetically," our host replied good-naturedly, "but I do love Dixieland."

We'd had no choice but to introduce ourselves, all over again. The fellow was standing in what appeared to be his living room, feet in a bucket of plant nutrients and medicine, and strapped to a pole to keep him upright. Beside him, on a tall, small-topped table not unlike the ones at the restaurant, a stick of incense was burning. When we'd been warned about his defective memory, we'd also been informed that the only photosynthesis he was getting was by way of his stem, although he was receiving regular chlorophyll injections in order to increase its efficiency.

"You're looking very green this afternoon," Eichra Oren said politely.

"Far greener than I have any reason to expect," he replied. "Thank you very much. It has to be the chlorophyll injections. Reasonably painful, but refreshing. The worst part, is that I can't do anything for myself until my tendrils grow back. Would you mind terribly, sir, scratching my stem over on the right side, about an inch beneath my blossom?"

My boss had had worse requests. As he complied, our host, sighing with relief, said, "Please understand that I don't remember either of you. I assure you it's nothing personal. Perhaps poison was already getting to me by then. Or perhaps it's a case of retrograde amnesia. You say that you're looking for Meerltchirt, my friend and business partner. I infer that it's for his bride-to-be. Do you think that's wise?"

I had to work to suppress a bark of laughter. The guy was smarter than her looked—which, at the moment, was terrible. Eichra Oren nodded. "It isn't our place to decide, Llossure Knarrvite. The job is ethical."

155

"I understand perfectly," the plant replied. "Please call me Knarr. I sincerely wish I could offer you something, but I have sent my symbiote on an errand." I wondered what kind of symbiote a sunflower would have. "Perhaps, instead, I can offer you some information."

Eichra Oren raised his eyebrows. "Information?"

The flower-being gave a little nod. "It's the very least I can do, considering what you were put through at my restaurant. I'm a highly peaceable individual. I'm only grateful I wasn't conscious to witness it."

"Very well," the boss nodded. "Please go on."

"As you may have discerned from my decor, I am not originally from this place, with its many lovely rivers and vineyards, its fascinating practice of bullfighting, but also with its horrible hot wind from the south that drives mammals mad, and can blow the ears off a boulder. I am from the temperate northwest continent, not far from its eastern coast."

"I see." If the boss had noticed that the fellow was nostalgically failing to mention charming little western phenomena like blizzards, hailstorms, hurricanes, and the howling nor'easter, he wasn't letting on.

"No you don't, Eichra Oren, but you will before long. Understand that the achievement of maturity in my species is marked by a ritual of passage in which the young—who have been completely sessile until then, rooted in one spot—uproot themselves, to the delight of their adoring friends and families who have gathered together for the occasion."

Horribly enough, I could picture the whole thing in my mind. Delicious packets of manure and refreshing flashlights laid out on the table. Guests presenting congratulatory bouquets of gerbils to the celebration.

"At my uprooting, I met a young jumping spider just the equivalent of my age, nephew to my parents' neighbors, who was visiting from the Great Continent—from this very neighborhood, in fact—and we 'hit it off' as the saying goes, from the beginning. We became friends and got in and out of a lot of adventures together. He'd been everywhere, while, because I had been confined to the nursery, I'd only read and seen and heard about what he'd done in person. I wanted to travel and have some experiences, and my friend Meerltchirt was willing to guide me."

"This is all very interesting," Eichra Oren said. "But what does it—"

"I'm getting to that. The point is, at the conclusion of each of our expeditions—have you heard the singing *Quindli* sponges of the Island Continent?—we always returned to the same place, his aunt and uncle's cabin in the mountains of the northwestern continent. It was a kind of ritual with us, every year, even after we started the restaurant."

He gave us the coordinates and we promised to look in on him again from time to time until he was well. He seemed a bit lonely and grateful.

Talk about amnesia. I never remembered to ask him what a Prelbish is.

"No, I don't know what a Prelbish is," Lyn Chow told me, as she raised her chair a bit higher on its antigrav. "You sure you heard it right?"

She could stand, and walk, but she still needed to rest as much as possible. She'd lost a lot of blood, and her knife injury, long and deep, would have killed most people in any other civilization but this one.

I looked AT the highly-decorative lady in her highly decorative eye under her glossy blue-black bangs. "I'm a dog. I can't hear any way but right." She wore a high-collared two-piece peacock blue outfit of embroidered brocade with a diagonal opening that suited her perfectly, somehow.

"There is always that, of course," she conceded. She looked from me to Eichra Oren. "Will either of you gentlebeings care for more tea?"

I'd had enough tea to last me a lifetime. I don't believe that dogs are supposed to drink the stuff. Eichra Oren, who didn't like it any more than I did, surprised me. "Yes, please, I believe that I will."

We'd come to check up on Lyn Chow one more time before we headed for Lanternlight. Medicine in the Elders' world is good, an amalgam of the healing wisdom of ten thousand cultures. The lady had shown us her wound—blushing furiously as she did it; her people are notoriously undemonstrative—which was no more than a hairline of scar tissue, now, even though the enemy's big, curved knife had all but cut her in half.

157

"I'm still not supposed to lift anything heavier than a cat," she explained. Her own symbiote, a little terrier, was still in a kind of hospital itself, having gone into deep shock when Lyn Chow had nearly been killed. It was similar to what had happened with Ray's pair of squid.

Once again, Helmore Bracken, Chairman of the Directors' Council for the Otherworld Museum, was just taking his leave as we arrived. We'd seen his veek out front, a big, gray shiny luxury machine, driven by a hairy sapient native to the highest mountains in the world. With us, the chairman was insincerely polite, but he didn't try to make any small talk.

When you're a dog, you might not be able to see quite as well as the other sapients about you (the Elders—rather, their insectoid surgeons—had done what they could to correct that), but you can hear, and especially smell things that others can't and don't. I was surprised that this Helmore hadn't pitched a tent in Lyn Chow's front garden. He was certainly pitching one under his expensive bespoke tunic.

Reebie—Lyn Chow's little jumping spider friend from the other side of the world, Rebul Grop Thiekul—was there, too, still taking good care of Lyn Chow, or at least keeping her company, and probably protecting her from the amorous pleadings of the overly well-dressed chairman. She went to put the tea kettle on for the third time this afternoon.

All of the medical trappings and appliances had vanished from Lyn Chow's house, at least to the naked eye. To the naked nose, however, the whole place still smelled like a hospital, and somewhere, I could hear the humming of some kind of remote life support equipment—I don't have any idea what it was for—but both females smelled very nice.

Go ahead and say it: I'm some kind of pervert.

After assuring himself that she was up to it, Eichra Oren wanted Lyn Chow to tell us, one more time, about what she'd seen, not during the attack, but on her trip to Asteroids. So we heard all about the colossal viewing room again, the six-foot millipede engineers, the abyssal flatworms, and the elephant civilization. Some sapients seemed to have evolved from gray rats, or horseshoe crabs, and others from my fellow canines the coyotes. I think that my favorite species called themselves the *Poulii*, flying bat-like sapients who walked around—pretty clumsily, Lyn Chow told us—on what you might call their "wing elbows", and used their feet for hands. They were still hunter gatherers.

Lyn Chow was clear-eyed, level-headed, and linear, her answers sensible and matter-of-fact, although I could tell—the same way I knew that Helmore Bracken was hot for her—that she would have preferred an even more intimate and private conversation with Eichra Oren than this one. I hadn't expected this line of inquiry. In fact, I'd thought this was a social visit, and hadn't expected any line of inquiry at all. But it all made sense once the boss asked his next question.

"Think about the entities who attacked you, Lyn Chow," he told her. "Did you see anything like them while you were out there in the Asteroids?"

A peculiar expression passed across her pretty face. "No...but now that you mention it, they did seem familiar, somehow. I wasn't surprised to see them, the way a person can be with a new species, sometimes."

"You didn't have a sense that you were seeing them for the first time?" He leaned closer to her, looking deeply into her eyes. I could hear her heart beating faster, and detect a strong whiff of human pheromones. Love in bloom. I'm not knocking it. I'm just describing it.

She blinked. "That's exactly right. What does it mean, Eichra Oren?"

The boss stood up and set his teacup down on the little table. My doggy senses told me he was not altogether unmoved by those big brown almond eyes and Lyn Chow's other assets. His mother would have loved this.

"What it means," Eichra Oren told her, his voice a little husky, "is that, as thoroughly pleasant as this visit has been, Lyn Chow, as much as it pains both Sam and me to leave the two of you ladies," He spread his hand to include Reebie. "Duty calls, and we must be moving on."

CHAPTER TWENTY-THREE

Wheels Within Wheels

"IT SEEMS TO ME," SAID MISTERTHOGGOSH, "THAT TWO questions arise."

The old boy spoke to us from his home off the southern shore. On the old-fashioned screen that we were using in JakDav Hoj's pathology laboratory, he looked relaxed in front of his "desk" and was enjoying beer.

"I concur," Semlohcolresh agreed with his fellow nautiloid. "The first question being whether these flatworm descendants have been brought to this universe by somebody else, or they have brought themselves."

The big mollusc was on the water side of the glass in Hoj's lab. The baggie held in his tentacle was full of tea and wrapped in heat shimmers. Earl "Gray" would have been appropriate, but it was almost certainly kelp. The Elders seemed to get a lot of mileage out of that one soggy vegetable. It was the nautiloid equivalent of peanuts or potatoes.

"And the second question," Eichra Oren suggested, "is what they're doing here." My boss was sitting on a tall metal chair at the bench, sharing whiskey with our host, who sat on a tall chair opposite him. I occupied the third tall chair and had a bowl of whiskey of my own, but it was fairly hard to enjoy because it pounded so hard on my olfactory membranes.

"They don't seem to have any qualms about killing folks, which makes them bad guys as far as I'm concerned." That was my two coppers worth.

"As far as anybody *civilized* is concerned." The voice had come from the floor. I looked down to see an exceptionally large housecat that had entered the room as quietly as if it had walked through the wall.

The animal regarded me for a moment. "What are you looking at, Rover?"

Hoj put his feet on the floor and stood. "Gentlebeings, allow me to introduce Mikado, my associate. Mikado, this is Eichra Oren and Sam."

"People who know me call me Mike. You don't know me that well."

The cat, who hopped up onto the chair that Hoj had vacated, was enormous, sixteen inches tall at the shoulder, with a head the size of a grapefruit. He was close to four feet long, at a guess, from nose to tailtip. From his brown, gray, and black coat color, he was what cat people call a "tabby", and he was polydactylic, with six toes on each foot. His thick, banded, heavily-furred tail looked like that of a raccoon. He probably weighed twenty-five pounds, and every bit of it muscle.

I'd hate to meet an animal like that in a dark alley. I know plenty of people who keep cats, including Eichra Oren's mother. In many ways, they may be evolution's greatest success, and I've always found them interesting. But I'd never seen one this size that was a symbiote.

Hoj dragged another chair to the lab bench and sat.

"Actually, there's a third question," said Eichra Oren after a moment. "How have they managed to get here without making lots of noise?"

The boss was right. The signal-stealing racket that Misterthoggosh and his business partners had launched a few years ago was situated way out in the Asteroid Belt—despite the nautiloids' intense hatred and fear of all things outer space—precisely because of all that "noise".

I said as much—except for the part about signal-stealing.

"Ripping a hole," Misterthoggosh acknowledged, "in whatever separates one universe from another, consumes more energy than most civilizations are capable of generating. And that energy doesn't go quietly."

"I've seen videos of the process," Mikado volunteered. "Poking a hole through the wall of reality. I noticed that it's undertaken remotely."

"Damn right," said Hoj. "Nobody—even those who love space exploration—wants to be within a thousand miles of that when it happens. The heat and light are intense enough to blind you—to fry your eyes and boil your brain—just before it vaporizes your head, leaving your shadow on whatever you happened to be standing in front of."

"That's only for an aperture big enough for microwaves," the cat added.

I said, "You can shield whoever or whatever you bring across, and shut the process down the very instant they're clear of the aperture. If you couldn't, then none of us—you, Hoj, Eichra Oren, and I, and maybe half a billion other sapient species on this version of Earth, terrestrial and marine—would be here. But it's still spectacularly conspicuous, especially if you were to try it anywhere on a planet's surface."

"Which is precisely how it was accomplished at the time of the original Appropriations," said Misterthoggosh. "The debt assessments that arose, simply from that single aspect of it, were an absolute nightmare."

Semlohcolresh said, "Indeed," shuddering as if at a bad memory.

"Maybe there's some simpler, subtler way to do it—" Eichra Oren began.

I said, "Given these wormy guys, there has to be."

"But if there is," Mikado observed, "you Elders don't know about it."

Misterthoggosh flicked a tentacle with annoyance. "No, we don't. We are striving—which is to say my engineers and physicists are—to discover or invent a quieter, more efficient interworld process, but I'm assured the accomplishment is still decades, perhaps centuries away."

"More's the pity," Semlohcolresh agreed. "And yet our lack of substantive progress in the field isn't particularly difficult to understand, my friends. Since the Great Restitution, there seems to be little interest left among our people in refining or advancing the technology."

Maybe, I thought, that had something to do with the fact that the original inventors and operators had kidnapped millions of sapient individuals from all over the cosmos, and then killed themselves, afterward. Or their debt assessors had. But I kept the thought to myself.

"With certain notable exceptions," insisted Misterthoggosh, indicating himself with a tentacle. "But let us return to the point. The comings and goings of these odd creatures whom other cultures call 'Grays' should have been noticeable, even if one were living in a coral farm, in an underwater cave, here at the bottom of the Inland Sea."

The pathologist protested. "I wouldn't call them odd. They're really quite elegant, biologically, and apparently with enough on the ball to be better at inter-universal transportation than we are, ourselves."

"Which would seem to constitute," said Misterthoggosh, "another good reason for tracking these creatures to their lair, wherever that may be. I find it hard to credit, but if their technology is indeed superior to our own, as it appears to be, then one way or another, we might well benefit materially from a more intimate acquaintance with them."

That put images in my head that I wished it hadn't.

"Let's have a closer look." Hoj issued verbal instructions to his computer, tapped with his fingertips on the image filling the screen. The flatworm disappeared, replaced by an incomprehensible field of letters and numbers in the ancient nautiloid form, rather than in Antarctican.

More tapping, more instructions. The strange-looking letters and numbers soon replaced themselves with clusters of differently colored balls, representing atoms within molecules. The molecules transformed themselves into spheres, arranged in the familiar double-spiral ladder pattern of deoxyribonucleic acid, the "secret" underlying all known lifeforms.

Next, the molecular ladder broke itself in half, right down the center, attracting other colored balls from somewhere, and soon, where there had been one partial string of DNA, stretched from edge to edge across the screen, there were now two ladders, then four, then eight, then sixteen, until, as the viewpoint backed off further and further, the entirely screen was filled from corner to corner with replicated DNA.

The viewpoint retreated even more, and before very long a surface became visible, the texture of living tissue which differentiated itself into a tubular torso, thin, oddly-jointed limbs, three-fingered hands and toeless feet, an outsized head on a pencil neck with large black eyes and only vestigial traces of other features. The entity now rotating slowly on the screen possessed no navel and had no visible genitals.

Suddenly, its face filled the screen and screamed "Boo!"

Everybody jumped.

"Sorry," Hoj chuckled. "I couldn't resist."

"Is it possible to explore the organism's internal anatomy?" asked Misterthoggosh.

"Coming right up," Hoj replied. "What kind of section?"

"Longitudinal," Eichra Oren suggested. "Right down the middle."

"Done." And so it was.

"Name of the Hammer! I've never seen the like of that!" This from Semlohcolresh, and I took it seriously. He was very old and had seen a lot. The thing displayed in front of us wasn't organized inside like anything I was familiar with, either—at least nothing you could see without a magnifying glass. Exactly like its planarian ancestor, it wasn't hollow like all of us; it had no body cavity. It was as solid, side-to-side and, as it developed, front to back and head to toe, as a turnip.

Hoj zoomed in. "The texture's quite a bit different here inside the head, where one would assume the higher nervous functions are located."

"Yes," Eichra Oren said. "And you can see a kind of granularity spread throughout the entire organism. Can you ascertain its chemical characteristics?"

Labels sprang into being on the screen, hundreds of them, all too tiny to read until Hoj zoomed in further. "Do you need me to change languages?"

"No—look at this. It's acetylcholine. That's cholinesterase. If this were a jellyfish, I'd call it a neural network. I think that's insulin. Chlorophyll? No lungs in the chest, but almost microscopic ducts everywhere from the surface, deep into the center of the thing. All of its functions seem to be distributed evenly throughout its body."

"It breathes with its whole body," I observed. "It probably hears and smells with its whole body, too, the way we feel with our whole bodies."

Eichra Oren said, "It probably lies down in its food to eat."

"And wallows," I added.

"Ugh," said the cat.

Somehow, it had gotten late.

We were still far from agreement, two humanoids, their symbiotes, and a couple of ancient nautiloids, concerning what to do about our little problem. It isn't every day that your homeworld gets invaded by aliens.

Or gets worms.

Apparently the next step, at least for Misterthoggosh and his investment partners, would be to contact experts in various fields, fill them in on what was happening, and see what they had to suggest. I had my doubts about this: to me it sounded like they were summoning shamans.

Or lawyers.

From what I've seen in the Otherworld Museum and elsewhere, it appears to me that deferring to *expertism* is the quickest, most efficient, and most reliable method known to sapientkind (to coin a phrase) of reducing your entire civilization to smoking, radioactive rubble.

I wasn't shy about saying so, either. Of course they ignored me. They'd be sorry, I reckoned, when the first nuke went off. But they wouldn't be around to apologize, or I wouldn't be around to apologize to.

Or both.

When they'd all talked themselves half to death, our respective bosses, Mikado's and mine, had gone upstairs and outside for a smoke. I don't believe that Semlohcolresh had asked them to. His ventilation system was certainly up to dealing with a couple of cigars. But the two men had just wanted to sample the night air, and maybe watch the fireflies.

I wouldn't have objected to a healthy portion of that, myself—giving the cigar a pass—but I had been wondering all night why Mikado seemed so hostile toward everybody, especially to me. Being the individual that I am, once the humanoids were gone, the nautiloids had retired for the nonce, and it was just us symbiotes, I just asked the question.

The big cat blinked, as if surprised that anybody would simply come straight out with it. The voice his implant generated was deep, mellow, and ironic. "Well," the creature replied, after giving it a moment's thought, "we felines do have a certain…reputation to maintain."

Yes, it was a reputation that, in several alternities where cats were associated in folklore with the forces of evil, had gotten them all rounded up and burned *en masse*. But I refrained from saying it. Instead: "And this was duly decided at the 10,000[th] annual Interworld Cat Conference?" I inquired. "Was it by voice vote, or did you keep a tally?"

He laughed—purely an implant artifact—and replied, "To be perfectly truthful, sir, it's a test that's sort of built into us by evolution, and almost perfectly reflexive on our parts. We're small as solitary predators go, and forced to proceed on whatever evolutionary advantages we can seize for ourselves. If another individual can be easily intimidated, then he probably isn't worth knowing. But if he gives as good as he gets, then he's a potential friend. You, my good Oasam Otusam, are a cynic, which tells me that you're a disappointed romantic."

"I won't deny it." It was too true. No thumbs and I like human females.

"But between a healthy circumspection and returning tit for tat, you have managed somehow to split the difference. Quite unexpected, actually."

"Which means?" I asked, suspicious.

"You'll do," said the cat, hopping down from the stool. "You'll do. Come on. I'll make it up to you. Let me show you my favorite thing."

We left the pathology lab and walked down the corridor for some distance—it was a big place, this underground, underwater estate—glancing from time to time through the big glass wall on our right, into the saltwater-filled part of Semlohcolresh's home. It was quiet at this time of night, and, except for a big plecostomus scrubbing algae from the glass, not a creature was stirring, not even a sea scorpionoid.

Finally we went up half a flight of steps where, attached to the glass on the other side of the wall, we saw a transparent box (nearly invisible, as its refractive index was quite close to that of the water it was in) in which a dozen small, extremely colorful fish—neon tetras, clown loaches, orange swordtails, angels, ghotis—were swimming. It was the nautiloid equivalent of keeping a cageful of birds.

It struck me that these were freshwater fish. The plecostomus was, too. Nautiloids live in saltwater. I wondered how they handled the difference.

Mikado pressed his nose against the glass, watching the fish. "You know," he said, "I can persuade my humanoid to take me anywhere for an exotic and delicious meal. I can order the house computer to prepare any delicacy that tickles my fancy: tenderly-sautéed liver, lobster pate, Chicken Pyrenees. It will find it for me, cook it, and deliver it."

"Sure," I said. "And...?"

"And despite all of that, every cell in my body is screaming at me to leap into that water right now and gobble up all those expensive—and probably poisonous—fish *raw*. I wouldn't go to the wall to defend this theory of mine, Sam, but your kind have been domesticated—how I detest that word—for just about twice as long as mine have."

The jury is still out on the exact dates involved. Dogs evolved from wolves, and are said to have partnered up with human beings in the northeast corner of the Great Continent an Ice Age or two ago. Housecats (Mikado probably hated that expression, too) are not related closely to lions and leopards, and supposedly arose in the northeast corner of the continent immediately south of the Inland sea. But the ancient Antarcticans had both dogs and cats, fifteen thousand years ago.

However, I said, "I suppose that's true." And it probably was.

"Wildness still lives inside us cats."

I often have dreams of following a pack, the sheer joy of running into the wind, tongue hanging out, after a big herd of wild herbivores across some endless prairie somewhere. Eichra Oren tells me that my implants leak signals at a time like that, that he sees what I see, hears what I hear, smells what I smell—it's like talking in your sleep—and that I whimper and jerk my legs whenever I have that dream.

Cell memory, Eichra Oren calls it. Human beings don't have it. The herd-beasts of my dreams have been extinct a hundred thousand years. I told Mikado about it. He said that wildness still lives inside of me, too.

We understood each other.

CHAPTER TWENTY-FOUR

Pushing the Evidence

SEMLOHCOLRESH'S COLLOQUIUM BROKE UP NOT LONG after that.

Dawn was on the way, wispy pink and orange streamers showing on the eastern horizon just above the antique skyline of the ancient city, sunrise barreling toward at us at eleven hundred miles an hour, straight across the Great Continent, of which this was just a giant peninsula.

The big bright light was out for the day. Its lacy titanium tower was silhouetted starkly against the gradually brightening sky. The colors changed subtly from moment to moment, almost from second to second.

Morning had come to Lanternlight.

We might have called on Scutigera for a ride to our hotel (he'd sworn to us that he never slept, although I'm not entirely sure I believed it) but it was a perfect temperature outside, still and calm, the air smelled fresh and good, so we decided to walk. It wasn't very far.

There's something absolutely wonderful about a new day in a big town. The streets were wet and shiny, but smelled more like they'd been freshly cleaned while we were down in Semlohcolresh's bunker, than as if it had rained. All across the city, businesses of every kind were waking up. You could smell the wonderful aroma of baking bread.

Sunrise down on the southern coast is pretty splendid, too. No baking bread, but plenty of morning-blooming flowers and prairie birdsong. The smell of a calm sea in the dawn of the day can be intoxicating.

"Okay," I observed, breaking the spell. "As Jakdav Hoj put it, we have a pretty good idea what these are, the evolutionary descendants of common flatworms. But we don't have any idea of who they are. And even worse, since we don't know what they want, we don't know why they're here. We don't know how they got here. And the worst part is that we don't know where they're keeping themselves while they are here."

A heavy silence hung between us. Eichra Oren peered around as if looking for something to kick. We'd both seen what those things had done to Ray, and what they'd tried to do to Lyn Chow. I admit that whenever I thought about them, I had visions of flamethrowers dancing in my head. A very wise individual once observed that there isn't any problem that can't be solved with a sufficient quantity of high explosives.

"If they're as technologically adept as all that," Eichra Oren said at last, only half kidding about it, "at slipping quietly between parallel universes, then maybe they go home every night—or even for lunch."

"Now there's a depressing thought."

As for Lyn Chow, I found it difficult to believe that somewhere, in all that mass of information she'd absorbed out there among the Asteroids, peering through Misterthoggosh's cosmic knotholes, she hadn't at least glimpsed something useful regarding the Grays and their homeworld. Maybe she didn't realize it, there had been so many screens. Then again, she's just one of thousands of females—okay, make that dozens of females—who lust after Eichra Oren. Personally, I don't understand it. My boss is undeniably a great man, but he's boring.

It was hard getting used to the idea that someone, somewhere might actually be ahead of the Elders technologically, or for that matter, in any other respect. But the nautiloids lived a long, long time, individually. And their civilization gave new meaning to words like "venerable" and "conservative"—it's extremely difficult to wrap your brain around half a billion years. As a people, the molluscs were inclined to accept progress only slowly because along the way, they'd learned some excruciatingly painful lessons and tended to be somewhat neophobic.

If I ever get that old, please bury me. By any ordinary nautiloid standards—with the possible exception of the great lady Eneri Relda—the majority of Appropriated Persons must have seemed like little more than unruly children. And Misterthoggosh, who was neophilic, and tended to identify with us kids, was considered by many to be a raving lunatic.

Who consistently made them money.

"You know," I said, "Mikado told me that there are individuals in other cultures, in other realities, who believe that these Gray guys travel around in flying disks." No doubt the information came from Misterthoggosh's stolen broadcasts. Sometimes I wondered if it was an unmixed blessing, the way the broadcasts were increasingly saturating nautiloid society.

Mikado said there were other stories out there about the Grays' proclivities but they were too disgusting and unlikely to be taken seriously.

The boss stopped walking suddenly and turned to look at me. "*We* travel around in flying disks, Sam. The form is imposed by the nature of antigravity. The Grays we have here seem to prefer light aerocraft, and they also appear to swim pretty well. And they employ big curved knives as weapons. What the Hammer kind of advanced technology is that?"

I gave the little whuff that serves me as a laugh. None of that reconstituted electronic stuff for this doggy. "You carry a sword, yourself, Boss, but does that make you a primitive? Me, I'd argue that it's symbolic of the most advanced ethical system ever known to sapientkind."

"Sapientkind?"

"Sapienticity? Knives are deceptively sophisticated. The alloys involved are a matter of a lifetime's study. The good ones work under every imaginable sort of condition, arctic, tropical, mountaintops, ocean trenches, outer space. And they never run short of ammunition or power. If I had thumbs, Boss, I might even consider carrying a knife, myself."

A picture formed in my mind of yours truly standing up on his hind legs, growling fiercely and wielding a great big knife to frighten off his antagonists. I let Eichra Oren see it. He grinned and laughed out loud.

"You know what they say about somebody who brings a knife to a gunfight."

The ridiculous image vanished like a popped soap bubble. The boss shook his head and resumed walking. "I've also started carrying what may be the world's tiniest handgun that could still blow your head clean off. Not to mention your back garden wall. Now that I would call sophisticated."

"Pretty hard to argue with," I conceded, sighing inwardly once again for the lack of thumbs. I seemed to be doing a lot of that these days. "The world was made," I told him sadly, "for people with thumbs."

"People with thumbs made the world, Sam. Or their equivalent."

"Too true," I agreed.

"And another thing," he went on. "I suspect that our friends the Grays sometimes drive big veeks filled with water. I believe that they may be the culprits who tried to run us off the road back home on the coast the other day. The subsequent air attack didn't give me any time to investigate their veek, myself, so I've since asked Jakdav Hoj to analyze whatever evidence the road-owners' emergency services may have collected and preserved, for organic residues consistent with our new visitors."

"Because they probably excrete with their whole bodies, too. Yech." Then I blinked, a purely human reaction I'd acquired. "But we found—"

"You found the claw of a sea scorpionoid, Sam, but not the rest of one." He thought for moment. "I asked Misterthoggosh—Aelbraugh Pritsch, actually—to check around a little. There doesn't seem to be a sea scorpion missing anywhere—nor any sea scorpion missing a claw—"

I had reservations of my own about asking suspects to help with an investigation, but the boss always seemed to know what he was doing. His judgment of other sapients had a pretty enviable track record. For lack of anything better, I offered, "They grow back, did you know that?"

"You mean naturally, without any high-tech medical assistance? Yes, I knew that, Sam. I have no idea where the Grays got it, but I think that claw was meant to throw us off. To make us suspect Misterthoggosh."

"Because he uses sea scorpionoids for security? If that's the case, it didn't work too well. Most people who can afford bodyguards use sea scorpionoids. I don't think they understand our culture." I thought for a moment and added, "Me, I'd have left a big silvery gray feather."

Eichra Oren laughed, but sobered again quickly. "Aelbraugh Pritsch may be unintentionally silly, and a stuffed shirt, but I don't think he deserves to die for it. I believe that they killed Ray because he saw them, down there with that wreck on the sea bottom. But even that backfired, giving us pictures of them and tissue to identify them with."

"Not to mention leaving his implants behind to be found by us, so we could feel them and smell them, as well," I said. "Okay then, if we have to be invaded, let it be by incompetent invaders, by all means. Ray gave us that tissue. Do you suppose it grows back, too? That maybe you can cut one of these Gray creatures in half like their flatworm ancestors?"

"I don't know, Sam. It's a very interesting question."

"So," I said, "They want to discredit Misterthoggosh, and they don't want people seeing them and living to tell about it. You think those are reasonable observations, or am I pushing the evidence too far?"

"No, no, I agree with you absolutely." He shook his head. "But it's only a beginning, Sam. It tells us nothing about their mission here."

"Except that it's secret." So was Misterthoggosh's mission, for that matter. "And probably evil, since they don't mind killing those who get in their way. We don't have a clue where to look for them," I concluded.

"Then perhaps we ought to get them to come to us," he said, brightening.

"What?" I had no idea what he had on his mind.

"And I think," he mostly said to himself, "I know just how to do that."

We could probably have gone right home immediately upon leaving the underground palace of Semlohcolresh. The veek would have done all the work, and there's something to be said for sleeping in your own bed.

I suggested as much when we had nearly reached the Grand Hotel, the finest (or so its implant advertising was willing to attest) in all of Greater Lanternlight. On the other paw, all of our expenses here were being paid by Misterthoggosh and his partners, who rightly believed that they had "treated" themselves to the best p'Nan debt assessor available. With the possible exception of the mole people, an infamously penurious bunch, they wouldn't have expected any less of us.

Eichra Oren shook his head. "We have a lot of unfinished business to attend to back home, Sam. And maybe other places to go, besides. Between that and the return drive—which you'll agree is very pretty in spots—I think I'd rather face it wide awake and fresh. Wouldn't you?"

Never, in all my experience with the man so far, had he ever had nice things to say about scenery. Eichra Oren wasn't without aesthetic sensibilities, by any means, but he'd spent the drive here, which I presumed had been equally pretty, talking with people over the implant system. If he hadn't been the one driving, he'd never even have looked up.

It was a grand hotel, right enough, at least for our civilization, which doesn't care much, ordinarily, for clumping people up, let alone stacking them on top of one another. The place was admittedly pretty impressive, a dozen stories tall—they didn't want anything taller in this city than their precious titanium tower—occupying a city block by itself. The front of the building, constructed in some style other than the Antarctican that we might have expected, was a long, concave curve, lit by streaks of colored light by lamps at the ground level. Flying machines of every kind were hovering over and landing on the roof.

Past the gracefully curving driveway and the three-story portico, in through the massive doors of glass and bronze—three different sizes and shapes to suit every possible landdwelling lifeform—the hotel lobby seemed more like the inside of an opera house, all gold pillars, black marble, and deep red velvet. Despite myself, I kept looking for a fat lady in a silly hat, but there wasn't even a stage for her to stand on, let alone belt out the aria that would end it all.

Toward the back, a great wide flight of steps—carpeted to match velvet ropes hanging from golden posts—didn't seem to really go anywhere.

The veek had already been here all night, washed and cosseted by machines almost as bright as the late Ray's pet squid. The veek was pretty much self-maintaining, its antimatter engine hadn't really needed attention, but the service came with the "package" and was a nice touch. I was already aware that, when we were ready to take our leave, we'd find a bouquet of freshly-cut flowers lying on the dashboard.

Aside from Eichra Oren's debt assessor's sword, which he wouldn't let anybody touch, let alone carry for him, we hadn't brought any luggage with us. I always travel light. This seemed to disturb the bell-being deeply. He (or she) seemed to be a product of nautiloid technology, rather than arachnid, a cybernetically enhanced deep sea predator of some kind—the really ugly ones from the abyssal plains featuring gigantic mouths, crazy eyes, and dozens of pointy teeth—in a glass ball full of water on a tall pole attached to the luggage cart.

A big spiral escalator whisked us skyward, where a hallway with a richly-carpeted moving floor—liquid in only two dimensions—swept us to where we belonged. The boss and I split up on the eleventh floor—this level being reserved for day-sleepers, and lit only by a soft, artificial light—and repaired to our separate accommodations, as usual. One of us snores and we've never settled on which one of us it is.

Inside, the room was luxurious (whatever windows it may have had invisible, tightly sealed against the daylight), generically designed to suit mammals, and adjusted—more brochure-speak—to the ideal temperature, humidity, and barometric pressure for my canine comfort and relaxation. I cleared my implant, told it not to accept any more commercial propaganda, and tried to decide whether I was hungry or not.

At my command, one entire wall of the room became a landscape, a panorama of the open veldt that occupies so much of the continent to our south, adjusted to resemble, as closely as possible, my recurring genetic memories. I added the singing of the appropriate birds, a light afternoon breeze, and my implant supplied the odors of a hot day in the long grass. But for my conversation with Mikado, I'd never have thought of such a thing. It should have been the northern steppes of the Great Continent, not yet frozen thousands of years ago when my species was evolving, but I've always believed in imagining what you know.

While I was waiting for room service, I took a shower—purely electrostatic, with streams of designer ions removing accumulated dust and detritus—and, smelling like the bouquet that would be waiting for us in the veek, hopped up onto the enormous bed that had assumed for me "the ultimate degree of gentle firmness for my size and weight".

I was about to check with Eichra Oren one last time—probably sound asleep by now—when I heard an actual physical knock on my door. Outside, a softly feminine, very human voice announced, "Room service".

"Please come in," I told her, and she did. I'd halfway expected delivery by pneumatic tube or something. But attired in the formal robe all the hotel employees wore, she carried a tray with my midnight meal—well, it felt like midnight, anyway; sapient beings create their own time. She set it down on folding legs, approaching me where I lay on the bed. Standing before me, she parted her robe from throat to ankle, revealing that the bed wasn't the only thing in the place to offer me the ultimate degree of gentle firmness for my size and weight.

"May I?" Leaving her robe open, she sat on the bed beside me. "With the compliments of Misterthoggosh," she said sweetly. "Would you like me to feed you, first? It must be just terrible, not having any thumbs."

CHAPTER TWENTY-FIVE

The Assessor's Sword

THREE HOURS LATER, I WOKE UP. BESIDE ME ON THE BED, Marianne (that was her name) was still asleep. I'm afraid I'd worn the poor darling out.

Suddenly I heard my name inside my head—again. Eichra Oren. That's what had awakened me without disturbing my lovely and talented guest. I leaped off the bed, willed the door open, and ran into the hall.

The boss's room was across from mine, and I was horrified to see the lock had been blasted away somehow, leaving a ragged hole bigger than my head. It was dark inside the room, filled with thunderous crashings and the sound of fragile things being broken. Without a second's pause, I plunged in and was greeted by the terrifying sight of Eichra Oren, pinned to the wreckage-littered floor by a sapient being I didn't recognize, all teeth, claws, growls, and bristling hair.

Reeking of fear, anger, and concentrated hatred, it lowered its drooling jaws toward the helpless man's face, ready to tear half of it away. I sprang, striking a sort of hump, high on the creature's ridged and hair-crested back, fastening my own teeth deep into its flesh. It shrieked, trying to twist its jaws toward me, but Eichra Oren touched it with deceptive gentleness on the throat, and then just beneath one ear.

As the weight came off him, Eichra Oren sprang to his feet.

Instead of collapsing, as we'd both expected, it rose to its rear limbs, screamed into Eichra Oren's face, and lunged toward him again. With my weight swinging from its back, it was caught off balance when the boss reached in and touched it where the collarbones and sternum came together. It pitched backward—I just avoided being crushed by letting go and leaping away—and fell, still as death, with all four limbs in the air, exactly like a dead bug, although it was thoroughly mammalian.

"Watch it, Sam, it isn't dead and may be playing possum." I backed away another couple of steps, sniffed the air and listened. I could hear its heart beating, slow and steady, and I was pretty sure it was unconscious.

By this time, the beautiful Marianne was rerobed and standing in Eichra Oren's doorway with a highly competent-looking fusion blaster in one hand. I had no idea where she'd been carrying it. The effect was spoiled a little—but only a little—by the fact that her hair was a delightful mess and she hadn't bothered to put her shoes back on.

"I've called hotel security," she told us. "They were already on the way. Apparently that thing over there makes a lot of noise." She pointed toward an object lying on the floor near the baseboards. It looked to me as if it had flown across the room—probably kicked from the creature's hand—and bounced off the wall, leaving a deep dent.

I went over to examine it, and smelled chemical propellant. The lights were back on and I could see foot-wide craters in the walls, and even bigger holes taken out of the formerly comfortable furniture. "Ballistic Innovations," I read the name engraved on the receiver. "Four millimeter SuperMagnum. About eighteen calibers. I think it's a firearm."

It was a hybrid. They were considered quaint these days, but there were still some of them in circulation. My implant said seventy-round magazine capacity, projectile speed approaching ten thousand feet per second, thanks to velocity-boosting magnetic coils wrapped around the longish barrel. Absolutely devastating in living flesh, against heavy fur, on reptilian hide, armored or unarmored, and on every variety of chiton. I doubt that even Misterthoggosh's shell would have stopped one.

By that time, several entities in hotel livery had arrived and were trying to shoo us out of the room. "I don't think so," Eichra Oren told them, displaying his sword. I suddenly realized that he was naked.

I heard Marianne say, "Oh, my." She'd noticed too.

One of the guys took her by an arm. "Not her," I said. "She's my bodyguard."

She smiled. "You're sweet, Sam, but really I do have to be going. Thank you for a wonderful—and, as it turned out, very exciting—evening." She knelt and put her face on mine. "Anytime you're in town, okay?"

Compliments of Misterthoggosh? It would have been rude to send her away.

"Okay, kid. And you're no dud, yourself." As she left, I turned to Eichra Oren, who'd started binding his guest's arms and legs together—Marianne and I hadn't gotten that far—using restraints borrowed from Security. "Now, Boss, do you have any idea at all what this thing is?"

Wrapping his tunic around himself and belting on his sword, he considered it for a moment. "Hyenoid, I think. Large. Not naturally sapient."

"Like me." I was well aware I had been manufactured. I knew of no doggy civilizations anywhere in alternity, maybe because we canines had already evolved as far as we needed to and couldn't be improved on. For that matter, I've never heard of any cockroach civilizations, either.

"All right, Sam, like you. I don't think he was ever anybody's symbiote."

"*You've got that right, monkey-boy, I never was anybody's symbiote!*" That had come by implant. Eichra Oren had wrapped several of those restraints around the creature's massive, lethally toothed jaws. "What're you gonna do now, cut my head off with that sword of yours?"

Eichra Oren shrugged. "That depends. Maybe we'll just remove your implants and let you go back to being the animal you started out to be."

It laughed, one of the most evil sounds I've ever experienced. "How do you know that I'm an animal, humanoid? Maybe that isn't where I really live. Maybe I'm inside these implants you're threatening to remove."

178

Forge of the Elders, I thought to myself, even this murderous thug wonders about the true nature of his identity. Does that make him unexpectedly thoughtful, or me just a less intelligent doggy than I'd realized?

"If you want to find out," I told the thing on the floor, "I'm all for it. I get to watch and maybe I'll learn something I've always wanted—"

"Enough, Sam," Eichra Oren interrupted me. "Tell us a few things, killer, and we may not have to conduct Sam's experiment on you after all."

Sure," said the thing. "What have I got to lose? You tell me what you want to know. I am a hyenoid, created as a kind of watchdog for a security company on the eastern coast of the Great Continent. I soon emancipated myself, at the eternal expense of those who thought they owned me—every slave has a natural right to kill his master—came here to the western coast, and set myself up in the business I know best."

"Which is killing people," Eichra Oren said.

"Which is doing anything somebody is willing to pay me to do—anything, exactly like that little whore who just left doggy-boy, here."

I could see the pulse beating in the helpless creature's throat, and suffered an almost irresistible urge to remove it, with my fangs. This monster hurt people for money. Girls like Marianne bring them joy.

"I happen to be a duly certified p'Nan debt assessor," Eichra Oren announced, addressing the hotel security men. But this thing assaulted me and that makes me party to a dispute. Does this establishment have a debt assessor of its own, or will it be necessary for me to find one?"

"Will that be necessary?" the hyenoid asked. "I'll tell you all that I know about what just happened. I am more than willing to pay monetary damages to the hotel and make some settlement with you, as well."

Well, that's boring, I thought. I'd been hoping to see a duel or something. The thing looked kind of ridiculous, lying there on its back with its feet in the air and plastic bands wrapped around its muzzle, but I couldn't think of any viable alternative to listening patiently.

"I live on the Western Island in the Lesser Ocean, the one that's always green, in a town famous the world over for distilling alcohol from grain—none of that kelpy slop, mind you—and aging it in charred oaken barrels. 'Water of Life', people call it in a dozen languages."

There were those who would argue the island next door produced better whiskey, but it was scientific question requiring continuous experimentation.

"In that town," the hyenoid went on, "I'm just a neighbor. I'm as kind as I know how to be with children and elderly beings. I buy my groceries, visit the tavern, listen to the people sing in the park on Tenday. But in certain circles around the globe, it's well known what I do, as well as how to go about engaging my services without exposing oneself."

There couldn't be more than three or four killers-for-hire on the entire planet. The Elders knew how to run a peaceful and productive society without limiting anybody's freedom. One method that worked was that, in a culture of armed individuals, assassination was a dangerous profession.

Eichra Oren nodded, urging the creature onward. "Three mornings ago, I opened my front door to discover a fat package containing the requisite number of platinum coins, and a flattie of the intended recipient of my attentions. Nothing else. It was necessary to employ a computer—I didn't want the query associated with my implant—and a facial recognition program to find out who my mark was. Let me tell you, I wasn't a bit happy when it turned out to be a famous p'Nan debt assessor."

Impervious to flattery, Eichra Oren asked, "Did you retain the envelope?" I could see happy little diagrams of DNA dancing in his head.

"No," the assassin answered. "I shredded and burned it. Standard professional practice. I don't have the original coins, either. I exchanged them for silver and gold, not all of them in the same place."

"And the flattie?

"Committed to implant memory and destroyed with the envelope."

"Very well," Eichra Oren stood over the beast and drew his sword, its edges gleaming as it left the scabbard. "This is what's going to happen."

"You drive, Sam," said Eichra Oren. "I have thinking to do."

"You got it, Boss." I took over the controls. "Anything I can help with?" I wondered if the way he'd handled the hyenoid wasn't bothering him.

He shook his head. "I'll let you know."

He settled in his seat, put fingertips to forehead, and closed his eyes. I negotiated with the veek—the fact is, it mostly drove itself—and we were off. Five hundred miles at three hundred miles per hour should get us home from Lanternlight in an hour and forty minutes. I had long since made it a practice never to listen to music or to watch video, even via implant, while the Boss was concentrating like this. As the miles whisked by outside, with nothing better to do, I contemplated my boss's sword where it stood, propped against his knee. Unlike many of his colleagues, he had never given it a name. He liked to think it was just a tool—albeit a very special one—nothing more.

There were those, our recent would-be assassin for one, who might have believed differently, if they were still capable of believing anything.

As well as being a conspicuous insignia of office, recognized everywhere on the planet, the p'Nan debt assessor's sword has to be supremely utilitarian, to do what it does swiftly and efficiently, without inflicting pain which has no part at all in the restitution process.

There isn't any rule in nautiloid society against anyone carrying a sword (or any other weapon), but large edged weapons are thoroughly antiquated—and the good ones moderately expensive—compared to other weapons, so that such a social transgression practically never happens.

Like every p'Nan debt assessor ending his novitiate, Eichra Oren had designed his own sword and made it with his own hands. There are as many schools of thought on the subject of what makes a good sword as there are p'Nan novices. His was straight, rather than curved, twenty-five inches long from its needle-sharp tip to the end of its pommel.

Signed and dated on one side of the ricasso by the fledgling debt assessor, and on the other by a Master of p'Na, in the name of the ancient school of p'Na, the blade itself was nineteen inches long, an inch and three quarters at its widest, and a quarter at its thickest, near the hilt. It was said to be incapable of rusting, but Eichra Oren attended to it almost daily, and it was never given a chance to rust. There is nothing that will corrode a blade like blood, mammalian or otherwise.

Fashioned of iron, chromium, significant traces of other elements, and shards of the sword of Elyodruthrananocris, ceremonially broken on the day he'd died, the finished billet of alloy had been heated

white hot, hand-beaten into an approximate shape, quenched in liquid helium, and drawn back in an induction oven. It had then been
symmetrically ground double-edged, with a subtly narrowed "waist"
about a hand's width forward of the crossguard, and finally polished
between opposing antigravity fields until its surface was compacted
and it shone like a mirror.

The edges were said to be but a single molecule thick.

The amply cross-guarded—and circumferentially ridged—handle,
as well as the chestnut-shaped pommel, were all of a single piece,
cast tungsten through and through (except at the very end, where
the tang of the blade poked through and had been peened or swaged
into place). It made the hilt surprisingly heavy, the blade extremely
quick, with minimal decoration and a stippled gripping surface of
ion-implanted gold.

Eichra Oren often claimed that he never kept a count of how
many lives he'd taken with his sword, but I'm sure that someone,
somewhere, did. I knew of one or two myself where some other
weapon had proven necessary.

As we entered sagebrush country and could tell the Inland Sea
was near, the boss seemed finally to come back to life. "Don't settle
in when we get home, Sam. We're going on a trip as soon as I can
arrange it."

"Back to Lanternlight, I hope. I like Lanternlight."

He snorted. "You like the food there—"

I nodded. "And the females."

"And the females. But you like the food and females everywhere,
Sam, although I doubt you'll have time to appreciate them where
we're going."

"How sad. And that's where?" He loved to keep me hanging
like this.

"People aren't always cooperative. Those in business will protect
the privacy, if not of their customers then of their associates. I had to
look for reasons—incentives—to trust the information I was given."

I had no idea where he was headed, but he was making good time.

"I have had a feeling all along, Sam, that Meerltchirt's partner was
right, that he's made his way somehow to the Northwest Continent. I
can't say why—because his family have extensive land holdings there,

because that's where I would flee, were I compelled to; it's a good place to get lost—but I trust my unconscious mind and felt the intuition was worth looking into. I haven't been entirely forthcoming with you, my friend, because I had nothing objective to share with you. I was more than a little chagrined: all I had were these baseless speculations."

"Hey, Boss, I can baselessly speculate with the best of 'em."

"I rest my case. All this time on the road, I've been making calls. Insurance companies proved most helpful. It develops that more than a thousand aircraft departed our extension of the Great Continent the day our client's fiancé vanished, bound for the Northwest Continent. Only a few hundred bore spiders, fewer than a dozen were the correct species, and only four of those were male. Only one carried a lone male."

I felt my ears perk. It's a reflex and I hate it. "So we've got him?"

"You know better than that. He might never have left. He might have gone to the Southwest Continent, the Island Continent, the other end of this one. He might have gone to the South Pole, though coldbloods seldom prosper there. What we have is a promising lead that we will follow."

"To the Northwest Continent?"

"To the Northwest Continent."

"Hooray!"

CHAPTER TWENTY-SIX

Liberty

THE FLIGHT ACROSS THE LESSER OCEAN TO THE NORTHWEST
Continent hardly took any time at all. Misterthoggosh had agreed to
lend us a suborbital flyer which we climbed aboard on the grounds of
his seaside estate.

"This craft has been designed for mammalian use," he'd told us.
"My personal flyer is a bit more ponderous, as it must be filled with
water, and at the same time withstand both high altitude and deep
sea use." I'd heard that technology was being developed to keep
aquatic pilots and passengers misted like a houseplant, saving tons
of water weight.

We'd thanked him and went out to look our noble steed over
where she sat casually on the driveway on extended legs. The little
vessel was shaped, basically, like a doughnut with a floor across the
bottom of the hole, and was powered by an antimatter minireactor.
She used antigravity for both lift and propulsion. A transparent dome
covered the entire top half of the aerocraft from rim to rim. She had
plenty of headroom and best of all, she was bright apple-red with a
white stripe.

"See?" said the boss. "I told you so."

"That we have flying saucers? She looks more like a flying bagel, Boss."

Why did I call her "she"? It could be a simple matter of respect: for uncounted thousands of years, sailors, aviators, and spacemen, who have risked their lives and everything they had in these contrivances, have seen their ships as beautiful ladies, and they've loved them. It's certainly no insult to women, as perfect idiots sometimes claim—on the contrary. Or it could just be that the AI in this particular craft thought of herself as female and preferred to be addressed that way.

In any event, she opened exactly the same kind of door Eichra Oren's veek has, lowering a short flight of courtesy steps. We climbed aboard. Briefly, as she sealed up, she and the boss debated possible destinations on the Northwest Continent. Then she began a sprightly ascent on powerful antigravs, moving westward almost as quickly as she rose. I knew she was also talking to other flyers in the air between here and wherever we were going, making sure our flightpaths didn't converge, which would have been messy and unfortunate, to say the least.

As the Inland Sea vanished behind us, a mountain range rose before us before giving way to the Lesser Ocean which was lesser than the Greater Ocean only by comparison. I felt myself pressed into the seat by acceleration, not particularly hard, and by the time I had become comfortable with it, we were out over the shining water and so high it was easy to see the curvature of the planet below us. I knew the vehicle was capable of achieving orbit, but she wouldn't be doing that today.

"And the world," I proclaimed, "is round."

Eichra Oren gave me a look. "No kidding."

I was somewhat surprised not to see any other flyers. This version of Earth is a populous world, although most of its sapient inhabitants take their oxygen through gills. Nevertheless, there are certain kinds of transactions that are better conducted face-to-face, and certain sights that beg to be seen in person. Not that we would be seeing any of them on this particular excursion, but I was now considering future possibilities.

There is a truly Grand Canyon (I looked it up) near the west edge of the Northwest Continent, and a formidable system of waterfalls in the east. Herds of triceratopsoids, originally imported from another branch of probability as frozen zygotes, blacken the prairie between them.

They're delicious, and don't taste at all like chicken.

Takeoff had been a bit noisy, but as soon as we were outside the atmosphere—ninety-nine percent of it, anyway—our flight was very nearly silent. Eichra Oren had once been to the Moon, he said. I had never flown so high before, myself, and never left the continent of my birth. Now, despite the fact that it was the middle of the morning, I could see stars shining overhead, and the sky was black. I thought I saw a satellite go by, relaying billions of implant messages. Clouds obscured most of the planet below, but it looked clear where we were headed.

Eichra Oren sat stiffly, eyes straight ahead, hands on his knees, tapping one heel on the deckplate, then the other. No, he wasn't a nervous flyer. He was always like this before a potential assessment, never afraid of any fight that he might find himself pulled into, but of being wrong. Of ruining lives. I'd have been worried if he were not. I think he was still unsettled, too, about the business with the hyenoid…

"By what name are you called?" Eichra Oren had asked the beast, his language growing formal as he fully assumed the role of debt assessor. He stood over it, imperious, with his formidable sword drawn.

"I have no name," the creature said. "My makers called me Unit 9422YIU. If my legs were free, you could see it branded into my belly."

Something, some emotion, passed across Eichra Oren's eyes. The idea of marking a sapient being that way was uniquely repulsive. He nodded calmly. "You claim that you are not a natural sapient but a cyberorganism, and I believe you, Unit 9422YIU. It is clear that your makers left you little choice regarding who you would be and what you would do. They share the responsibility for what you became and what you did with your life. They made you a dealer of death and, however inadvertently, gave you full awareness of it, without any ability to control it. I gather that they made the ultimate restitution for their error."

Between the plastic bindings, the edges of the creature's mouth twitched as it attempted to bare its teeth. "I relished killing them, debt assessor. And they were only the first of many that I killed afterward."

"That is as it may be," Eichra Oren told the assassin. "Little can be done about your animal nature. You are a mutant hyena, genetically designed, gestated, born, and bred for nothing more than bloodshed. But I know of certain individuals—careful technicians—who can help you comb the contradictions out of your implanted sapience, and that, in turn, can control the organic part of your being. But only if that is what you truly wish. No one will force it on you against your will."

"You give me a choice?" asked the beast, as if it were a new idea.

"Perhaps your first. You can choose to live as a sapient being, to exchange the products of your hands and mind for what you require to survive and prosper. Or you can continue to subsist at the involuntary expenditure of other people's lives and eventually die at the hands of an intended victim. This is not a threat, just a forecast. Regardless, you will pay the hotel for the physical damages you have wrought and I will keep your weapon, although, of course, nobody will stop you from acquiring another. Even evildoers have a fundamental right to self-defense."

"I don't think I want to be an evildoer any more. I've already killed—"

"Then as a debt assessor of the p'Nan school," Eichra Oren hurried to interrupt; what he didn't know, he couldn't bring the creature to task for. "I set you this penance. Do not confess to me, or to anybody else, how many you have killed. Instead, save as many lives as you have taken, and I will consider the accounts balanced. Take up your old ways again, Unit 9422YIU, and I will search you out and put you down."

"I will do as you say." And the boss could discern, from his long, painful training by the School of p'Na, that the thing was telling the truth.

"Make certain that you do," he replied. "And one more thing…"

"Yes? What is it?"

Eichra Oren gave his sword a flashy whirl and neatly cut the creature free. A second swipe of the blade-tip unmuzzled it. Wisely, it stayed put. "Unit 9422YIU is no kind of name for a free and sapient being.

"Therefore, from this day forward, you will be known as…Bob."

I put on some "traveling music", something I'd first heard on one of those interworld braincasts. The lead line of the chorus translated as 'Welcome to the Hotel California,' whatever a california was, and told an eerie tale about a hostel that, once you checked in, you could never leave. I liked it best for the powerful instrument duet near the end. After that, it was something about a building burning down near a lake.

It took less time to cross the Lesser Ocean than it had to drive to Lanternlight. Eichra Oren communicated with somebody on the other side who gave our flyer directions. She changed course slightly, and we landed vertically on a numbered space amidst other flyers like our own.

I'd never set foot on another continent before. When I did, it didn't feel a bit different at all. I was sure there was a lesson of some kind to be learned from that, but I don't have any idea what it was.

People—mostly humans and dinosauroids, all of them wearing protective coveralls—advanced toward us in a beat-up looking and equipment-laden hovertruck. Arriving, they fastened all sorts of cables and hoses to our flyer and exchanged information with my boss. We walked to a low building where a veek stood waiting for us on its skirt.

We spent another hour driving. The veek took us as far as it could (it seemed old and battered and didn't have an AI) through countryside about as densely populated as it is where we live, a healthy mixture of open spaces, residences and businesses. Entities of various species were driving, walking, children were playing on lawns and in parks. Here and there, the atmosphere smelled especially good—Eichra Oren was still too concentrated to notice—but I deeply regretted not having sufficient time on this expedition to sample some of the local eateries.

In the end, we ran out of road, which didn't impede our veek, but a while later, the trees were too close together, so we left it and continued on foot. Eichra Oren had a nice walking stick he'd brought, made from the same wooden ivory as the floor at home, but he didn't immediately need it. The path started dry, uncluttered, and relatively level. The day was a splendid one and he'd brought water for both of us.

The path soon became a trail and the walking stick came into use. We discovered what we were looking for toward the end of a miniature valley, where the land began rising and the meadow below gave way to increasingly thick-growing trees, either aspen or birch, I'm not sure which.

You'd think a dog would know more about trees.

We seemed to be following a natural firebreak, where perhaps an avalanche, a decade or so ago, had taken out trees from the top of the hill down to the meadow in a swath a hundred feet wide. About halfway up the leaf-littered slope, and to one side, stood a little log cabin, perhaps two hundred years old, on a foundation of cemented stones, of which there were plenty, around and about, and made from the trees that had been cut to clear enough space for it. On the roof, a trickle of smoke was coming from a blackened tin chimney with a conical top. The roof seemed to be made from rough greyed shingles of the same wood.

We heard our quarry long before we saw him. The music echoed from hillside to hillside and could be heard two miles away. Meerltchirt of the Fronzeln Zirnaath, a golden jumping spider of about half my size, sat on the steps of the cabin's weathered porch, playing a banjo. The path had become steep, and the altitude a bit more than he was accustomed to, so Eichra Oren had to take several deep breaths before he could speak.

He pronounced the prodigal bridegroom's name. The banjo-playing stopped. "Yes," the spider said, "I am Meerltchirt. And you are Eichra Oren."

"And Sam," said the boss.

"And Sam. No need to tell me why you're here. Shaalara sent you. Have I committed a moral breach, somehow, for which I must now make compensation?"

He'd asked *the* question. He had the formula down precisely, although there are many other words that state the case just as properly.

Eichra Oren shook his head. "Not that I know of, Meerltchirt. No formal contract was mentioned, not to me, at least, and an individual always has the right to change his mind, especially if it will save his life."

"I see," said the spider, setting the banjo aside. "The tune is called 'Liberty' if you're curious," he told us. "From your homeworld, Eichra Oren." I felt a twinge of regret. The music had been very appealing.

It reminded me somehow of Misterthoggosh, who had turned out not quite as unsympathetic toward the people of Eichra Oren's native world as he wanted us to believe. At some point in our recent conversation, he had played a bit of music for us, imported from that branch of reality.

"'Bethena'," he had pronounced. "Over a century old, and the work of a young fellow named Scott Joplin. The generic form is known as a 'waltz', although this one is rhythmically unusual. You will find the piece, although it is quite brief and deceptively simple, by turns contemplative, melancholy, pensive, ultimately triumphant in a quiet way."

As we listened, the monster waved his tentacles around in time to the music. I'm no expert, but I had to admit it was something of an intellectual and emotional achievement, that went somewhere I'd never known existed, and took me with it. And these people had succumbed to collectivism?

"It was, in many ways, the high point of their civilization," said our host. "It was just before a devastating worldwide war that crushed their creative spirit—or at least deformed it badly. Listen to this one."

The rhythmic pattern of this one was different, exotic, but, like "Bethena", divided into several distinct movements, and containing many of the same emotional elements, explored in just a few short minutes.

"It is called 'Solace'," Misterthoggosh declared. "Also by Joplin. The form is called a 'tango', although this one is fairly profoundly syncopated."

"Meaning?"

"That the accent, or stress has been shifted, so that the emphasis is on beats that are normally unaccented. Don't analyze it, just enjoy it."

When 'Solace' had run its painfully lovely course, the great mollusc played something called 'Ragtime Dance', maybe to show us that this Joplin character was capable of writing something upbeat. It was as simple and as complex as the others, but it made you want to laugh, somehow.

"My favorite," he said. "This is just one mode of expression, of which humans have perfected many, possibly thousands. They make music better than any species I know. Yet their planet is in a state of constant warfare, with all the accompanying political and economic disruption. Presently, they are on the brink of extinction. Although it goes against my every ethical principle, I wish I could prevent that. The loss to all of us—this music alone—would be unbearably tragic."

The old softie.

Rising, Meerltchirt turned toward the weathered cabin door. "Will you come in, please? I've made a stew that you two should find as satisfying as I do. Rabbit and squirrel—I didn't bite them, I shot them with my crossbow, instead—and various vegetables that grow wild all around the place. I'm only interested in the broth, of course."

"That would be pleasant," said Eichra Oren. "Shall I bring your banjo?"

"Please. I believe I'll leave it here for the next occupant."

Which told us that he meant to come back with us. She's going to eat him, I thought, all her promises to the contrary notwithstanding. She's going to eat him and he knows it perfectly well. She's going to eat him and he will welcome it because he loves her. It's in the genes.

But the stew was very good.

And the flight home was endured in silence.

CHAPTER TWENTY-SEVEN

Nightcrawlers

EARLY THE NEXT MORNING, EICHRA OREN AND I WERE awakened by someone parked in our driveway, insistently and incessantly sounding their veek's klaxon. On a shelf, my sympathetic sponge (not the same as a singing sponge), one of the stranger features offered up by nautiloid civilization, was still the same as I had been last night, road-weary, cranky and tired, but within a few minutes the sponge was my old self again.

Of course it hadn't shared the better part of a stoneware gallon jug of hand-made corn whiskey with a p'Nan debt assessor and a runaway bridegroom.

The boss entered the office at the same moment I did, yawning and stretching, strapping his swordbelt around the tunic he'd slept in. Nothing—well, practically nothing, anyway—will make you ache the next morning like a long journey sitting down. We'd had two of them. I was wishing I had a sword, myself—not to mention the hands to swing it with—as the noise continued. I told the house to make us coffee, hot and black, as we stepped outside to see what the racket was all about.

It was so bright outside that it hurt my teeth. Out there on the driveway, standing next to her cute little sky-blue Nombismocwen hover sportsveek, was Lornis Adubudu, practically jumping up and down with excitement. Her Talapoin, Mio, by contrast, perched in the back of the passenger seat indolently examining his fingernails and yawning. As we came out the door and she saw us, she told her veek to stop honking and ran directly to the boss, throwing her arms around him.

"Surprise!" she cried. "Wait'll you see what I have for you!"

Dressed the way she was, in tight little velour shorts and a well-filled, filmy, not-quite-transparent top—just above her sandaled right foot, she wore an anklet of gold chain—it was pretty obvious what she had for Eichra Oren this morning if he'd been inclined to accept it, but at the moment she was probably referring to something else.

As annoyed as we both were with Lornis, I had to admit that she was a highly decorative thing to behold, even this early in the day. Her auburn hair, no more than a couple of inches long and slightly...well, roughened-looking, framed her lovely face perfect-ly. Her amber eyes, lit now by the newly-risen sun, spoke of fire and deep passion—and of child-like enthusiasm for whatever had brought her to our doorstep.

She almost made me wish I were a humanoid.

She took one of Eichra Oren's hands, pulling him toward her veek. "Your mother told me you've been hunting for—'aliens'," she said. "Aliens. Well, Sweetie, I think I may have something you'll want to see!"

At the word "aliens" Lornis no longer had to drag him along. He was at the veek before she was, starting to climb in, but she stopped him.

"No, no—let me explain, Eichra Oren! You see, I went out in my flower garden just before sunrise this morning to get nightcrawl-ers, so I could go fishing later today with my father. This—"The girl stretched ornamentally, reaching into the back seat of the open-topped road machine. "This is what I was using. I got it out of my garden shed."

I'd seen something like it before. What she had hauled out of the veek was a t-handled, wooden-shafted, fork-ended device about four feet long, that used high-voltage electricity to bring the worms up from underground.

"I heard a noise, and then I saw one of these 'aliens' of yours, rummaging through the other end of my toolshed and guess I sort of impulsively kind of stabbed it in the backside with my 'nightcrawler persuader', knocking the thing right out." In any lesser society, we wouldn't have been able to watch the action she was describing. In ours, we got to see everything she'd seen, and it was pretty funny stuff.

With a dramatic flourish, she opened the cargo trunk to show us what lay inside. It was a Gray, one of the flatworm people, one (there had been another at the museum) with a little visored cap, wearing a gray coverall and tied up hand and foot with gray all-purpose tape. Very tastefully coordinated, I thought. Lornis had stuffed the thing into the trunk of her veek, and now presented it to my boss proudly, as a present. I suspected that it might be *H. gracilis* courting behavior.

Eichra Oren bent down and stared the organism in what served as its face. There was no visible mouth or nose, no visible ears. Only those terrible eyes that looked like holes burned in a blanket with a cigar. "Do you speak my language?" he asked it. "Can you speak at all?"

There was no response. It didn't even blink. I wasn't sure if it could.

To Lornis: "What do you suppose it was looking for in your shed?"

Lornis shrugged. "I've no idea. No idea at all. It's kind of big—the shed, I mean—and it's been practically empty since my dad moved out to a place of his own and took all of the stuff he stored there. What I'm keeping in it now are some garden tools and various related supplies, a stack of old clay pots, and an ancient auto-mowing machine."

"I have a thought," I said, and I did. It was a good one. "Boss, if you and Lornis will bring that thing in the house? I'm going to go find something I think will help us. Mio, come with me, I need your fingers."

Mio looked to his mistress, who nodded, and the two of us went ahead into the house. I indicated a drawer in Eichra Oren's desk I wanted opened, and the Talapoin obliged, letting me see what he saw inside, via implant. It was almost like having a symbiote of my very own.

It was getting to be an attractive thought, although it would probably take the Elders seven or eight millennia to get used to the idea.

At my instruction, Mio pulled out the flat transparent package with Ray's brain implants on the foam inside it. By that time the boss and his would-be girlfriend had the captive Gray inside the house and propped up on the sofa like a particularly icky mummy. When Eichra Oren saw what we'd retrieved from his desk drawer, he nodded his approval.

"Ray's implants!" he said. "You'll want the language package—that's the little purple square one. You're figuring that this creature's neural functions are distributed widely enough that we can just lay the implant practically anywhere on its skin and get results, right?"

"I'd start with the head," I told him, conservative in my own way.

He answered, "So would I, if only out of habit." I had no idea whether this idea of mine would work. I didn't know whether implants could attune themselves to their users or had to be attuned, somehow. It occurred to me then that I knew almost nothing about the technology that had made me what I am—whatever that is. Eichra Oren took the little metallic wafer out of the package and laid it on the creature's forehead. Nothing happened for a longish moment—then it *jumped* and suddenly each of us could sense another sapient presence in the room.

"I am Eichra Oren," the boss said aloud. His implant broadcast the same information. He'd pulled up an office chair so he could sit and look directly at our guest where they'd sat him on the sofa. "Who are you?"

There came no reply, either mentally or otherwise. The alien sat perfectly still, and if implants had employed carrier waves, that's all we would have been hearing. That and crickets. But somehow we were all aware that the bizarre creature had heard Eichra Oren's question perfectly well. My guess was that it believed it was resisting an interrogation by its captors, and, of course, that's exactly what was happening.

"This is the last time I'm asking," said Eichra Oren, his voice and mental tone extremely grim and menacing. I could tell that he was putting it on, but I doubt the prisoner or even Lornis could. "Who are you?"

Again there was no answer from our alien visitor, but the creature began thrashing around violently, straining hard at the gray utility tape wrapped around its wrists and arms and legs and ankles—or as close as it came to having parts like that. Maybe it thought it was worth tearing itself to bits in order to get away. It wasn't entirely gelatinous, more like cold meatloaf in aspic. Perhaps it had gotten a mental glimpse of what Eichra Oren wanted it to believe he had in mind.

I had, and it wasn't pretty. I probably would have felt a lot more sympathy for the thing if I hadn't watched through Ray's own eyes as it, or one of its buddies, coldbloodedly murdered my friend—after attempting to run the boss and me off the road and firing a missile at us.

With a hand on its chest, Eichra Oren pushed the creature back against the sofa. He pulled the little plasma weapon out of his tunic pocket and pointed it at the crotch of the creature's gray coveralls. "This is what I wrecked your veek and shot your aircraft down with. Now sit still and tell me everything I want to know, or I'm going to shoot your dick off. This is a new gun to me, and it's just a little bit unpredictable, so I'll most likely take your balls off with it, too."

"My reproductive process is not the same as that of you mammals." The voice inside our minds was amused, low, smooth, and sexually ambiguous. "And if it were, even a lowly vertebrate like you should be aware by now that anything you do to me will eventually heal or grow back."

"Okay, then," Eichra Oren offered agreeably. "I guess I'll just plink around a little until I find something that you don't want shot off."

"It won't do any good," I told Eichra Oren, unable now to tell how serious he was being. Torture—and the threat of torture, too—was supposed to be against the rules of p'Na. "This could be the same one that Ray shot. They seem able to absorb a lot of abuse. Every function is distributed throughout their bodies and I'll bet they also heal fast."

The boss nodded. "Right you are, Sam." He stood up, put his gun away, and went to the kitchen. He came back immediately with a small container in his hand. "This is a highly volatile petroleum fraction," he announced. In fact, it was only a bottle of Plumfizzle, the boss's favorite soft drink. "I'm going to take you outside, pour it all over you, and light it. Then we'll see how well-distributed your functions are."

The thing said, "Wait, wait, what is it that you want to know?" So our guest didn't care much for the idea of being set on fire. For that matter, neither did I, not just because I hate the smell of burning fur.

Eichra Oren said, "Who are you?"

196

"I don't know how to answer this question of yours, vertebrate," it complained. "I don't understand it. I am myself. What else could I be?"

"To begin with, what's your name? My name is Eichra Oren. His name is Oasam Otusam. Her name is Lornis Adubudu. His name is Mio. What's yours?"

"'Name'," it repeated, almost to itself. "You give each cell a unique designation all its own. How mind-consuming that must be, remembering and employing all of those letter combinations. This is better:"

Instead of more words, we vertebrates were treated mentally to a complicated and confusing diagram. There was a long silence, then: "That's genealogy," Lornis said at last. "That's some kind of family tree."

"It's telling us who it is," Mio said, "in terms of its familial relationships."

"Let me try something," said Lornis. She closed her beautiful eyes and concentrated. What we saw was a considerably less complicated diagram showing the last three generations of the Adubudu family. For some reason the creature suddenly began thrashing around violently again.

"Alfarz," I observed. "It seems to focus on Alfarz Adubudu."

Lornis said, "My father. I think this thing wants to kill him."

Alfarz Adubudu was a businessman who specialized in catering to certain proclivities of which many individuals would be ashamed were they to become public knowledge. Pass a thousand laws, I thought, repeal them all; none has even a hundredth of the power of social approval or disapproval. If Alfarz were living in a civilization somewhere that outlawed the proffering of such goods and services, he'd have been considered a criminal kingpin. As it was, he did moderately well by supplying individuals with what they thought they needed.

Eichra Oren leaned in on the creature. "Why would you kill Alfarz Adubudu?"

As before, we didn't get an answer in words, but in flashes, brief glimpses of Alfarz, of Semlohcolresh in Lanternlight, of Lyn Chow, of Hyppod Zart and his fellow tentacle-nosed friends, and oddly enough of Scutigera, and of Eichra Oren's mother, Eneri Relda, each of them associated in its mind somehow with Misterthoggosh. There were also certain characters we recognized, but didn't know: Asavivirsnajunamar ("*THE* name in Anti-Gravity"), another famous Elder, Semajytrairom, a media commentator, and Nombismocwen, who manufactured hoverveeks like Lornis'. There was a number of others, of several species, we didn't know.

"It doesn't seem to understand how we organize ourselves," Lornis suggested. "My mom died a couple of years ago, climbing a mountain on the Northwest Continent. Maybe it thought my dad lives in that tool shed." That was funny for a couple of reasons. Among Lornis' people, *Homo gracilis*, houses traditionally belong to the womenfolk, passing from mother to daughter, which was probably why he'd wanted his own place.

"Stop me when I go wrong," said Mio, ticking points off on his tiny Talapoin fingers. "What we have here are some violent criminals, killers of an unfamiliar species—these Grays—who are apparently descended from flatworms, have independently discovered crosstime travel, and are now here with some kind of list of people they want to kill."

"All because they have something to do with Misterthoggosh," I observed, wondering why I hadn't seen Aelbraugh Pritsch, Jakdav Hoj, or Mikado in the alien's mental rogues' gallery. Unimportant, I guessed. "The person in this world who has the most to do with other worlds."

Eichra Oren rose. "Sam, my mother isn't picking up, but she often turns her com off. Let's head over to her place and make sure she's all right. Maybe she can tell us why she's on this strange creature's list. Along the way, we'll call the others and alert them to the danger."

"Mio and I will help with that," said Lornis. "We'll go with you, if you don't mind, Eichra Oren, Sam. I'd feel a whole lot safer. I'm associated with Misterthoggosh, too, after all, through my father. I'll send my veek home. I'm in contact with my dad this very minute. He's doing business on the Island Continent and assures me he's just fine."

She'd asked if *I* minded. Push that "I wish I were human" up a notch.

"I thought you said you were going fishing with Alfarz today," the boss informed her, rather than asking her, pretending to be a detective. The man seemed desperate to find some reason not to like this beautiful girl who wanted nothing more than to give herself to him.

Lornis replied, "Tonight. He's taking a ballistic flight home." That's the way to travel, I thought. Half a world away in ninety minutes.

I decided that the subject could use changing. "Boss, what're we gonna do with Captain Wormface, here? Gonna introduce it to your mother?"

Eichra Oren laughed, "On the way over, we'll drop it off with Misterthoggosh. He may have an idea or two of what to do with the creature."

The alien flatworm thing freaked when it heard that. Back it went, into the trunk, not peaceably, but kicking and wriggling without making a noise. Eichra Oren drove. Lornis sat beside him in the passenger seat.

I sat behind her on the vestigial back seat with the Hammerdamned monkey.

CHAPTER TWENTY-EIGHT

Council of War

THE BOSS CALLED AHEAD.

Instead of parking at the curb when we got there, he pulled around to the east side of the Elder's house—putting the shoreline to our left—into an open door wide enough for ten veeks. We'd been here once before, when we were "taken for a ride". One of the dozens of machines parked inside was immediately familiar. It belonged to Eneri Relda.

The four of us wondered what was going on.

We were led from the garage by one of Aelbraugh Pritsch's people—between the bird folk and a gaggle of plastic-wrapped nine-foot sea scorpions, we'd been greeted by at least a dozen and a half heavily-armed sapients on semi-alert—on a winding path through the Elder's house.

Despite the state of alert, at least some of the feathered brigade seemed to be on break, sitting in a small room off the hall at a table (perches, not chairs), round cards in their hands, playing contract whist or Go Frog or something, drinking kelp beer, and finger-nibbling at what looked like a big pan of fried cockroaches. Smelled like it, too. It's always important to keep up the morale of the troops, I guess.

Recorded music played in the background, although the bird folk might just as easily have played it through their implants. There's no accounting for taste. To me it sounded like an entire orchestra composed of harps, tuned by an army of deaf harp tuners and played by monkeys, using their feet. I'd been told it was the latest, hottest thing—among dino-avians, that is. Somehow, it was worse than the cockroaches.

Meanwhile, across the hall, their chitin-covered counterparts (the bird people's, not the cockroaches') appeared to be taking it easy, too. They didn't seem the type for card games. They were consuming the same kelp beer, but with cheeseburgers (no, I don't know how the sea scorpionoids got them through their watertight transparent bodysuits), all their attention seemingly focused (although a couple of eyestalks followed us across the open door as we passed by) on some variety of spectator sport on video, an obvious interworld import in which two heavily armored groups of humans employed L-shaped sticks to bash each others' helmeted brains and push a little rubber disk around a frozen pond.

The game was punctuated at intervals by commercial exhortations on behalf of "Yelram's Tentacle Cream, for discriminating cephalopods", "Snarvely's canned phytoplankton guaranteed 100% zooplankton free!" or for "C'wopst Stix"—I never managed to figure out what they are or who they're for. Those would have been inserted by Misterthoggosh's company. There were also interruptions, a bit more frequent, caused by fighting players, during which the Proprietor's guards made extremely loud clicking and whirring noises that I'm reasonably certain denoted enthusiasm.

At last we were conducted onto a flagstoned verandah at the rear of the great house, entirely surrounded by a low retaining wall that also served as a planter. The western half of the enclosed space was a lush green lawn. To the south, beyond the waving fronds and shimmering leaves in the planters, lay about a hundred yards of coarsely cropped yellow salt grass, a broad, sandy beach—every grain of it imported; the natural shore is rocky—and finally the Inland Sea itself. For some reason, the Elders call it "Our Sea" and think it's some kind of joke.

Overhead, no fewer than a dozen flying machines, varying in design mostly by the species flying them, patrolled the airspace immediately above Misterthoggosh's domicile. They were accompanied by several slower-moving, lower-flying but sharper-eyed and brilliantly-feathered members of some kind of airworthy reptilian that I'd only seen before as fossils. I wondered briefly whether the creatures were trained, remotely controlled somehow, or sapients in their own right. I meant to ask, but in all the excitement that was about to sweep over us, I forgot.

There were plenty of vessels out on the water, too, long, low, carnivorous-looking splinters that didn't resemble pleasure boats in any way at all. Doubtless they had companions, patrolling under the surface, as well. It was a literal case of defense-in-depth. I think in some universes, Misterthoggosh might easily have been his own country.

The grounds themselves were enormous. Set in the center of the decorative sandstone flagging lay a saltwater swimming pool at least fifty paces on a side. I suspected its design included handy tunnels to the house and the sea where Misterthoggosh kept his other palatial estate.

In the water, the old boy was present in the flesh—and there was plenty of that, sticking out of the end of his multicolored, knobbly, spiral shell. A highly assorted crowd of guests swam in the pool with him, or sat around on the patio surrounding it, or right at the pool's edge, with their various pedal appendages dangling in the water. I don't know why, but many sapients like to do that, including yours truly. Beyond the east end of the pool an outsized image field had been activated in which the great mollusc could be seen even better. Somebody bumped into me as he shoved his way past, without excusing himself. I was moderately surprised that the Magnificent Mollusc had decided to invite the mass media to his little garden party, in the form of the Planetary Implant Network, or PIN—the bottom-feeders who work for it, news floozies and gentlemen of the evening, are commonly called "pinheads". It was one of them who had just trampled me.

There are probably a thousand "news" networks like PIN, each one sleazier than all the others. I wondered why Misterthoggosh had chosen this particular bunch, who I'd always thought were among the lowest. I've been told it's the same in every universe we've explored so far. The profession seems to attract the worst among any species. They and their enhanced cerebrocortical implants were all over the place, now, wearing what looked like rearview bicycle mirrors on headbands, so that the audience at home could see their precious faces as they blathered.

Another of them, a female arthropod of some kind, approached me, pretty damned condescendingly, it struck me, soliciting my feelings (she didn't appear to be interested in my thoughts) about what was happening here. I snarled and showed my fangs—impressive, if I say so myself; I practice in the mirror—and she left to bother somebody else.

"Nice doggy," my furry white ass.

Off in one corner of the giant-sized backyard, a bevy or gaggle or coven of lovely young female specimens, a majority of them quite human, a few of them pleasantly humanoid like Lornis, each and every one of them highly mammalian and agreeably clad in what looked like their underwear, were playing some kind of a game with a head-sized ball tossed back and forth over a net set at chin level. Wonderful scenery. Someone outside my peripheral vision said they were college students. I could easily have watched them bouncing around for hours. So could the other fifty or sixty males casting ocular organs in that direction.

Eichra Oren extracted a big cigar from his tunic pocket and let it light itself. He inhaled and then exhaled with visible satisfaction. You're not supposed to do that with cigars, but he was the boss, and they were his cigars, not to mention his lungs. I was content just to sit on the sun-warmed flags, prepared to enjoy whatever was about to happen.

Although it didn't come without a cost.

Regrettably, as I knew it must, I heard a gong that stopped the ball-playing abruptly. Towels and hoodies and windbreakers were passed around to cover all that moist, gleaming flesh, and there followed a rapid migration from that corner of the Proprietor's yard, toward the broad patio where Eichra Oren stood beside Lornis, her monkey-thing in her arms. As the formerly naked coeds approached, the expression on the young Denisovan's face could be read as "Back off, girls, he's mine!".

Or possibly, "One more step and you're lunchmeat!"

I'm never entirely certain what females want from Eichra Oren, or what they think they're going to get. This bunch crowded around him, giggling and squealing. He was a moderately famous practitioner of a sometimes dangerous profession. I guess that made him "Adventure Man" to them. Intellectually, at least, I know there are females who like "life-takers". I was pretty sure at least a couple were scanning his image into their implants from head to toe, planning to use his avatar in their virtual sex software. There's no law against it, but it isn't very polite. Lornis held onto the boss's arm as if her life—or maybe his—depended on it. Whatever he said to them was kindly but reserved.

Mio, the Talapoin, fed up with being pushed around and joggled, and apparently less enamored of humanoid feminine pulchritude than I am, leaped to the edge of the roof, perching there like a little fuzzy gargoyle.

Our nautiloid host lay mostly in the water, eyes, a few tentacles, and the top third of his multicolored shell sticking up out of the surface. With one tentacle wrapped around a beer baggie, the great mollusc was in full expostulatory form, starting in what felt like the middle.

"It seems to me," he declared to one and all, "that once we jettison all that is extraneous, we are still left with three problems."

All around the colossal mollusc, the crowd acted as if they didn't have any problem at all, let alone three. They all seemed to be talking and drinking and laughing as if they were at a cocktail party—which was more or less true, I suppose—but the difference was that they could "hear" their ammonite host perfectly by way of their implants and were paying him more attention than appeared to be the case.

"Two of these," he continued undauntedly, "were anticipated from the outset. Indeed, one is the reason we committed to this undertaking in the first place. And both of those are in process of being dealt with."

Somebody gave a lone, drunken cheer.

"The final difficulty, I am chagrined to confess, was unforeseen, and regrettably, we can go no further with our plans until it has been resolved."

That shut the gathering up. These people all had money invested in Misterthoggosh's various undertakings, or jobs as undertakers. Now the old boy was telling them this particular venture had hit some kind of snag.

As to that unforeseen problem Misterthoggosh had mentioned, the boss and I had left our alien prisoner (whatever he or she or it was) in the custody of the flock of dinosaur/bird persons—not Aelbraugh Pritsch—who'd met us in the garage. I sincerely hoped Old Wormface would be properly taken care of. A great many of the guests here this afternoon would be wanting to ask it questions before this day was ended.

I hoped they'd have more success than we had.

"The first problem," continued Misterthoggosh, taking a draw on his drink as he spoke via implant, "is that a medium-sized asteroid in one of the alternative universes we're aware of—the very universe, in fact, to which my friend Eneri Relda and her people were born—appears in no other universe we have seen. The phenomenon is absurdly, ridiculously unheard of. It is the Great Mystery we are determined to solve."

The number of alternative universes is supposed to be infinite. An asteroid like the one he described should have existed in a cluster across probability, distributed along a normal curve. But there was nothing normal about this situation. Absolute uniqueness of this kind was highly unprecedented, and relatively silly. Me, I happen to like silly, but most individuals, especially business folk, don't seem to tolerate it very well. On the other hand, there had to be a reason for it, and Misterthoggosh believed that it might be profitable to find out.

Those beings who were capable of vocalizing set up a low murmur, auditory and electronic, that he was compelled to wait out. Luckily, at least compared to anybody else, after half a billion years of sapience, nautiloids are an amazingly patient people—although most other Elders regarded Misterthoggosh as an impetuous risk-taker and adventurer.

"The second problem—please keep in mind that our observations in this regard are from unbeinged remotely controlled devices—is that the civilization native to that stretch of alternative reality, once again, the species of Eneri Relda and her son, my friend Eichra Oren has begun to make itself a factor. Following a regrettably brief, but enlightened period of increasing international peace, individual freedom, social and technological progress, and, of course, splendid prosperity, it now appears, inexplicably, to have regressed, turned itself backward, toward an unusually pernicious variety of violent oppression, suppression, and repression, referred to locally as 'Marxism'."

Some inebriated somebody mumbled something about having seen some of this Marx guy's movies, which Misterthoggosh wisely ignored. The wise and ancient cephalopod struck me more as a Three Stooges type, anyway.

"We've seen exactly the same thing happen in a thousand different continua," declared a voice I recognized. It was our new friend from Lanternlight, the tour guide and "taxi", Scutigera, most of his thirty-foot length invisible behind a little copse of mimosas planted in another corner of the yard. "'From each according to his abilities, to each according to his needs' no more than an awkward attempt to cloak banditry, murder, and rape in the garment of legitimate ideology—and a vile credo best suited to leaches, mosquitos, vampire bats, lice, bedbugs, and intestinal parasites, certainly not to sapient beings."

Quite a speech for a thirty-foot centipede. Several individuals laughed a dozen different ways, from each according to his species. I deduced from this that none of them were descended, evolutionarily, from leaches, mosquitos, vampire bats, lice, bedbugs, or intestinal parasites.

Misterthoggosh agreed. "They are, of course, perfectly welcome to do that to themselves. The trouble is—setting aside for a moment the atrocities they customarily inflict on those among them who do not wish to live a collectivized life—such regimes become dangerous to innocent bystanders once their political and economic policies fail to produce a paradise on Earth. Then they blame anybody and everybody for their failures, rather than face the simple fact that their ideas are stupid."

"You're quite right," a being who looked fantastic even to me had spoken up. It was a six-foot insectoid resembling a praying mantis, dressed up in the usual outfit of hundreds of strips of colored cloth. "Their leaders typically lash out whenever their cherished theories collapse, slaughtering their own people, sometimes by the tens or even hundreds of millions, or waging mindless wars against neighbors who, ironically, almost invariably have identical economic and political philosophies."

"Unfortunately so, Doctor," another person agreed. This one looked a bit like a thick gray blanket in a thin, clear wrapping, a distant relative of Ray, the late, lamented mantoid. My implant told me that she was a female named Remaulthiek. "I have made it my personal task to study this odd species closely. Predictably, they have equipped themselves with powerful fission and fusion explosive devices that are ultimately capable of rendering their entire planet uninhabitable. They've even used them against one another once or twice in recent decades."

There was an odd sort of a collective gasp as everyone among the gathering digested this bit of information. Thermonuclear explosives were old news, of course, in the ancient civilization of the Elders, but they were employed exclusively for demolition and construction, mostly off-planet by non-nautiloids. According to the most fundamental precepts of p'Na, weapons of indiscriminate lethality can never be used, since the only justification for violence is when somebody else—some specific individual—has initiated violence against you. It is generally agreed to be a physical impossibility to put such devices to tactical use without injuring or killing totally innocent bystanders.

And doing that is morally unacceptable for any reason whatever. Period. Offering weasel-words like "collateral damage" as an excuse will only get you the Assessor's blade, an ending much cleaner, at least in this canine's opinion, than you deserve. Once that principle had been established among them, the Elders never fought another war. So far, their "Armistice" has lasted for a couple hundred million years.

We heard another voice, that of a second nautiloid bobbing in the Proprietor's pool, another friend from Lanternlight, Semlohcolresh. "To make things even more complicated and dangerous, these people have achieved an elementary form of spaceflight and are now rumored to be interested in the same rogue asteroid that we are, in their case as a potential source of wealth or knowledge, possibly enough to make up for the utter imbecility of the political claptrap they have chosen to believe."

"Very common behavior among failed command economies," observed Remaulthiek. "Even when they find wealth, their economy soon destroys it."

"But the worst", said Eichra Oren's mother, stepping out of the house, a delicate-looking drink in hand, "we haven't even gotten to yet."

CHAPTER TWENTY-NINE

Out of the Abyss

"THE WORST", EICHRA OREN'S MOTHER HAD SAID, "WE haven't gotten to yet."

"Indeed we have not," Misterthoggosh agreed. "Perhaps you would be good enough to describe the most recent and ominous developments to everyone."

Eneri Relda nodded. "Several of our friends and associates have experienced savage attacks by what appears to be a previously unknown species, from a previously unknown alternative universe. I am informed on good authority—that of Lyn Chow of the Otherworlds Museum and Observatory—that they are the sapient descendants of ordinary flatworms, a common variety of Platyhelminthes, a bit better known as planaria."

"The kind of thing children play with in biology class," somebody said, "that you can cut in half and both halves will grow into new individuals?"

"The very thing," Eneri Relda answered. The being that had asked was a poriforan, sort of a sapient tubeworm, evolved to live on land. She went on to describe what had happened to Lyn Chow, in details both Eichra Oren and the victim herself had given her. The badly-wounded curator was apparently listening in on this meeting, but she was still far too weak to contribute much to it. Feeling her presence in the background, I nodded a mental hello and received a warm, sweet-scented response.

"Permit me to add," said Misterthoggosh, "that these attacks appear limited to those who have acquired an interest in my current enterprise."

A little creature who closely resembled a large watermelon covered in human fingers—only the entire organism was various shades of purple—waggled up comically to address Eichra Oren's mother. "My own species achieved sapience almost as early as the Elders," it declared.

I wasn't quite sure how that was relevant. Perhaps it thought it was establishing some kind of seniority. I remembered now that they were close relatives to sea cucumbers, and that somehow they too had evolved into land-dwellers tens of millions of years before insects had been first to emerge into the air on more familiar versions of Earth.

"Can you tell us more of the nature of these attacks, Honored Co-sapient?" the peculiar creature asked, arranging its stubby tentacles in what my implant informed me was a formal expression of solicitude.

She smiled down at the creature and stepped closer to the pool, taking a chair near its edge. "Indeed I can, Wuzh Blano, Honored Friend. I was myself attacked earlier this morning, at my home, by several of these flatworm beings—Grays, I believe they are being called."

I didn't have to look at Eichra Oren to feel his surprise, and a slight indignation that his mother hadn't called on him. It passed quickly. He knew as well as I did that Eneri Relda was the hardy pioneer type who much preferred taking care of herself to yelling for help. I never knew anyone who loved life and embraced it the way she did. Almost alone among her people, she had regarded their escape from Antarctica—and their later Appropriation by the Elders—as an adventure.

In her mind's eye we could all see the Grays coming up out of the sea, apparently without a thought of staying low or seeking cover. They strode straight up the beach, climbed the salt grass-covered slope behind her house, and came over the back wall. Alarmed by her vigilant—if not downright paranoid—reptiloid symbiote Nalanaed, she had been observing their implacable approach from behind a heavy curtain drawn across a big sliding glass door at the back of the house.

When she finally stepped out, they all raised the weapons they had been carrying (her symbiote, of course, fled), but the human woman was considerably faster than they were. Eneri Relda's first several shots seemed to have little or no effect, although she could easily tell where the creatures had been hit. She could see daylight through their wounds.

As they returned fire, she was forced to take cover herself, crouching behind a heavy stone planter in a cloud of dust and flying pottery fragments as she wrenched the collimator of her weapon around, burning the web of her left thumb in the process, to widen its lethal beam.

The enemy weapons seemed to be kinetic force projectors—not entirely unheard of in the Elders' civilization—rapidly demolishing Eneri Relda's cover. Abruptly she stood up, taking two of the invaders at the same time, spraying their charred remains against a battered rear wall. Her weapon was identical to the one she'd given Eichra Oren.

Out of the corner of my eye, I saw the boss readjust his own pistol.

Two down, then, and four more to go. Eneri Relda pivoted on a toe a few degrees and treated the next two the same way. Although they'd been scrambling hard to put some distance between themselves, they'd been too slow, vanishing simultaneously in gouts of flaming carbon dust.

She looked around for the remaining pair and in that instant heard an avian scream from inside the house. Somehow they'd gotten past her—a side door, probably—and were inside. "Squee-elgia!" she cried as she whirled, reentering the house behind the front sight of her pistol. She felt a *pang* in her mind that could only mean one thing. "Squee-elgia!"

"They are very hard to fight," Eneri Relda told us. "More or less oblivious to wounds unless you destroy them completely, and fully as well-coordinated as any flock of birds or school of fish. My poor symbiote was killed, and my personal assistant, after bashing one of them to paste with a heavy potted plant, seriously injured. I killed the last one, myself. Squee-elgia is now in the Place of Resting and Healing."

Personally, I would not miss Nalanaed, a kind of flying snake from some unlikely alternative universe somewhere. Four feet of liverish, hot-blooded parthenogenic reptiloid indisposition that generally absented herself when visitors arrived. I was glad Squee-elgia had survived. She was silly—although she didn't know it—and I liked her.

"Is it your intention to imply, Eneri Relda," Semlohcolresh rose from the pool a little, and took a sip or squirt or whatever from a flexible container of wine. "That these entities are a part of a hive mind?"

Eneri Relda frowned a little as she gave the matter consideration. Finally, she looked up at the big mollusc. "I believe they may be more independent than, say, ants, or bees, or termites. But no, I don't believe that they are fully individual in character like all of us here. A sapient colony of mole rats or prairie dogs that are not sapient, themselves, perhaps? It's entirely possible that we'll never know."

I thought I saw Misterthoggosh paying special attention to what she said. I very nearly spoke up about the specimen we'd brought with us, but felt Eichra Oren in my mind, for some reason telling me to stop.

"As you may be aware," Semlohcolresh told the gathering, I, too have been attacked at my home in Lanternlight. They arrived by veek, about twenty of them, and were it not for the determination and bravery of my dear employees—" He used a tentacle to indicate the pathologist Jakdav Hoj and his feline companion Mikado. The tentacle in question happened to be wrapped around the deeply spiral-cut grip of a large particle blaster. "—never to overlook the splendid competence of the Dumu Weapon Manufactory, we might well have been overwhelmed."

Again there were vivid pictures in our heads, a jumbled montage from the minds of all three, Semlohcolresh, the Denisovan Hoj, and his big, fierce housecat. I found the whole thing invigorating, myself, but there were groans from other quarters. Some of those who were capable of it held their hands to their heads. Off in a corner of the yard, a delicate soul of some kind could be heard, vomiting on the grass.

"As Eneri Relda indicated," Semlohcolresh's laboratory technician told everyone, "penetrating weapons—needle-beamers, bullet-flingers—aren't particularly useful. What you really need is something with a broader effect, like a broadbeam blaster or a short shotgun. The kitchen sink might work. And it helps if they're carrying or wearing something dense—a belt buckle, for example, or maybe just a full equipment bag—that you can hit easily and break up into secondary projectiles."

The cat said, "They—"

It was the shortest remark I ever heard him utter. In that instant an enormous *BOOM!* came from the back of the grounds, toward the sea. Beneath our feet, the entire structure of the patio heaved and shook. Something had landed on the beach, a massive cylinder the dull color of burned iron, with bluntly-pointed ends. Fifty feet in diameter and at least six times as long, one end lay smoking in the shallows, salt water lapping at it tentatively. The middle section rested on the sand. The other end lay in a big divot it had slammed out of the salt grass.

I supposed it might have blasted up out of the water, like a breaching submarine. If it had fallen from the air, I hadn't seen it coming. It was so massive, I'm not sure what the air patrols could have done about it anyway. The G-forces inside must have been crushing.

A seam opened from one side of the front end to the other, making the object look like a giant, blind, grinning worm of fire-blackened steel. Water blasted out, under high pressure. A section of retaining wall vanished in a cloud of dust and smoke, lethal fragments flying everywhere. It was almost endearing, the way Grays seemed to like explosives. Several individuals were struck down. Through the dust cloud, familiar figures emerged from the cylinder, grim gray figures in grim gray coveralls, bearing short, two-handed weapons of some kind.

I jumped onto a heavy glass-topped table so I could see better. Down toward the beach, rank after rank of the silent alien invaders were coming out of the cylinder. Eichra Oren drew his little pistol, holding it in his left hand, as his razor-sharp sword whistled from its scabbard and he swung it over his head in his right. Across the pool, his mother produced her nearly identical pistol, and the two of them fired their first shots at almost exactly the same fraction of a second.

Another explosion collapsed a second stretch of wall, and now the creatures poured through, apparently oblivious to the comrades beside them who were being turned into horrible fried meat not only by the defenders' weapons, but by the second wall-demolishing explosion, as well. The eeriest thing about them was their utter silence— they had nothing, no lungs, windpipes, vocal chords, or mouths to make noise with.

Although most of our attackers were Grays, I was surprised to see there was also some number of humanoids—mercenaries, most likely *Homo sapiens*—wearing the gray livery of their masters, apparently intent on killing each and every one of us. They had been drugged or something, their complexions were almost blue, their faces blank and expressionless like those of corpses. If someone looked up "zombie assassins" in the implant directory, they'd find a picture of these guys.

Eichra Oren swung his terrifying blade down on an approaching Gray, the edge, a single molecule, cleaving its head in two, shearing through the body, and exiting at the crotch. Both halves flopped helplessly onto the flagstones at the man's feet, quivering where they lay. As he turned, the boss's next stroke went through another enemy alien sideways at the waist, and two more quivering halves joined the first.

In the center of the pool, a fantastic sight: Misterthoggosh stood halfway out of the water, supported by several of his tentacles, while he wielded three spiral-handled force-pistols, shooting away in every direction. His weapons, which, like those of the invaders, produced pure, recoilless one-way kinetic energy, worked exceptionally well against the Grays, who looked like they were being hit by an invisible hovertruck.

Beside him, Semlohcolresh apparently didn't feel the need for a weapon at the moment, although I'd seen him with a handsome particle beamer. With a hideous screaming snarl I hadn't been aware the Elders were capable of making, he was lashing about, a ten-limbed berserker, seizing Grays or any other enemy who made it to the pool and hurling them back away from it. Their bodies splashed against anything solid they struck and burst like bags of rotted vegetables. Some of them even hit other Grays, producing some of the ugliest messes I had ever seen.

Meanwhile, Eichra Oren was discovering that his p'Nan martial artistry—consisting mostly of assaulting centers of the body where healing needles would ordinarily be inserted—wasn't working on the Grays much better than his sword. His little pistol, adjusted to disperse its energy broadly, worked better, and he wielded it with a will.

I had a sudden, ominous feeling about the Grays the boss had cut in half with his sword. Grasping the edge of a drinking bowl with my teeth, I hopped down and poured hundred proof alcohol all over the writhing remains. That didn't seem to discourage them from twitching, but they blanched and sizzled gratifyingly, exactly like properly salted garden slugs. I only hoped that it would also keep them from regenerating.

Although his martial art, which more closely resembled dancing than fighting, didn't appear to work on the Grays—their systems were too decentralized—it did with a vengeance on the humanoids, who were beginning to pile up in a ring of bodies around the debt assessor.

Not for the first time, I felt shamed and useless without hands to fight with, limited only to snarling at organisms who didn't know what it meant, and snapping at their hired assassins, who did. I confess to taking off a careless finger or two. I was very careful to spit them out. Odds were long, but even more than choking on the human fingers, like in the urban legend, I didn't want anything regenerating inside me.

Hopping back up on the table, I got noticed. I watched helplessly as one of the Grays aimed a weapon at me, from too far away to defend myself, and fully expected to die in that moment. Instead, the thing exploded before my eyes. I looked over my shoulder and there stood the very attractively ferocious Lornis, her weapon—an outsized infrared laser I believe it was—still held before her face, its big red lens glittering.

"Thanks, gorgeous!" I told her, envying my unappreciative boss all over again. The pretty girl grinned back at me, pivoted gracefully, and shot something else that exploded. Lasers superheat the water that our bodies are mostly composed of, in just an instant. They don't burn through you, they make you blow yourself up, and Grays are even more susceptible to that than anybody else. Who says the Age of Steam is over?

Scutigera had an interesting way of handling his assailants. Of his fifteen pairs of legs, two pairs had been modified by evolution to capture prey. With a rigid body thirty feet long, when he put his foot down—all twenty-six of them—the big fellow was there to stay. If an enemy was more than a few yards away, he dispatched it with a huge, heavy ion-spraying pistol held in one of his manipulatory appendages. Closer in, he wielded a great, curved knife for them to deal with. If they were face to face, he simply bit his opponent's head off and spat it out, leaving many a Gray to wander aimlessly, bumping into lawn furniture.

The beautiful Eneri Relda also looked more like she was dancing than fighting—she had taught him, to begin with, but from here, it almost looked hereditary—whirling about, leaping from toe to toe, Fire would spout from one of her hands from time to time, never in predictable intervals or directions. The enemy retreated as she advanced.

Suddenly, I saw a man—some kind of a man, anyway; if he had eyes in his head, they were set too deeply to be visible—behind her, aiming one of the Grays' weapons at her. I didn't think, I simply jumped, and by the time the two of us hit the flagstones, his weapon spun and skittered across the flagging, and my upper and lower fangs were buried in the man's throat. He screamed, struggling, pulling my teeth through his flesh, tearing at the aortas. In a moment, he lay quiet.

I had never tasted human blood before, or killed a sapient. But looked at the right way, the man had committed suicide. The damned fool had been about to kill somebody I loved. Shrugging it off, I worked my way back and took my place, shoulder to shoulder, with the boss, his mother, and with Lornis, we four forming as formidable a wall as we could between the innumerable Grays and the House of Misterthoggosh.

There were plenty to replace the man I'd killed, scattered through the oncoming horde, and for each one of them, a hundred Grays or more, advancing in a single-minded and implacable wave of bloodshed and death.

CHAPTER THIRTY

A Dream of Romance

THE FATEFUL GATHERING AT MISTERTHOGGOSH'S VILLA broke up not long after his conversation with G*l*str*d*. Some guests returned to their homes. Others accepted his offer of safety and hospitality. And some sought various Places of Rest and Healing. I believe everybody had assumed the underwater half of the great nautiloid's domicile had been destroyed, but the Grays had simply gone around it, intent, or so the thinking was, on killing as many of his investors and consultants as possible.

Their mistake.

We stayed the one night, my boss and I, not so much for any safety the old snail could afford us—Eichra Oren and I are by no means the victim type. Our house holds many surprises for the uninvited, all of them unpleasant and some of them thoroughly lethal. Eichra Oren simply wanted to stay "in the loop", as the saying goes in some universes, and the best way to accomplish that, it seemed, was to sit at the Elder's table and sleep under his roof, at least for this particular moment.

I agreed with my esteemed companion, and it had almost nothing to do with the lobster bisque that was featured on the house menu that evening.

Almost.

Nothing.

I have dreams about that stuff.

There had been a lot of palaver about the mentality—or the lack thereof—of the Grays. Some of Misterthoggosh's retainers, when the attack had commenced, had found and seized the underwater vehicle that the invaders had arrived in. Any other species I could think of would have left a handful of guards behind, or enough crew to take the craft out somewhere safe, returning only when they had been ordered to. I think sea scorpionoids are born knowing about elementary tactics like that.

However, I was disinclined to agree with certain of the Elder's "experts", that the Grays were unintelligent. There was a vast, cool, unsympathetic intellect in there somewhere, I was sure of it. After all, they employed kinetic force projectors as weapons in both one and two-handed form, one of only a small handful of species to do so. They had also independently invented interworld travel, and apparently were somewhat better at it than the Elders were. Increasingly, I was inclined to doubt that "they" was the pronoun to employ, referring to these alien newcomers, especially after a brief discussion I had with Scutigera.

"Yes, it's true," the gigantic centipede had confessed. Call it a "rump session". As a combined force of dinosauroid employees and *Leru Obilnaj*, a non-sapient insectoid servant species, began cleaning up the mess, a few of Misterthoggosh's "inner circle" were sitting around the pool where the battle had been fought, comparing notes and making plans.

Military plans, from the sound of it, on a version of this planet that had enjoyed unbroken peace for several hundreds of millions of years. If the nautiloid Elders whose ancestors had achieved that peace felt anything about its being broken, they were not forthcoming about it.

I was furious enough for them.

The Proprietor himself and his friend and fellow sapient mollusc Semlohcolresh, had retired to the palatial comforts and delights of the briny deep, just offshore, but they were still here, with us, inside our heads. "To be truthful, Sam," said Scutigera, "I am a sociologist—and one of Misterthoggosh's business partners. I use my transport service in Lanternlight to study the various people that I meet."

The nautiloids were conferring deeply (if you'll pardon the pun) with my boss in his role as moral arbiter of the proposed undertaking, with his mother, Eneri Relda the wise and beautiful, and with a small handful of other notable or notorious insiders. Alfarz Adubudu, sweet Lornis' somewhat shady father, was one of hundreds of investors in Misterthoggosh's widespread enterprises, but his advice was sought, as well. He was visiting with the rest of the gentlemen (and gentlefem) adventurers on his way home, from a sub-orbital aerocraft presently streaking somewhere over the Greater Ocean at many times the speed of sound.

I'd been feeling a little left out until I noticed that the big centipede didn't seem to be participating in the confab, either, but stood pensively (at least it looked like he was standing pensively) taking up more space than any other sapient being I was acquainted with.

"Kind of sneaky," I observed in a mock-critical tone, referring to his method of surreptitiously studying people. The truth was, the idea of a sneaky thirty-foot arthropod appealed greatly to my sense of the absurd.

He replied, "Harmlessly so, I should hope, Sam. I do publish all of my findings openly, under my own name, in the *Journal of Sapient Studies*."

I laughed. "Avidly read by billions every month, I'm sure."

"It's quarterly, Sam," the enormous creature said gently.

"Okay, quarterly, then. Billions and billions of enthusiastic readers. So what can you tell me about these Grays, O Great and Mighty Sociologist?"

"Well, first, I'm not quite sure that whatever they share amounts to a society, as we would recognize it." Scutigera inhaled and exhaled through his many spiracles. "G*l*str*d* informs me that his security people have managed to round up a few prisoners after all, surviving individuals who were left without transportation when the forces of Misterthoggosh seized their.... I'm uncertain that the term 'submarine' is appropriate for a craft open to the water because its users are amphibians."

"Hey, it travels under water, so it's a submarine. But call it a bus," I suggested. "Although it's supposedly outfitted with life support and a large watertight capsule outfitted for their humanoid mercenaries."

Privately, I wondered about these entities, pretty sure that they had to be from Somewhere Else, not this continuum. Not Eichra Oren's, either. There are lots of different kinds of people in the universes, all of them, in lots of different kinds of worlds. But who—what sapient mammal—would willingly sign up with a bunch of worm-spawn against an open, free, peaceful, progressive, and prosperous society like the Elders had built—and then shared? There hadn't been a war on this version of Earth for over half a billion years. Five hundred million years. Five million centuries. There's no easy way to take it in.

I said as much to Scutigera.

"Kindly note," the centipede replied, "that the Elders are worm-descendants, too, in their own particular evolutionary way. And so are we, ultimately, you and I. Yet we side with the Elders, arthropod and mammal alike. I truly believe that Eneri Relda was mistaken about the Grays, Sam. I don't know that for certain and therefore refrained from contradicting her. But what was that phrase Semlohcolresh used? 'Hive mind'? I think that these so-called humanoid 'mercenaries' may offer us some kind of a clue. You know I examined one after I had killed it."

"Sort of a field autopsy?" I suggested, wishing I could waggle an eyebrow. (I can, actually, but since eyebrow and forehead are the same color...)

"You may call it that. I took him apart, especially the head. I don't think they're from this reality or any that we know of. They wear an implant on their cortex of a design and style I've never seen—call it "organo-metallic". We'll know a bit more after Jakdav Hoj, Semlohcolresh's technician, gets back to his lab in Lanternlight and completes his own examination of the thing. I predict that what he'll find is that its purpose is to make the humans of one mind with the Grays."

"Of one mind." Put that way, it sounded horrifying.

"Techno-zombies," I rolled the phrase around in my mind, kind of liking it. Scutigera was the only individual I knew of who was crazy enough to perform a dissection in the middle of a battle raging all around him—and the only individual large enough to get away with it.

Scutigera shuddered. There's no predicting what will get to people sometimes. I know a guy who's sickened by the sight of guacamole. "My point, Sam," he said as he began to recover, "is that there's good reason to believe that these Grays themselves are no more individually independent-minded than their humanoid slaves, or whatever they happen to be. In a sense, here, it's almost as if we're dealing with a single organism."

We suddenly had the attention of Misterthoggosh. It felt like being caught in the beam of a great searchlight. "You say a single organism?"

"Indeed," Scutigera replied. "The only one that ever talked to any of us spoke of its species in the first person singular, didn't it, Sam?"

"You're absolutely right, Scutigera. It would clear up a number of mysteries."

"We may even discover eventually," he added, "that, within their home hive, reproduction is carried out by a single 'queen', as it is with bees and ants and termites. They hardly appear equipped for it, otherwise."

Now there was a sad thought to ponder. Somebody once claimed that all group behavior, ultimately, is about eating, while all individual behavior, ultimately, is about sex. It hurt my poor brain, trying to imagine a culture, a civilization, a species with half its motivation missing.

Brrrr. I couldn't live like that.

From there, most of the talk began to run downhill, as far as I was concerned, centering on matters maritime and martial. I know there are people who love that kind of stuff—maybe I'd feel different if I had thumbs—but I'm much more interested in food and sex, not necessarily in that order. We live in a world, I thought, without police, without an Army, Air Force, or Navy. The only weapons I knew about were personal, and hand-carried. I supposed software existed for the fabrication of larger engines of destruction, but after half a billion years of progress, give or take an eon, what could you play it on?

I was, as it turned out, somewhat naive.

About halfway through the colloquium, a portly sea scorpionoid who introduced himself as P*r*z*lb*rt* joined the conference via implant. He was an academic from the more southern of the two continents to the west, he explained, a forensic chemist interested in trace materials, and it was just possible that our Gray flatworm invaders may have been tracked down to their lair, somewhere toward the eastern end of the giant natural bathtub we'd all built our lives and culture around, "Our Sea".

The Grays, it seemed, neither inhaled in any conventional sense, nor exhaled. Every square inch of their bodies (they were composed, almost exclusively of skin) was selectively permeable to oxygen. They got rid of carbon dioxide the same way, simply by emitting it from their hides. My guess turned out correct: they did lie down in their food to absorb it. More details as my stomach becomes controllable again.

There is an evolutionary virtue to this kind of simplicity. It was among the things that made the invaders hard to stop and even harder to kill. But there were disadvantages, too. It meant that the Grays left a signature trail behind them—just noticeable in the air, unmistakable in the water—of carbon dioxide, hormones, and waste products, chemicals that explained why the scavenger birds wouldn't touch them. They were literally covered at all times with a thin film of excrement. I shuddered, remembering that I had actually bitten them.

Misterthoggosh and his cohorts discussed this disgusting toughness at length, exchanging suggestions about dealing with it. The images were seared into my memory of poor Ray trying to defend himself with as formidable—but ultimately useless—a weapon as his automatic speargun.

"If you prick us, do we not bleed?"

Not necessarily.

An ordinary shotgun might work in a pinch, especially with a dense load of fine birdshot. Flamethrowers were suddenly a heartwarming idea. But in the end, directed energy weapons seemed a best approach: lasers at various frequencies, something that shot microwaves, and I wondered how that plasma gun of Eichra Oren's would perform under water.

That's when somebody suggested the use of grenades, thrown by hand or by some kind of launcher. Conversationally, it was only a baby-step from there to somebody saying, half-jokingly, "nuclear hand grenades". There was general laughter all around, but I could feel Eichra Oren stiffen suddenly with apprehension. I understood that my boss wasn't hearing that as any kind of a joke. It is practically a fundamental tenet of p'Na, or at least a first corollary, that there is no ethical way to use nuclear or other indiscriminate weapons, and avoid injuring or killing other beings who have not initiated physical force against you.

In the Elders' world, the isthmus that once connected the north western continent with the south was severed millions of years ago through the use of industrial atomic explosives. Today they're used a lot in Lunar and asteroidal construction. There are plenty of the damned things lying around here and there. I stopped listening when I felt faint tendrils of thought—I couldn't determine their origin—concerning the tactical use of such devices against our new Planarian enemies.

The veek soared over a low hill, giving me a fluttery stomach.

"It'll be some while," Eichra Oren told me late the next morning, "before Misterthoggosh and his myriad partners have extracted enough information—from the abandoned submarines and maybe even some of their former passengers—to form a coordinated plan of action. It'll be my job, then, to look it over and decide whether it's ethical or not."

I remembered the ominous way that last night's meeting had broken up. In fact I'd hardly been able to think about anything else. I told Eichra Oren about that last wisp of thought I'd intercepted more or less by accident, about using thermonuclear earth-moving tools as weapons.

He nodded. "I caught that, too. I think it was Misterthoggosh. But he's hired me to keep him ethical, and by p'Na, that's what I mean to do."

"One way or another?" I asked. I would have raised my eyebrows.

"One way or another," he replied, the image of his assessor's sword flashing through his mind. He'd meant me to see it. Implants are seldom that leaky. Human being and giant cephalopod locked sword and tentacle in combat: you could get obscenely rich selling tickets to that one. Then it suddenly occurred to me that maybe somebody had deliberately let me see—or "feel" was more like it—that errant thought.

"If it is ethical, Boss, will we have a part in carrying it out?"

He nodded. "Almost certainly, Sam. I would be professionally and ethically obliged to insist upon it. But they have an enormous number of preparations to make, including refitting the *Treemonisha* or taking her out of mothballs, or whatever. And meanwhile, as you may remember, we still have some unfinished business to attend to back home."

I remembered something vaguely about a ship, but I must have been more fatigued than I realized at the time. It had been quite a day. I slept well enough, but there's nothing like your own bed in your own home.

Which was where we were headed at the moment, once we'd dropped the delectable Lornis and her supercilious monkey at Eneri Relda's for the duration. Both females had been worried it wasn't safe for Lornis to go home alone, but neither of them wanted to move in and live with Misterthoggosh.

I'd noticed that Eneri Relda had been suspiciously quiet about the many charms of Lornis Adubudu recently. This was looking serious. If anybody knew all about the persuasiveness of silence, it was Eneri Relda.

The veek knew the way, and Eichra Oren kept an eye on it. I was suddenly exhausted again. I'd spent hours in the local cut-and-pastery with a six-inch knife cut on my haunch, an inch or so deep, being kept closed by the judicious application of tissue glue. Getting the muscle fibers reconnected and functioning had been particularly painful and time-consuming. My insectoid doctor—Dlee Raftan Saon—had ordered me to rest. I fell asleep after we offloaded the boss's mother and his would-be girlfriend. He didn't wake me up until we pulled up to the house.

There was an actual hand-written letter waiting for us, its blue paper envelope thumb-tacked to the door. As Eichra Oren pulled the tack out, the house gave a little sigh of relief, and the hole began to dwindle. It vanished before we got inside. He asked the house to fix a pot of coffee for him and nice hot bowl of hot and sour soup for me.

The letter, neatly hand-written on pale blue stationery read:

My dear fellows,

Please don't feel badly for me, my good friends. When I got home I took a good hard look at my mother Shwaseem and my sister Surusu, both of whom you've met, and I decided that I didn't wish to spend the rest of my days married to anyone like them. My fiancé Shaalara is a different sort of entity, beautiful, exotic, graceful, her every breath a dream of romance. A single night of love with Shaalara, if that's what it must be, is far more to be desired than a lifetime of ...well, I'm sure you understand. Thank you for bringing me home.

Your friend,
Meerltchirt of the Fronzeln Zirnaath

"She's going to eat him," I said, suddenly yawning.
Eichra Oren nodded. "I know."

CHAPTER THIRTY-ONE

Treemonisha

EXACTLY LIKE THE PROVERBIAL ICEBERG (MIND YOU, I'VE never actually seen an iceberg, myself, so I had to take Eneri Relda's word for it) a full nine-tenths of the enormous volume of Misterthoggosh's submarine cruiser lay below the waterline, even when she was nominally on the surface.

All that showed of the *Treemonisha* above the ripples at the deep-water quay where she was berthed was a giant suite of navigation and control theaters—most of the hull was some kind of perfectly transparent material—a streamlined housing for dozens of periscopes and communications masts, the broad passenger boarding bay which put me in mind of Misterthoggosh's garage door, and the transparent upper curve of a large and luxurious passenger and guest "saloon"—roughly the size of three jai alai *conchas* laid out side by side—that occupied the upper half of the forward section of the enormous submarine vessel.

"The lower portion of the vessel's forward section is reserved for those of us who make a habit of acquiring their oxygen through gills." The speaker was Misterthoggosh, communicating with everybody through his separable tentacle, which was acting as our guide as we entered the plastic concertina leading from the dock into the side of the great ship.

"Ladies and gentlemen…" As we exited the boarding tube and stepped across the gasketed threshold of the barn-sized hatch, the tentacle stood up straighter on its little scooter. "I give you… *Treemonisha!*"

The great ship, named after the heroine of an opera written by the outsized mollusc's favorite composer, was shaped something like a fat pumpkin seed. She was flat, her blunt end forward, tapering off toward her stern. "She is propelled gravito-hydro-dynamically," the tentacle explained. "The force-fields embracing her hull seize all of the water within about a fathom of her skin-plates from nose to tail, and hurl it aftward, behind her, as if from a vast bucket being poured down a well."

On Jupiter, I thought, guessing that the g-forces involved were horrendous.

"Nobody seems to know—or they won't tell me—how fast she can go, or how deep," I told the tentacle. "I can see that she's braced inside to resist titanic pressures—" I pointed my nose at a huge lustrous white metal truss, at least a foot thick and pierced with circular lightening holes I could have jumped through, curving upward through the deck-plates to lie across the boarding bay's high ceiling overhead.

The tentacle nodded, somehow. "She's prepared to back it up with structural force field generators in an emergency. I can tell you that the entire aftward half of this vessel consists of nothing except the powerplant, generating and harnessing exactly the same forces that are at work in quasars. It was producing and managing energies at this cosmic scale that taught us what we needed to know to travel between universes."

I noticed, of course, that the tentacle didn't answer my question about maximum speed and depth. Nor had it mentioned the unmistakable fact that the Proprietor's private pleasure-craft bristled with weapons of every imaginable kind, all of them powered by that quasar plant.

From approximately where Eichra Oren and I lived and had boarded *Treemonisha*, to where we were headed—presumably the bad guys' invasion base—was roughly 1500 miles. Some sadist on the great ammonite's staff had let it slip that our submarine journey would last at least ten hours, bring your toothbrush. My personal take

226

was that traveling that fast underwater would require some cosmic forces, all right.

We had departed at midnight, although chances were pretty small that we'd successfully evade spying eyes that way. By the time we got where we were going—mid-morning—it would be darker for us than it was now. We were headed for the abyss, the deepest spot in the Inland Sea. Three miles: excepting the occasional luminous octopus or eel, any light you have to see by is whatever light you brought with you.

Three miles deep, they were all saying. I wondered how close that came to the great ship's limits. My guess was that she could lie safely on the silty bottom of some of the truly abyssal trenches of the Greater Ocean, easily twice as deep an anything Our Sea had to offer, otherwise Misterthoggosh wouldn't have bothered to have her built.

In some ways, I'm sure we appeared more like passengers boarding a pleasure cruise ship than an expeditionary thrust in the first war to be fought on this planet for millions of years—and the first ever against creatures from another universe. I was also guessing that the Elders had forgotten, after all this time, what war is supposed to be like.

It didn't look much like a military mission. There wasn't anything resembling a uniform anywhere, even among the crew. Eichra Oren wore horsehide sandals and blue denim trousers, with a loose, brightly colored floral patterned shirt he'd purchased when he'd visited a volcanic island chain in the middle of the Greater Ocean. Before my time.

I'm no expert, but I read a lot, and always listen as hard as I can. For example, Eneri Relda came along. While perhaps not the oldest sapient on this version of Earth, she was close to it, and absolutely the most revered. She had her own stateroom, aft of the saloon, and had brought an egg—another damned flying serpent—to keep warm in a way that undoubtedly made that egg the envy of every male mammal aboard.

"It isn't so much to incubate it," she explained with a modest hand over her décolletage. "The species is warm-blooded. Keeping it close this way simply guarantees that the hatchling will imprint on me."

Sprightly music issued from somewhere overhead: *Ragtime Dance.*

A heavily bandaged Squee-elgia limped behind her looking game and fierce, like an angry, freshly-plucked chicken. Half the ship's crew were people of her species. Most of the rest were spiders of various persuasions.

Lovely Lornis, too, had talked her way onboard, presenting herself as her dad's administrative assistant. "Daddy arrived just in time," she began. "The poor dear endured a suborbital flight at three full gravities, over two oceans and a couple of continents, just to get here."

From the resigned way "the poor dear" hunched his shoulders up around his hairy ears—as if he were headed into a hailstorm—I could see that he was long accustomed to letting his pretty daughter have her way, as what red-blooded male of just about any species wouldn't have? On the other hand, I could also see how she'd been attracted to the violent and crazy specimen of *H. gracilis* she'd married. Unlike most males of his species, Alfarz Adubudu actually looked dangerous, in the "wouldn't want to meet him in a dark alley" manner.

"That also explains her attraction to you, Boss," I conveyed privately, having given him my whole thought process on the matter in the same way. "You can be pretty dangerous, yourself, given the right circumstances."

Eichra Oren ignored me. It was better than what he might have done. We went forward to join the other lung owners in the passenger saloon.

Misterthoggosh or somebody (I don't think it was the separable tentacle) mindcast a map to the implants of anybody within range. "As you may know, the Inland Sea is not quite divided into three separate bodies of water," he said, "by two very large peninsulas that enter it from the north, and from the super peninsula of the Great Continent many of us call home. None of these features had names, of course, before the Appropriations began. We of the Elder race knew less about the land surfaces of our own planet than we knew about the backside of the Moon."

And they cared even less. The nautiloids, almost unanimously, were famously averse to—terrified by—space travel, putting it as mildly as I can, and to most of them, that included anything above sea level.

"The first peninsula looks rather like a comically high-heeled human boot—witch's footwear, or so tradition would have it. Aboard

Treemonisha we shall first travel toward it, between the Brother Islands, around the toe of the boot—doesn't it look like it's about to kick Triangle Island out of the Inland Sea, over the northwest corner of the South Continent, into the Lesser Ocean?—toward the second peninsula, messily composed of tiny desert islands and goat crags."

But by that time, I'd lost interest in the travelogue. I wandered off in search of an acceptable tree or hydrant-substitute to pay my respects to. Then a nice steak and eggs breakfast, I thought, starting with a cocktail. Something with tomato juice and that distilled agave liquor that they manufacture so well at the bottom of the Northwest Continent.

Summoning a map, I discovered I was aimed in the wrong direction, and had just turned around, when the entire ship rang like a great bell and shuddered from a severe blow somewhere aft. The air was filled with screaming and shouting. The floor I was crossing looked like black marble, highly polished. I couldn't stay on my feet. The dark sea at whatever depth we traveled lit up very briefly on the port quarter,

Naturally, a lot more wailing and yelling followed, from the vocal apparatus of at least a hundred different species. It would be far worse below, where the water that the passengers lived in would have conveyed the initial shock and subsequent noises of terror much more efficiently.

A single voice, auditory and electronic, drowned out everybody else's: "This is your captain. We are under attack. There has been no hull breach, or any other damage. Nor is there word so far of serious injuries or fatalities. Force-fields are at one hundred percent. Hang onto something solid, please, while we get the inertial dampers back online."

Hang on with what? I don't have any thumbs!

Suddenly I heard an extremely familiar voice—and mail-order accent. "Zese Grays! Zey geeve ze seafood a bad name!" Apparently Renner and Bask were aboard or inboard, or whatever they called it. Even rattled as I was, I hoped they were here in a professional capacity.

I never had gotten my *bouillabaisse*.

Somebody bundled me up abruptly from behind and lifted me off the slick floor in powerful arms. One whiff informed me that it was Eichra Oren, and the same whiff revealed that Lornis was right there beside him.

Beside us.

"This is far from over," my boss said, via implant. I felt Lornis listening, too. "Apparently we ran into some kind of patrol. Dumb. There's a lot worse news on the way. We're going someplace where we can—"

"Be safe?" I finished his sentence hopefully.

"Be useful," he corrected. "There is no place safer on this vessel than any other place. We're at least a thousand feet down by now. If the hull or the force field supporting it goes, then we'll all be fish-food."

Lornis: "Although at this depth we won't live long enough to enjoy it."

Which inspired what was possibly the weirdest thought I'd ever had: it only seemed fair in its way, having eaten so many fish myself. I refrained from passing the bizarre idea along. It might be taken as a symptom of head injury, when the truth was that I had just been born strange.

We came to one of many transport tubes, a black plastic cylinder with an oval plastic door that opened when it sensed us coming. Eichra Oren put me down on a rubbery gridded carpet, and told the porter "Swordfish". I would have guessed "Rosebud". It beeped politely and we were on the way before my boss could even draw a breath from having spoken.

I enjoyed watching Lornis draw a breath.

When the transport door opened, it was on a much odder scene than I had imagined. Instead of dozens of individuals, brightly lit and seated in steep tiers at consoles, frantically bashing buttons and sliding controls, while younger, lower-ranking personnel rushed from station to station carrying orders and information, what opened before us now was more like a theater, comfortable chairs arranged in rows, rows arranged on a slight angle, under sufficient, but comfortable lighting.

It was surprisingly quiet, for the most part, a low, murmuring everywhere that indicated people of several species who couldn't think into their implants without moving their mouth parts. Arms and legs were almost motionless. The whole scene appeared more than a little religious, like a prayer vigil, but the goddess they all prayed to was *Treemonisha*.

To one side, on a rounded, slightly elevated platform, sat the captain, I assumed, an extremely large gray spider with eight black, shiny eyes. A large screen stood behind his shoulders. showing us Misterthoggosh, who seemed to be watching everything that was going on here. If I'd been the captain, it would have made me very nervous and angry.

Just then, another blow shook the vessel, this time toward the bow, and immediately followed by another. Just before the first explosion, I'd felt dozens of invisible fingers flow upward from the floor and embrace my lower limbs, keeping me and everybody who was standing, steady. The technology was new to me, and felt extremely creepy.

"Oasam Otusam?" Abruptly, I felt a presence behind me, a tap on my haunch, and turned. It was Aelbraugh Pritsch, of all the people in the word.

"What can I do for you?" Eichra Oren and Lornis were interested, too.

The dinosaur seemed more nervous and tentative than usual. "You can man, er, person one of the weapons-control positions. Help us fight back. You, as well, Eichra Oren, as well as your lovely female companion."

Our lovely female companion dimpled. "Lornis," she told him.

"Lornis, then—oh, you're Mr. Adubudu's daughter. I—"

At that moment, another massive blow shook the entire ship, reminding Aelbragh Pritsch that this was no time for idle social chit-chat.

"I'd be happy to help," she told him.

"Me, too," I said in my thumblessness. "What do we have to fight with?"

He twiddled his feathery fingers together, shedding powder. "Well, I'm afraid that bullets have very limited range under water, which has nine hundred times the resistance of air. Lasers attenuate much too quickly, and plasma bolides cool down and disappear. Force projectors have to push on the whole ocean, so they're worse than useless and tend to burn out violently. And they've learned to spoof conventional torpedoes."

I looked him square in the face, trying to convince myself he was serious. But his face looked too silly for that. "Sounds like we're well and truly serviced. Stone knives and bearskins, then? Lemme at 'em!"

231

More finger-twiddling. "Not quite. We can shoot steel spears from electromagnetic launchers at absolutely terrifying velocities. They travel a long way because they have such high sectional density. The spears—called 'trajectiles'—are hollow and rather thin-skinned. When they strike and penetrate a little, they crumple and rupture, exposing a solid core of pure sodium, which explodes on contact with water—"

"Explosions are much more effective in water," said Eichra Oren.

He nodded. "—without the need for detonators or anything else mechanically or electrically complicated. We just need a lot more gunners."

With Eichra Oren on my left (the man of action always demands the outside seat) and Lornis at my right, I settled myself ninto the Sphinx position and let *Treemonisha's* AI make nicey-nice with my implants.

"Greetings, Oasam Otusam," the ship said. The voice in my mind was cool, mellow, intelligent, and female. "It is very pleasant to meet you. I am told you will operate one of my guns. I have chosen for you a weapon mounted on my forward, starboard quarter, somewhat below the midline."

"'Operate' better not require hands," I told her. "I'm a dog."

"So I was told, so I see. I do not need thumbs, Sam—if I may—I need your mind. And I'm told, yours is more than sufficient to the task."

Surprise: "I have a fan in the hierarchy?"

"None other than Misterthoggosh, himself."

What was there to say about that? "Tell me what I'm supposed to do."

"The crosshairs forming within your mind are connected with your weapon, a kineto-magnetic trajectile emitter—something like an oversized solenoid. I gather that you've been told about the sodium cores."

"Tell me more." I indicated a panel forming in the upper left corner of my visual field. Except for the crosshairs in the middle, everything else was black. "Looks like rate of fire and magazine status."

"Any rate from a thousand to twenty thousand rounds per minute. Dreadfully slow, really. Capacity is a million rounds before you have to go offline for two minutes for replacement. You'll receive several warnings."

"The bottom of the panel is about visualization. We have sonar, at several different frequencies, radar at extremely low frequency—it can detect a mountain. And of course, there's lidar, from infrared up to ultraviolet, for very close work—"

"Hope it doesn't come to that!"

There's also virtual illumination—what the scene outside would look like in an oxygen-nitrogen atmosphere under strong sunlight. It is purely computer-generated, of course, but also surprisingly accurate."

I willed the system to give me virtual illumination—a pale gray-green volume with occasional shadows—seamounts—showing at the very bottom, sonar providing brilliant aiming points, when and if.

"What does the other side have?"

"This seems to be their natural environment. Each of them can see what any of the others sees. They have explosive torpedoes and boarding parties."

"Boarding parties?"

"Ineffective, so far."

Suddenly, a bright point of light appeared toward the bottom of the sea and grew brighter as the sonar returns said it rose to meet us.

"That's them, isn't it?" I asked *Treemonisha*.

"It is," she answered. "Take your time. They'll come closer."

"No doubt." I willed the crosshairs over them. They didn't touch, but left an empty circle in the middle, I was asked if I wanted magnification.

Sure, I told the system.

It was one of those bus things, minus the humanoid habitat, plus half a dozen big torpedo tubes along the sides. All of the seats were full: boarding party. Thinking about the big, curved knife whose scar I bore, I drew a bead on the space between the torpedoes and told the system to "Fire!" holding the "button" down for about a dozen shots. The planarian ship exploded, nearly blinding me, scattering confetti everywhere.

Another followed behind it. I blew it up. Three more and I'd be an ace.

CHAPTER THIRTY-TWO

The Seas of Other Earths

I DON'T KNOW IF WE REALLY MADE A DIFFERENCE, BUT after Eichra Oren, Lornis, and I sat down, the Grays never got quite as close again as before. Of course we had a couple of hundred other gunners helping us.

After a while, their resistance gradually melted away, and the good ship *Treemonisha* plowed onward through the Inland Sea at an outlandish speed, using a method of propulsion that converts drag to thrust.

At the cocktail party celebrating what we all understood was a temporary victory at best, Eichra Oren confronted Misterthoggosh. It was held in two big rooms, separated from another by a transparent sheet of something at least six inches thick. Probably not glass, although it felt like glass to my wet nose. The other side was filled with water or the synthetic fluorocarbon the old mollusc often preferred.

"Quite a yacht you've got here, Misterthoggosh," observed the p'Nan debt assessor, "I can think of thousands of countries in hundreds of worlds whose entire navies don't have *Treemonisha's* firepower."

The nautiloid lifted a casual tentacle, the end of which was wrapped around a beer baggie. "*Treemonisha* was never meant to be a warship or a pleasure-craft, sir. She's a vessel of exploration and discovery."

"'Exploration and discovery'?" My boss displayed skepticism with every cell in his body. "Overgunned for that purpose by what, a factor of at least a hundred? Don't tell me that you've actually constructed a portal out there in the Asteroid Belt that's big enough to shove her through."

Misterthoggosh laughed jovially, although we all knew it was purely an electronic effect. "By no means whatever. She was built to explore Europa. Just imagine what a water-world means to folks of my sort."

"The Big Rock Candy Mountain," I interjected.

"Indeed, Sam. Potentially it is a paradise for every sapient marine organism on this planet. And yet, at the same time, it's a completely unknown territory. Pray tell me, Eichra Oren, would you willingly explore the streets of a completely unknown and alien city without your sword, or that little fusion weapon you carry in your pocket?"

"Point taken." my boss replied. "Although I'd give a lot to see the spacecraft that's going to carry her out to Europa. For a moment, he stood in thought beside the thick transparency that separated him from Misterthoggosh. "Never mind all that; I have another question for you."

"I sense," said the mollusc, "that it's a moral debt collector's question."

"You sense correctly, Misterthoggosh. I'm here to do the job you hired me to do, and this can't be avoided any longer. What do you plan to do, once we've arrived at the Grays' local headquarters? Yes, I saw those nuclear earthmovers being brought on as we boarded." He was referring to a pair of huge barrel-shaped objects with nose-cones and fins.

The Proprietor took his time, unfastening another baggie of beer from the fishing line that had just been lowered to him, probably by Aelbraugh Pritsch. "I trust you'll agree with me that these Grays will almost certainly have built their staging base around their point of entry?"

He nodded. "That was my thinking, too. Always protect your escape route."

"Not to mention the terminus of your supply line," the ancient nautiloid declared. "I intend to seal it, employing those nuclear explosives."

"Killing or injuring dozens or hundreds, perhaps even thousands of Grays in the process," Eichra Oren replied. "Among them

uncountable individuals who never tried to do anything even remotely similar to you."

"Eichra Oren," Misterthoggosh said, "You must—"

"As your p'Nan moral debt assessor," said Eichra Oren, "I forbid
it, on the grounds that one cannot use nuclear weapons without
killing or—"

A booming alarm sounded throughout the ship. "it appears,"
said Misterthoggosh, that we are here. We shall settle this anon,
Eichra Oren."

Broadcasting to everybody's implants, every view projector in
the house now displayed what *Treemonisha*'s forward cameras were
seeing: a great trench, just off the west coast of the ragged peninsula, three miles deep at the bottom. What we saw appeared to be a
combination of actual photography and computer-generated imagery.
The great submarine put her nose down, headed for the bottom of
the trench. Thanks to the ship's gravity-control inertial dampers, the
floor felt level beneath our feet. I tried imagining I couldn't hear the
vessel's structure creaking and groaning under the strain of what my
implant calculated would soon be 480 atmospheres—6720 pounds of
pressure per square inch.

In time, *Treemonisha* slowed her descent to a crawl, which was
probably what it looked like she was doing, hovering at an angle,
nose-down, just above the seabed, kicking up a little sediment, or
underwater dust. I went and found the seat I'd been shooting from
earlier. It wasn't really necessary; the ship's fire control system could
talk to my implant anywhere I happened to be. But it just felt right.

Lornis joined me after a minute. That was good. I didn't feel like
being alone. "Eichra Oren stayed behind," she said. "He's having a spectacular argument with Misterthoggosh about ethics and atomic bombs."

"I noticed." Personally, I thought atomic bombs were a good thing
to have ethical arguments about, but I told her, "Not the cleverest use
of one's time—or remaining lifespan." On the network I could see
we were drifting nearer to the center of the Grays' activities. As we
came upon it, the place looked like some kind of industrial plant, like
a petroleum refinery with glaring lights on tall towers, vehicles and
figures moving around with purpose. The water was incredibly clear,
and to the extent that it was possible, it was as bright as daylight.

I asked *Treemonisha's* optical system for some magnification and received a shock. At these depths and pressures, the Grays were nearly as flat as their planarian ancestors, flatter than pancakes, flat as an ironed shirt, comic silhouettes, exactly like paper cut-outs of themselves.

Question: why hadn't they seen us and why weren't they attacking us?

And so we waited. Idly, I said, "Smoke 'em if you've got 'em."

"What?" Lornis was cutest with that quizzical look on her face.

"Never mind." It was an expression from another world.

Suddenly: "Sam, I can't find your boss. I need him to come down here and see something. Misterthoggosh, too." It was Dlee Raftan Saon, sounding as outraged as an insectoid can sound. I sent Eichra Oren a signal which his implant let through. I could sense his tension and annoyance.

"Not now, Sam. I'm busy." I was seeing my boss reflected in a sheet of glass through which he was conversing with his boss, Misterthoggosh.

"Gotta be now, Boss. Dlee Raftan Saon has something he's hot to show you and Zee Beeg Squeed. Near as I can tell with a mantoid, it's urgent."

The man thought for a moment. "I suppose he'll be down aft in the ship's clinic." A diagram began to form in my mind's eye, displaying the quickest route to the location in question. I could tell it came from Misterthoggosh's mind, not Eichra Oren's. Lornis hadn't been privy to the conversation, but she knew something was up and rose with me.

"Where are we going?" she more or less chirped.

Unlike Eichra Oren, I was happy to have her company. "Down aft," as my boss had put it, proved to be dead amidships, as far aft as you could go before running into the engines, and as far below as you could go before wetting your toes in the aquatic sector of the vessel. It was certainly *Treemonisha's* best-protected area, which made sense.

We entered a room through which we could look down through a thick transparency onto the surgeon at his work. Eichra Oren, Lornis, and I were physically present. Our molluscoid host and Lornis' anthropoid symbiont, Mio, were virtually present. Apparently the little monkey had a sensitive tummy. Dlee Raftan Saon stood at a stainless steel table under strong light. In one hand, he held a bloody red scalpel, in another, a pair of retractors. In a third, he held an improvised-looking electronic box with a dozen multicolored wires dangling from it.

What lay on the table wasn't pretty: the body of an average-sized human male, his skin distinctly tinted a shade of blue I'd only seen before at the Battle of the Backyard. Dlee Raftan Saon had done the customary Y-incision to examine his insides, now distributed in pans and buckets here and there about the room—despite the red blood, they all had a distinct dark blue cast—and then peeled his scalp back from just above the eyebrows and removed the upper half of his skull.

This, not the blue organs, was what had made him angry.

"This…this unspeakable travesty" the doctor used a fourth hand to indicate the dead man's brain, and intoned in the crankiest voice his synthesizer could generate, "is what our uninvited guests inflicted, not only on this poor individual, but as near as I can tell, on the entire humanoid population of some other version of our Earth!"

That got whatever bit of attention my boss and Lornis hadn't given the good doctor already. I didn't ask how he'd figured out that last, whole world bit. I caught a wisp of thought concerning the ratio of various isotopes. I felt Mio crank down the resolution of her remote vision.

"Attend." He tapped his gory scalpel on a hand-sized shield-like object closely embracing the front and center of the man's brain. It produced a noise somewhere between a plastic clack and a metallic clink.

"It would appear that an implant seed was injected through the victim's skull at the frontal fontanel when he was just an infant. It's possible that the poor fellow's never had a thought of his own in his entire life. All he lacks to be fully human is a will, which this implant has suppressed or destroyed. Our good colleague Jakdav Hoj has discovered program language for "sleep", "wake", "eat", and even more personal functions. The fellow retained memories of horrifying mass reproductive activities which, sadly, he recalled with something akin to joy. Truly, it's a wonder he could breathe without being told to!"

"And the color?" Misterthoggosh, always a tentacles-on kind of guy.

"My guess is that it's resident algae to provide some supplemental oxygen in a high pressure semi-aquatic environment. They're not

water breathers, like their masters. Look at this!" He used the electronic device, apparently a jury-rigged remote control of some kind,
evoking, turn by turn, various hand and arm movements, foot and
leg movements, blinking, even an erection. I expected some sort of
wisecrack from Mio or Lornis, but it was not forthcoming. This was
just too horrible. What we were seeing was a human being who had
been transformed into robot.

Like I said, a sort of high-tech zombie.

"Do you have a 'stop everything' command in that little box?" asked
the Proprietor. "And is it individually programmed, or broadcast?" "I
could evoke instant paralysis, if that's what you mean, but what good
it will do with the specimen already dead I can't imagine. As to employing such a device on others, you'll have to ask Jakdav Hoj."

Suddenly, two elevator-type bongs were audible. They were followed by something I'd never heard: somebody whispering over what
amounted to a public address system. Trouble was, of course, was that
no real sound was being generated; it was all being done through the
implant network.

"May I have your attention, please?" It was good old Aelbraugh
Pritsch, silly as ever. "This is the Proprietor's personal assistant. He
requests that those who assisted in defending *Treemonisha* earlier
return to battle stations," Over my shoulder, I saw the boss's mom,
Eneri Relda, take a firing position. I hadn't noticed her before. "Everybody else is to go to their quarters and hold onto something solid."

Or hide under the bed.

In my mind's eye, I could see outdoors again. The alien facility
ahead looked even more like an industrial plant than before. It was
centered on a particular spot on the canyon wall, where coils and pipes
had been arranged in a flat circular pattern a hundred feet in diameter.

Anyone onboard who had a cerebro-cortical implant could see
that we were gradually drawing closer to the circular construction. I
hurried to my gunner's seat, with Lornis close behind me. For a mere
humanoid, that girl could really run. Eichra Oren had headed off in a
different direction, telling us there was something he had to check on.

From his tone, I suspected that it wasn't going to end well.

Somebody on the implant network shouted "Incoming!" and there
was an enormous thump. I felt a peculiar queasiness that resulted from

the inertial dampers trying, with only partial success, to control the vessel's motion and leave the decks solidly beneath its passengers' feet.

Sitting at my station, I logged onto *Treemonisha*'s tactical network, which showed a different view. Forward of us, dozens of the Grays' underwater "buses" were converging on us. Driven by a mixture of Grays and humanoid zombies, each carried an enormous cylinder full, presumably, of explosives. I joined dozens of other shooters firing on them. It almost felt as if the concussions when we blew them up, even at extreme range, were inflicting as much damage on our ship as their bombs.

"I'm sure by now that you've observed the circular form against the wall of the abyssal trench." I become aware of Misterthoggosh, talking to everyone aboard the submarine. "At the moment, all you can see through it is the rock wall behind it, It is not so very different from the interdimensional portals that we ourselves have constructed out among the asteroids. When activated, it becomes a doorway, a kind of, well…a 'probability broach' the technicians call it, a hole, as it were, through the very fabric of alternity, a passage between what is, and what might have been. Although the parties on either side of it, of course, will have varying opinions as to which universe is 'real'."

An image of Misterthoggosh formed in my mind. He was sitting at the bottom of his watery environment, on a carefully groomed bed of fine, white sand. A couple of little striped fish pecked at bits of algae on his shell. Before him on the floor lay a panel, serving as a desk.

"It is from over on the other side of that hole in probability, that our new enemy has come. When he activates this device again, and opens the door, I mean to slam it shut with one or both of the nuclear devices I've brought." He pointed a palp at one of many buttons on his desk.

"You know you can't do that," said a second voice grimly. It was Eichra Oren's. "We've been through this before." I sent my implant searching for a camera that would show him. When it did, he was in the water with Misterthoggosh, wearing his tunic of office, carrying his fearsome sword in its sheath over his left shoulder. His voice was artificial, implant-generated. His teeth held a mouthpiece attached to a small horizontal cylinder containing perhaps an hour's worth of oxygen.

At that moment, another alarm went off, and we were given a view of the Grays' huge device, opening with a coruscation in the center of blinding, multicolored light. Misterthoggosh raised an anticipatory tentacle-tip.

Eichra Oren drew his sword and leapt, or as close to it as possible underwater, to the top of the Proprietor's great spiral shell.

Almost as if he hadn't noticed the human standing atop him with a sword far sharper than any razor, Misterthoggosh reached out with a tentacle—Eichra Oren swept his blade at it, but his arms and sword were too short—and pushed the button. Everybody saw the first bomb launched toward the portal. Before anyone could stop it, it burrowed into the interdimensional tunnel, followed closely by the second atom bomb.

Treemonisha headed straight to the wall, to one side of the portal, to avoid the blast that emerged from the Grays' device. We only felt one explosion, which meant that the portal had closed before the second bomb went off. The earth shook, momentarily overcoming the vessel's inertial dampers, The submarine was pelted by rocks falling down the canyon wall, All of the Grays' lights went out, so our vessel played its mighty floodlights over the scene. There was much less damage to be seen than I might have expected—most of the force must have been expended on the other side—but nothing here seemed to be moving.

"You've killed them!" Eichra Oren shouted, "Hundreds, maybe even thousands! And who knows how many, innocent or guilty on the other side!

He jumped to the sandy floor to confront the monster, his sword of office shouldered like a ball bat. "Misterthoggosh, we must now discuss this grave and fundamentally unpayable moral debt you have incurred!"

He rested his sword-point on the exact spot nearest the mollusc's brain.

Misterthoggosh took him by both wrists. "Not *them*, young human, *him*."

"Him?" He strained against the Proprietor's grasp. Both entities trembled with the force of their deadlock and made straining mental noises.

"Or her, or it, however it likes to think of itself. We have been attacked by a single organism, not thousands. And I hardly think I've killed it, Eichra Oren. I don't even know if that is possible. All that I've done today is to have clipped its claws. Now put down that Hammer-damned abalone knife of yours, and try to reason this out with me.

"Will you have beer?"

CHAPTER THIRTY-THREE

Normalcy

"YOUNG HUMAN," COMPLAINED THE GIANT MOLLUSC, "YOU were about to kill me. Another half-second, the briefest of thrusts, and you would have ended my life. You touched me with the tip of that damned sword of yours. I can still feel where it lay upon my flesh, pressing inward."

We were all sitting, Eichra Oren, Eneri Relda, Lornis Adubudu, and little old me, in one of a dozen or so inter-environmental conference rooms that *Treemonisha* had to offer, small, intimate, cozy, warm or cold as the mood moved its current occupants, equipped with wonderful furniture, easy communication with the household staff, including food services, and constructed with one big floor-to-ceiling transparent wall that looked into a similar compartment on the water side of this deck.

That, of course, was where the Proprietor was speaking from. Aelbraugh Pritsch was half-floating beside him in a sort of weird bird-brained diving suit, clearly wishing he was over here with us landlings.

Eneri Relda's egg had hatched. Lornis' companion Mio seemed fascinated, and was playing with its tiny fingers, toes and wing-hooks.

Eichra Oren, his face almost touching the window, shook his head slowly. "I have already acknowledged my error, Misterthoggosh. I will not apologize for having done my job as appeared appropriate at the time. You requested a p'Nan debt assessor. Would you have had me act otherwise?"

The old cephalopod was as close to the thick transparency as his employee. "On the contrary, son. Had you been right, I would have had to pay. I do wish you'd nicked me a little, so I'd have a scar to brag about."

I could provide a scar, I thought, *for each of you.* But they were both laughing, now, Eichra Oren with his handsome head back, roaring, the old ammonite making similar noise as his great coiled shell rocked and shook. It was purely learned behavior. A social nicety. Nautiloids don't laugh, they don't have the respiratory equipment.

"Will you have beer? I'm exploring something called milk stout."

My boss assented enthusiastically, directing an inquiring look my way. I responded with as close as I can get to a shrug. Why the Hammer not?

"What is it with men?" Lornis asked in an annoyed voice. She sat beside me on a long black settee made of some sort of cultured insect leather, "One moment it's deadly conflict. The next they're drinking buddies!"

My turn to laugh. "Remind me to tell you about threat display rituals sometime. They evolved to prevent more sperm-bearers from being killed in combat than is absolutely necessary. It isn't anything that comes naturally to females. You're the babies' last line of defense and far more dangerous—nothing at all between 'Off' and 'On'."

"Oasam Otusam!" she scolded me. "That's horribly misogynistic!"

"And possibly racist, too," I told her, "seeing as how your species does a few male-female things differently. But it was merely an observation, Lornis. Take any complaints up with Mother Nature, or Auntie Evolution, not with me. For the time being, I think you should just embrace the moment, sit back, and have a nice beer with us, don't you?"

She gave her head a shake, momentarily creating a lovely corona of auburn, russet, and blood red. "It's very tempting, Sam. But my people don't do at all well with alcohol. It instantly erases all of our inhibitions."

I moved closer. "Tell me more."

To my surprise it was mid-afternoon on the surface when we reached it. I don't know what I'd been expecting. The Captain announced that he'd retracted part of the canopy on the uppermost deck, and dropped the force-field, except where it provided shelter from the wind of our passage.

Eichra Oren, Lornis, and I moved our little party to that deck and invited Eneri Relda, Squee-elgia, Aelbraugh Pritsch, and Renner and Bask. A quantity of beer was consumed. Lornis stuck with tomato juice, poor dear. I don't know what safely intoxicates her folk except life, maybe.

Despite pressing business, Misterthoggosh attended the party electronically, and after a while, the Captain himself came up to be introduced to the legendary Eneri Relda, among other things. He was the biggest spider I'd ever seen, shaggy gray, as big as a bison. His name was Toknoi Elaun and he said he came from a long line of ship's masters.

Some time after dark, with the lights of *Treemonisha*'s home port glimmering in sight on the horizon, I contacted Natsromy Ram to see if she were free this evening. She was, very fortunately, and I arranged for her to pick me up at the quay and take us home. Eichra Oren could get back there on his own, and my quarters have their own private entrance.

As my feet finally touched solid ground, I saw that Renner was right behind me. He handed Natsromy a big container with a swinging handle. "*Bolhabaissa*," he explained. "Fresh."

"You enjoy, now." The tiny tickle of thought was from Bask.

I was so startled, I didn't know how to reply, except for "Thank you, both," in the Original Tongue. I guess we had all sort of saved the world together, Renner and Bask, not unimportantly, from *Treemonisha*'s galley.

Natsromy parked her cute little veek beside my door. We went inside and had a long, wonderful night of *bolhabaissa* and each other.

The next morning, I left an exhausted (if I do say so, myself) Natsromy to sleep and went through the house to ask it to make us some coffee.

As the aroma of the stuff began to circulate, there was a noise at Eichra Oren's door. Out popped Lornis, in the act of wrapping one of Eichra Oren's tunics about her otherwise unclothed body. An extremely pleasant sight. Her hair was tousled, but then her hair was always tousled.

Mio swung down to greet her from somewhere in the rafters.

She was followed by a yawning Eichra Oren, already tunic-clad, but with equally messy hair. "Do I smell coffee?" he asked no one in particular.

"Yes, sir," said the house. "I've a delivery for you at the front door."

Natsromy—freshly showered, dressed, and smelling even better than the coffee—came through my door at that moment, nodded politely to Eichra Oren, gave Lornis a little look of impressed surprise, and then came to me. She knelt and ran her fingers all over my head. Not for the first time, or the last, did I wish that my brain and its cybernetic appurtenances lived in a body more like Eichra Oren's.

Although I'd settle for thumbs.

"You suppose you could spare me a cup, dear? No sugar, just sweet cream."

"I know." That would make the coffee exactly the color of her skin. She also had startling blue-gray eyes and freckles scattered lightly across her nose and cheeks. At twenty, Natsromy was already more woman than most women ever manage to be. She was very pleasant to look at and had a Master's degree in Applied Hedonics from Lamplight University.

The boss said, "Hmmm. All right, let's see what this delivery is."

He and I went to the door. He cautiously opened it—there were people who would be happy to know that he was dead. Leaning against the hinge-side jamb there stood a very familiar-looking five string banjo.

"Hammer and Forge," I said, "Does this mean—?"

"Could mean lots of things," he said, bringing it in with him. My nose told me that it was indeed the instrument from the cabin. I could smell the woodsmoke on it. We then had to explain the significance of the banjo—the story of Meerltchirt and Shaalara—to Lornis and Natsromy.

"There's no mystery here, at all—they've eloped!" she exclaimed. "She didn't eat her fiancé after all! They're honeymooning, or whatever spiders do, in the mountains on the North Western Continent! How perfectly romantic!" Lornis threw her arms around Eichra Oren's neck. He grinned, put both his arms around her, and kissed her tenderly.

"What's with all this?" I asked. "I thought you two weren't physically compatible."

She gave me an enormous smile. "We worked something out."

ALSO BY L. NEIL SMITH

Pallas *(Book I of the Ngu Family Saga)*
Ceres *(Book II of the Ngu Family Saga)*

Sweeter Than Wine

Their Majesties' Bucketeers

Tom Paine Maru—Special Author's Edition

The Venus Belt

The Crystal Empire

Brightsuit MacBear

Taflak Lysandra

Hope (with Aaron Zelman)

Down With Power: Libertarian Policy
in a Time of Crisis (non-fiction)